Jean, Duke of Berry 1340-1416
* (I) Jeanne of Armagnac
* (II), Jeanne Countess of Auvergne

Philip the Bold,
Duke of Burgundy 1342-1404
* Margaret of Flanders

Jeanne 1343-1373
* Charles II 'the Bad',
King of Navarre

John the Fearless,
Duke of Burgundy
1371-1419
* Margaret
of Bavaria

Jeanne of Navarre
1370-1437
* (I) Jean V,
Duke of Brittany
* (II) Henry IV,
King of England

Philip the Good,
Duke of Burgundy
1396-1467

René
1408-1480
* Isabelle
of Lorraine

Yolande
1412-1440
* Francis I
of Brittany

Charles
(of Maine)
1414-1472

Marguerite
d'Anjou
1430-1482
* Henry VI
of England

Yolande
d'Anjou
1428-1483
* Frederick
of Vaudémont
1428-1470

Jean VI, Duke of Brittany
1389-1442
*Jeanne de France

Arthur,
Count of
Richemont,
Constable of France
1392-1458
* Margaret of Burgundy

Francis I, Duke of Brittany
1415-1450
*Yolande d'Anjou
1412-1440

THE ROYAL FAMILY OF FRANCE AT THE TIME OF THIS STORY

Agnès Sorel: Mistress of Beauty

Also by HRH Princess Michael of Kent

Crowned in a Far Country: Portraits of Eight Royal Brides

Cupid and the King: Five Royal Paramours

The Serpent and the Moon: Two Rivals for the Love of a Renaissance King

The Queen of Four Kingdoms: An Historical Novel

Agnès Sorel: Mistress of Beauty

HRH Princess Michael of Kent

Constable • London

CONSTABLE

First published in Great Britain in 2014 by Constable

ISBN 978-1-47211-913-1 (hardback)
ISBN: 978-1-47211-914-8 (ebook)

Typeset in Palatino by SX Composing DTP, Rayleigh, Essex
Printed and bound in Great Britain by Clays Ltd, St Ives plc

Constable
is an imprint of
Constable & Robinson Ltd
100 Victoria Embankment
London EC4Y 0DY

An Hachette UK Company
www.hachette.co.uk

www.constablerobinson.com

For my daughter Ella who has the beauty and gentle intelligence of her ancestor Agnès Sorel.

Chapter One

The Queen of Four Kingdoms is dead. A weak sun shines through the windows on to the face of Yolande d'Aragon, Duchess of Anjou, Queen of Sicily, etc., as she lies in state. In the chapel of the massive medieval Château of Angers, capital of her sovereign territory of Anjou, her catafalque stands open to receive the homage due to her. Outside, snow is falling, gently, steadily. Until today, 24 November in the Year of Our Lord 1442, winter has been slow in coming to this part of north-western France.

Too late to see his mother before she died, René, her second son and heir, kneels alone by her coffin, its stand draped in black velvet to the floor, a banner bearing the royal arms of Anjou hanging across it and down either side. Finally, the son she adored can confess his sorrow for the pain he caused her. 'Do not let me die without seeing your dear face again,' she asked when they last embraced; it was all she wanted, just one more sight of him. With a grieving heart he remembers the plea in those deep-blue eyes, now closed for ever.

Agnès Sorel, beautiful, twenty years old and modest, a *demoiselle* in attendance on Isabelle of Lorraine, René's wife, stands in a corner of the chapel, her allure hidden by its shadow, watching as her kneeling lord weeps. His mother lies serenely on her bier as if asleep, swathed in white satin, hands folded – clasping a rosary.

She appears as perfect as her son remembered, a glorious, firm spirit, omnipresent throughout his childhood; wise, warm, ethereal and forever reliable.

Rising, René catches sight of Agnès. Wiping his eyes, he beckons for her to follow him out of the chapel.

'Welcome back, Sire,' she murmurs, eyes cast down as she curtseys.

'Come, child,' he sighs, 'sit with me awhile. Tell me about my mother's last year, while I was fighting in Naples – you stayed with her, I know.'

The girl moves quietly a little behind him, and at his bidding perches reluctantly on a window seat, unaccustomed to sitting in his presence.

'Well, what did she say about me when she heard I had reached Marseilles?' he asks almost brusquely, made impatient by guilt. René always considered Agnès Sorel to be the prettiest and most honest of his wife's *demoiselles*, and now he can see that she has grown into a striking beauty.

Naturally reticent in the presence of her sovereign duke, Agnès holds back the truth. 'Sire, she was most relieved to hear of your safe arrival in Marseilles,' she says softly, eyes fixed on her hands in her lap.

'Come now, Agnès, I have known you most of your young life. That's not what I expect to hear from you of all people. How disappointed was she that I didn't come straight to her after landing? What did she say on hearing I had lost my throne – after all the sacrifices she made for me? Did she protest when I did not come to her sooner? That I stopped at Pisa to see Florence? Was she upset, angry that I put my love of art before her? Oh, I should have come at once, I know I should.'

With that heartfelt lament, René d'Anjou gets up and paces back and forth before the girl. In Naples he was acknowledged by both the court and the people of his kingdom as the best of sovereigns: kind, sensitive to their needs, a truly heroic figure, and notably just. Now those same loyal people face the terrible wrath of their conqueror, Alfonso d'Aragon, the man they had spurned in favour of his cousin from Anjou. But René's thoughts are solely with his mother at this time, and Agnès hastens to reassure him.

'Sire, believe me, you have no need for such anxiety. Your lady mother was both relieved and content once she heard you had reached your port of Marseilles. She told me: "Thank God, he is safe – now you can return to Lorraine," and sent me back to Nancy to help with the preparations for your arrival there. Sire, I promise that is all.'

'Because she believed I would come north to Anjou at once,' and René wrings his hands, his face etched with sorrow, his voluminous black robe swirling about him.

Isabelle of Lorraine, crowned Queen of Sicily, had gathered her children, the ladies of her court and her many pets and, at René's insistence, sailed from their doomed Naples to Marseilles. No sooner had she docked than her party headed north to Anjou, to Queen Yolande's Château of Saumur and the two children Isabelle had left in France – teenaged Jean, her eldest, ruling Lorraine for his parents, and Marguerite, her youngest, brought up by her grandmother. Yolande welcomed her daughter-in-law, her other grandchildren and the court with open arms. She tried not to show that it was her son she yearned to see again before she died, a day she felt edging nearer.

Now at last he is here – and she has gone. Agnès suffers for him, the agony of his guilt plain in his red-rimmed eyes. She sees to the new arrivals almost absent-mindedly, absorbed in her reminiscences. She is moving among the guests when she notices Queen Isabelle beckoning.

'Have you seen him?' her mistress asks anxiously.

Agnès knows the queen means her husband. Curtseying low, she nods.

'Well, how is he? Is he distressed? Does he blame himself?' and Isabelle answers her own questions, muttering softly, 'Yes, of course he does,' as she fiddles with her cloak's fastening.

'Agnès dear, hold the cloak for me – it's warm with all these people and the fires – but be sure to dress me again before we enter the chapel. I must wear black and it will be cold in there. Is my hair in order?' she asks nervously, pinching her cheeks to add colour. *How she loves him . . .*

'You will see to the guests, won't you, and order mulled wine for them all – they will be frozen, the new arrivals especially. And don't stray far from me, please!' *So tense, poor lady, but excited to be seeing her husband again, despite the shame of his defeat.*

René stops talking the moment he catches sight of Isabelle entering the Great Hall. Its walls are covered with the castle's famous tapestries, their glorious reds and blues the perfect backdrop for the tall, slender young Queen of Sicily. Like her hair, Isabelle's fine wool dress is the colour of ripe wheat. It hugs her body and reaches to the floor; several rows of Yolande's pearls surround her throat, and a loose shawl of gossamer-thin burgundy wool hangs casually over one shoulder. René moves towards her with quick, light steps for such a large man, his face a mixture of joy, pain and relief, and his arms open wide as a bear's to envelop his beloved wife. It has been only a few months since they last saw one another, on the dock in Marseilles when he arrived from Naples, but she was obliged to leave after a few days and return to Lorraine. As he embraces Isabelle, René's heavy heart lifts, and he holds her in his arms for what seems an eternity. His return confirms what they both feared when she left Naples: the dream they once shared of ruling their Italian paradise is over. Their coffers are empty; they can never afford another attempt to oust Alfonso. Now they must face the challenge of building a new future at home in France.

Agnès, never far from her mistress, or her confidences, understands her joy – and her sorrow. It has been a long and painful journey for everyone who left Naples, but most of all for Isabelle, for she knows how much her mother-in-law sacrificed for her son, bankrupting herself and her family for a cause in which she never believed. So many memories have been left behind; of Isabelle's ten children, six of them buried in Naples, another source of her sadness.

As his family gathers to pay their final respects to his revered mother, René, Duke of Anjou, sovereign Count of Provence, former King of Sicily, Naples and Jerusalem, embraces each and every one with a sad smile and a few quiet words. While he and Isabelle stand side by side in the Great Hall of Angers, the colourful tapestries a dramatic background for the black robes worn by most of the mourners, Agnès discreetly keeps her place behind her mistress, watchful, absorbing everything, memorizing faces, helping with the guests. She whispers instructions to the staff and exchanges quiet greetings with those visitors and their servants who come from Saumur. Others she recognizes from earlier days spent with the Old Queen at Angers and the various estates of the Anjou family.

'Oh, my Lady Agnès, you cannot know how much Queen Yolande missed you when you returned to Lorraine,' several tell her. 'It's a pity she sent you back – you should have remained with her until our duke arrived,' says another. 'She mightn't have died if you'd stayed longer.' *What nonsense – how superstitious they are*, but Agnès smiles politely while she busies herself with the mourners, discreetly calling on servants to satisfy every request but never losing sight of her mistress.

She arrived with Isabelle the day before, riding hard from Nancy with her escort and a number of her personal staff. Since none of the Anjou family had been in residence at Angers for some time, there was much to do inside the château to prepare for the guests who would assemble in the days to come. As the capital of Anjou, the great fortress of Angers was kept fully staffed and ready to receive visitors at all times, but without its mistress in residence, the many rooms needed dusting, fires lit, flowers added – at this time of year, autumn branches with gilded leaves. Plates of sweetmeats and dried fruits were laid out on counters, goblets lined up, and gallons of mulled wine heated in the kitchens to warm the travellers arriving after long, cold journeys.

'Agnès, my dear, please see to everything, and make sure that guests are shown to the right rooms – you know what I mean,' Isabelle told her, looking at her meaningfully.

The girl busies herself unobtrusively doing her mistress's bidding to make the visitors comfortable. Wet clothes are removed to be dried, shoes changed, and guests taken to their rooms on Agnès's direction before they descend again to the great reception rooms. There, fires burn high in the large chimney pieces, one in the middle of each wall, themselves covered with the famous tapestries. How well Agnès remembers her first visit to Angers, when Queen Yolande explained how the hangings had been commissioned by the late King Charles V, father of her beloved husband Duke Louis II of Anjou; how they were the largest series of tapestries ever made in France, their *toiles* painted by a master from Bruges to represent the Apocalypse. On this sad day, their glowing reds, ochres and cobalt blues transcend the greyness of the skies and of the occasion.

Isabelle has placed Agnès at the entrance to the Great Hall to receive the guests on her behalf while she mingles with those already there. Among the first to arrive is

Charles, Count of Maine, the youngest of Yolande's children, a handsome twenty-eight-year-old. He knows his mother's *demoiselle* and greets her warmly.

'My dear Agnès, more beautiful than ever, and such cheerful company for my mother during her last year – for which you have the gratitude of the Anjou family for ever.' With those elegant words he kisses her hand – a most unexpected honour from a Prince of the Blood – which makes Agnès blush.

Like René, Charles is wearing the formal black robes of royal mourning, protocol allowing only the addition of a pearl or diamond pin. The brothers embrace, tears in their eyes. As they study one another, René sees how much his young brother has changed in their four years apart.

'Why did I not come north to her the moment I landed in Marseilles? Why did I imagine she would live for ever?' he pleads. Charles merely shakes his head while René continues: 'My heart was so heavy; the shame of my defeat kept me in Provence – kept me from facing her. Can you understand, dear brother?' And they embrace again, sobbing.

'For years she gave me all she had, depriving you and our sister in order to sustain my army against our cousin, that usurper Alfonso d'Aragon – how I hate him! But even her colossal efforts were not enough.' Charles remains silent, allowing René to expel his pent-up remorse. 'You and I know she never believed in what she called this *chimera* of the kingdom of Sicily, a fantasy craved by our father and our brother Louis – and which killed them both. And yet she not only let me go, she financed my quest as well. She knew that she could never stop me wanting to rule our rightful kingdom. Tell me you understand,' he beseeches.

Agnès sees Charles gently shake his head once more. What can he say, after all? He does his best to console René.

'Calm yourself, dear brother. She heard you were safely home. It was enough. She wrote to me – and to our sister Marie – the moment she had word you had landed at Marseilles. Her joy and relief at your safe arrival was overwhelming, and indeed, she *expected* you to stay a while in the south. Yes, it is true. Be calm now, I *beseech* you. *None* of us was with her at the end. We were each in touch with her, sending letters by courier almost daily, and we believed she was well. You must console yourself that she was content to join Papa in Heaven.'

There are no more tears; both men know that Charles's words were spoken to ease their joint sorrow. In Naples, Agnès often heard King René announce, with a combination of love and pride: 'My younger brother Charles has always been cleverer than me – his will be a great career at the royal court of France.' Looking at him now, this handsome, upright young courtier with his mother's beautiful eyes, she thinks her lord may well be right.

Chapter Two

There is no time for sentiment about Naples and the way of life they left behind. Those who sailed back to France with the young Queen of Sicily know that, just as do the remainder who arrived a year later with King René. This is their new reality, and here at Angers, René and Isabelle must take their places as the sovereign Duke and Duchess of Anjou and care for the many guests come to honour his mother.

When they hear their father has arrived, René and Isabelle's two middle children, Louis and young Yolande, neither of whom René has seen for a year, rush into the Great Hall, tears of relief and happiness flowing freely at his safe return. Politely they greet their many relatives and family friends, speaking in low voices out of respect for their dead grandmother lying in the chapel next door. To think it was little more than a year ago that they arrived in Anjou and were merry with her at Saumur, chattering and playing with her many dogs. Then, to her parents' delight, Marguerite, the five-year-old they left behind with Yolande when they sailed for Naples, enters the Great Hall. A tall and pretty twelve-year-old, she arrived from Nancy a day after her mother. Since Agnès's is the face she knows best among the company, she rushes to the *demoiselle*.

'It's all right, dearest,' whispers Agnès soothingly. 'Go and greet your father, and don't upset him by crying.'

Marguerite hugs Agnès before moving towards the father she has not seen for more than four years. Instantly he folds his youngest, darling daughter in his arms, choking with emotion. Words will have to wait.

What a strange way to meet again, thinks Agnès, through the death of one so loved by them both.

King René's first born, his son and heir, Jean of Calabria, also barely knows his father. As he enters the Great Hall, he too immediately greets his mother's *demoiselle*.

'What a pleasure to see you here, beautiful Agnès, you who brought my grandmother such joy with your company. Every time I came to visit her during the last year, she told me so.' And he embraces Agnès. *How these children have grown and changed in such a short time.*

René is startled to see that young Jean has grown into the image of Louis, his beloved older brother. Tall, blond, blue-eyed and strikingly handsome, Louis III, another victim of the Anjou family's '*chimera kingdom*'. How often did Queen Yolande lament to Agnès of its magnetic grip on her husband and two sons?

Jean, a bright lad of seventeen, has made his parents proud by the way he governed Lorraine in their absence. 'Ah, my son!' booms René, cocooning him in his robes just as he did his wife and younger children. 'I have heard nothing but good of your work for us. Do not think your labours are over with my return – I will still need you!' He smiles proudly. 'With Anjou, Lorraine and Provence to administer, I will require you to continue to play your part for me!' And as they embrace, his eyes fill once again with tears of happiness.

'Papa, dear Papa, it's been such a long time without you,' Jean says softly on his father's shoulder. *How tall he is – though not yet as tall as his father, nor has he his girth!* 'Papa, you do know, don't you, that I visited Grandmère quite often – whenever I came to Anjou on your business. You know, even when we discussed the most serious problems or difficulties, she would insert a light word or anecdote to lift the gloom of our proceedings.' He pauses in reflection, and then looks at his father. 'How I admired her.'

'I know, my boy, I know,' says René, stroking his son's head.

'Then I am sure you know that all she ever wanted was for you to defeat our cousin of Aragon. Our focus was solely on finding ways to send you more men, money and supplies.' Again they embrace. 'I loved her, Papa, and in your and Maman's absence, I relied on her wisdom.'

'Yes, yes, I know, my boy, I know,' René repeats almost absent-mindedly, 'and yet despite her many sacrifices, I did not – *could not* – succeed in my quest.' He turns away from his son's all-knowing gaze, so like his grandmother's. As an intimate of this family, Agnès has no sense of intruding on their personal grief. On the contrary, she shares it.

Once again the *demoiselle* has been alerted to stand by the entrance to the Great Hall, and on seeing the depth of her *révérence*, those nearby realize that the Queen of France has arrived with her son, the dauphin Louis. Queen Marie is René's cherished older sister, and they too embrace, another warm meeting between loving siblings after many years apart, although they have remained close and in regular correspondence. Marie is not beautiful, but she has a smile and a pervasive charm that supplants beauty and her wisdom and goodness are universally admired. She will understand René's misery better than anyone.

Discreetly, gently, Agnès takes Queen Marie's black cloak from her shoulders and is pleasantly surprised by her grateful smile and greeting.

'Are you not Agnès Sorel?' she asks sweetly.

Agnès bobs and inclines her head.

'Yes, my mother wrote to me often of you and the pleasure you brought her during her last year. I thank you for this with all my heart – and I know we shall see more of you when our court joins with that of Lorraine.'

It is their first meeting. Throughout the year Agnès spent at Saumur, Queen Marie never left Bourges, remaining near the king, who needed her, but Queen Yolande spoke so often of her daughter that Agnès feels she almost knows her. True, her face is long and narrow, her eyes small, and her nose too long, but the sweetness of her expression and the charm of her genuine smile attract her mother's *demoiselle*.

'Marie, dearest sister,' René says softly after embracing her, 'only you can have some idea how deeply her death affects me.'

'Dear, dear René, not only do you and I and our brother Charles suffer her loss, but so does Louis my husband.

As you well know, hers was the only voice he hearkened to, hers the only order he obeyed, throughout our shared childhood and after. Hers was the only wisdom he acknowledged. Whose wisdom can he count on now?' she asks plaintively. 'None of us have our king's love or trust, certainly not I, his wife and queen, not in the way he gave it to her. None of us can replace her guidance of him – nor stem his follies and excesses, as she did.' Then, to her surprise, Agnès hears Marie tell René quietly, sadly, 'And somehow he still attracts the worst kind of people to his inner circle, as you well know.'

'I expect my own position with the king will also suffer now that Maman is no longer here,' René tells his sister pensively, 'because you and I both saw how devotedly he loved our mother – far more than his own. Without her, he has less cause to care for us in spite of our shared childhood and relationship.'

'How I wish Louis and I had been able to visit her at Saumur during the last year,' sighs Marie. 'Although Maman was not at court in recent times, you know that she never lost her influence over him, and he would often consult her by sending a courier with letters to seek her advice by return.' René looks a little surprised, but she continues: 'Dearest brother, you had your own battles to concern you, and I did not want to trouble you,' adds this gentle Queen of France, his dearest sister, with resigned, downcast eyes.

Agnès knows much of Marie's troubles, pieced together from little comments and confidences made to her by Queen Yolande. At the age of ten, Charles, then third in line to the French throne, came to live with the family of

Anjou at Angers betrothed to the eight-year-old Marie. They have been friends throughout their lives, but Agnès knows they have never shared the passionate love of Marie's parents, or that of René with Isabelle.

René shakes his head. 'Yes, it's true, our mother's death marks the end of an era for us her children; although adult, somehow we were still hers to command, were we not? Where can we – and even more importantly, our king – find such guidance now?' Although Agnès keeps her place behind her principals, she can hear every word, and since their mother trusted her completely, they have no need to be careful in their speech.

'René, you are my dear brother,' says Marie firmly, taking his hands in hers, 'and you must heed my advice – which, sadly, my husband never does: he declares that my role is to breed, not to advise! To date, I have borne him eleven children, and buried most of them. Now I insist, listen to me! You must look to Isabelle your wife, for she has our mother's strength, and the wisdom I saw in her before she sailed for Naples has grown with time and experience. I have come to know her through her many letters, and I am confident she will guide you well.'

Their embrace is warm and touching. *How sad Queen Marie looks.* Since the beginning, René has been aware that his sister's marriage to their enigmatic cousin King Charles VII has not been easy – nor her relationship with their son, the dauphin Louis. This Queen Yolande had confided to Agnès, telling her how troublesome and spoilt she found her grandson, often lamenting that he had no brothers to knock some sense into him as a child.

During these intimate family conversations, Agnès has

been actively in attendance on Isabelle and her family, never far should they need her: passing with a jug of mulled wine and plates of fresh home-made biscuits; helping with the younger ones when asked, as well as seeing to the needs of the other guests, while candles are lit throughout the great rooms.

Slowly she has become aware of being observed herself – no, more than that: actually of being *stared at*, and unashamedly. When finally she looks up, to her surprise it is the dauphin whose eyes are appraising her, half mockingly, dark and expressionless as a snake's. She is not sure if he knows who she is – then sees him whispering to one of his uncle's courtiers, nodding in her direction. Ah, so now he knows her status, and then his sneer makes that clear: she is but a lowly *demoiselle*, an innocent maid – perhaps even a potential victim. She can read it in his eyes. But Agnès knows more about him than he can ever guess. She sees him approaching as she stands discreetly behind her mistress.

With a slightly insolent bow, he addresses her. 'The *demoiselle* Agnès Sorel, if I am not mistaken?' he says with raised eyebrows.

She curtseys with her own eyes lowered. 'Yes, my lord, and what is your pleasure?' she replies, as befits her position at court. At this he laughs in a way she has heard the fisher boys laugh at the street girls in Naples.

'My pleasure? My *pleasure*, you ask? Well, we shall see, won't we, my pretty lady come from Lorraine? I have marked you well and you will hear from me.' With that, he turns, still chuckling to himself.

Isabelle sees her shudder and comes to her rescue,

taking her hand. 'Agnès, my dear, come and greet a great favourite of Queen Yolande's, one of the children who grew with hers, and my husband's dearest friend. He is Count Jean de Dunois – surely she spoke of him to you?'

Jean Dunois, Lord René's slightly older childhood friend, the cousin he told them much about in Naples, the friend whom René so greatly admires he named his first born son for him, has arrived in the Great Hall. The illegitimate son of Prince Louis d'Orléans, beloved younger brother of the late, mad king Charles VI, Jean was taken in by Queen Yolande to join her children in the nursery at Angers following his royal father's assassination. Prince Louis and his wife Valentina were close family members and dear friends, and Yolande often told Agnès how much she loved Jean as a boy, and valued his outstanding character. He quickly became the best friend of her eldest son Louis, and then of René too, and he influenced and guided all her children in the most remarkable yet understated way. She marvelled that he never showed resentment or a hint of dejection on account of his birth, simply carrying on with his studies, undertaking the tasks he was given with diligence and good humour. He was a natural leader, yet careful and prudent, and Yolande felt comfortable whenever her sons were with him, whether on their mad childhood gallops through the countryside or out hunting in the forests.

'My dear cousin.' René's face shows his pleasure as Jean approaches, and they embrace like the old friends they are. 'I knew you would come, and I am truly glad. From amongst us all in the nursery, you always gave Maman the most reason to be proud. You know, her letters to me in

Naples were filled with your military successes and your efforts for the king. She knew she could trust you as much as either Louis or me. And I know how often you represented her in carrying out many services, both public and private' – at which point they exchange knowing glances.

Agnès is aware from Queen Yolande's own stories that she undertook a number of strategies and subterfuges for the king's benefit, generally honourable, though sometimes perhaps deemed by others to be less so. All, however, were for the good of the kingdom, as she repeatedly stressed to Agnès, and towards this worthy goal there were no limits to her intrigues. Dunois holds many of the late queen's secrets, and Agnès knows that Lord René is justly confident they will always remain safe with him.

With a face full of compassion, Jean takes his cousin aside, and she hears him say: 'My dearest and oldest friend, know how I feel for you, and accept, I ask you, my most sincere sympathy on the death of your extraordinary mother, who I admired intensely and loved as if she were my own.'

'I know that, my dear Jean. Welcome, and thank you for supporting me here today. Now, go to her in the next room. See how peacefully she lies, and pray beside her for her soul.' The unspoken harmony between them, no great need for words, touches Agnès, and their deep commitment and mutual trust impresses her.

When Jean Dunois returns from the chapel, he is wiping his eyes. Then he lifts his head and says to René, perhaps in an attempt to cheer them both: 'Our shared childhood seems long ago, does it not? Daily lessons with your mother supervising; our jolly games at bedtime – especially when your father would dress as an ogre and chase us through the nursery; our fights with the village boys; riding and hunting in the forests. What an enchanted time we had. When you left for your uncle's duchy of Bar, I will never forget my many visits to you there and later in Lorraine, before your marriage, the fun we had climbing in the mountains hunting chamois. What innocents we were!'

Jean puts his arm about René and the two men move to a corner.

'René, my friend, I want you to know that everything I understand today about human nature, how to conduct myself in the world, I learned from your mother. It was she who gave me pride in being the last of the House of Orléans left in France – in spite of my illegitimate birth. When my father was murdered by our despicable cousin of Burgundy, she wrote to my half-brother, the new Duke d'Orléans, still held in London's Tower since his capture at Agincourt, and requested that I be brought into the royal House of Anjou to learn how to live my life as the nobleman I was born. I owe her everything I am today, not least my cordial relations with our cousin the king – like me, another of her protégés.' And he smiles, his eyes far away in memories, his arm still on René's shoulder.

Count Arthur of Richemont is announced – another of the great queen's acolytes. Charles VII has given the count leave from the fighting in Normandy to come to Angers and honour his patron, to whom he owes his august position. Agnès looks towards Isabelle, who signals her to remain where she is. Richemont, France's outstanding Constable, chief of the armed forces, wears his mangled face almost defiantly, a relic of that dreadful

Battle of Agincourt, twenty-seven years ago. Yolande told Agnès often how hard she had struggled to have the king disregard Richemont's facial scars, to look beyond them into his heart and there to recognize his true worth. Another difficult task she achieved against the odds, particularly in view of Charles VII's known revulsion for disfigurement and ugliness.

'Arthur – welcome! How pleased we are to see you. Come, dear friend, come into the chapel, where your staunchest ally lies in state.'

Agnès watches as René leads the visibly moved Richemont to his mother's catafalque. Yes, the Constable's scars really are horrific, giving him an aspect so terrifying that another might have covered them with a mask. But Queen Yolande forced his acceptance at court, and rightly so in view of his remarkable military capabilities and loyal character. Had Agnès not been warned by the Old Queen, she too might have had difficulties meeting his gaze.

Guests are moving in and out of the darkened chapel. Four hooded knights, heads bent, stand at the corners of the open coffin. In front of each knight, a tall, thick candle burns in a heavy brass base, spreading a faint light. There is no other illumination, and the strewing herbs on the floor give the room a subtle, pleasant fragrance. Richemont goes down on one knee by the bier, his head bowed, clenched hand on heart, to pay his silent respects.

Many other mourners have come; somehow René exchanges a word with each of them, and Isabelle too, with Agnès standing alert behind her, observing, ready to do her bidding, fetching for this one, seating another. She recalls Queen Yolande telling her how she had devoted her life to her king and country, just as her beloved husband had taught her to understand was her duty. Only once had she dared mention to him how hard she found it to put the king before their children, and his glance had been enough to silence her and lower her eyes at once. Thereafter she had obeyed him in everything he requested, no matter what she felt or believed. Hers was a sobering lesson in duty.

Among the crowd of mourners and well-wishers, Agnès catches sight of a familiar face, this one from her time with the court in Naples, where he was a regular visitor. He is another of Queen Yolande's protégés, Jacques Coeur, Isabelle and René's friend and rescuer. 'That great magnate of Bourges, a merchant prince if ever there was one,' was how René described him to everyone in Naples, 'and the more deserving of respect considering his humble birth.' It was through Jacques Coeur's recommendation that René stopped in Florence on his way back from Naples to meet Cosimo de' Medici, who showed him the glories of his city. Through this introduction, René is now pleased to call that other great magnate his friend.

'Jacques, how good of you to come to us at Angers today, and from Marseilles. I will be forever in your debt for enabling us all to escape from Naples on your ships!' René says loudly for the room to hear and applaud the good merchant. 'Since my childhood days I know how highly my mother regarded you, and always put forward your name to the king.'

Jacques Coeur bows low, and when he raises his head, René honours him with an embrace – a rare sight from a king to a commoner, but to this man he owes a very great deal. Then more quietly he says:

'One day I will find a way of thanking you, dear Jacques, for sending your ships for us, and twice – for Isabelle and her court, and then again for me. When finally I embarked, your captain told me that those fully armed fast galleons had been anchored for weeks in the bay of Naples, disguised as harmless merchant craft, sails and rowers at the ready. I had no idea. But in your wisdom, you knew that we would be obliged to leave and that I would finally have to flee.'

Agnès watches Jacques Coeur nod slightly but sagely, holding René's eyes. The merchant is at least ten or twelve years older than her master, who is thirty-six, but to judge from their demeanour, their age difference seems more like that of a father and son. Is there nothing this wise man does not know? Together with the other *demoiselles* at the court in Naples, Agnès would often sit spellbound, listening to the thrilling tales he told them of his adventures sailing to the Levant and the Near East, forever in search of precious merchandise for the pleasure of connoisseurs and the delectation of the court of France.

'Since I owe much of my successful career to your royal mother,' he says, looking deep into René's eyes, 'I would like you to know that there is nothing I would not do or risk for her or her family. You, Sire, were her greatest concern during your time on the Italian peninsula,' and he says this last with sincere compassion.

'As you may be aware, I visited Queen Yolande at Saumur two years before her death. I came at her request to bring a selection of splendid outfits for your daughter, the Lady Marguerite.' René looks baffled. 'Of course, how could you know? You were engaged in your battles against Alfonso d'Aragon. I was summoned by your esteemed royal mother because the ambassadors of the young Holy Roman Emperor, Frederick, wished to meet with her to discuss a possible union with the Lady Marguerite.'

'I had no idea!' booms René in astonishment.

'Oh yes, Queen Yolande asked me to make her appear a fitting bride for an emperor! You can imagine with what joy and enthusiasm your gracious mother and I arranged robes for her of cloth of gold, and a flowing cape lined with ermine. She looked every inch an empress-to-be! Later, your royal mother wrote to tell me how impressed the ambassadors had been. However, our King Charles felt his own daughter would make a more advantageous match for France.'

René looks blankly at the merchant, then realizes that his mother had no reason to trouble him with such a vague possibility at the time. She knew him too well.

'When the Lady Marguerite returned with Queen Isabelle and her court to Lorraine, your royal mother wrote asking me to send a wardrobe for the *demoiselle* Agnès Sorel, who was to remain with her, her own wardrobe being more suited to the warm climate of Naples. Believe me, *mon seigneur*, it was an honour to return a year ago to Saumur and visit Queen Yolande again. She often invited me to recount details of my visits to you in Naples – how she loved to hear of your life there. And it was a pleasure to provide clothing for such a charming, beautiful *demoiselle* as the Lady Agnès, whom I had the honour to meet and know a little in Naples. It was she whom Queen Isabelle put in charge of the tame cheetah I gave her!'

'My dear Jacques, you were always a favourite of the ladies at our court on the peninsula, that I heard often' – and as René says this, Agnès sees him give the merchant a wry smile, his first since his arrival home. Yes, Jacques Coeur was indeed a great favourite at their court, with his stories and his beautiful merchandise, which Queen Isabelle could not resist.

'If I may be so bold, Sire, I have observed the Lady Agnès for several years on my many visits to Naples; moreover, I witnessed the contentment of your esteemed mother in her company . . .'

Jacques is unaware that she can hear him, and Agnès feels her colour rising. He pauses, and René takes his arm to walk with him a few paces away from the gathering, leaving Agnès blushing from his compliments. But René's voice carries and she hears him ask the merchant wistfully: 'Jacques, dear friend, tell me true, was there ever a chance that I might have held on to my wondrous Italian kingdom, my Garden of Eden?'

In a way Agnès came to recognize during his frequent visits to Naples, Jacques Coeur pauses, taking a little time to reflect before answering.

'Sire, as you know, your enemy and cousin Alfonso d'Aragon has the support of the Pope in Rome, whose coffers are bottomless. Unfortunately, not so those of your mother, nor those of the Pope in Avignon, who depends on the King of France for sustenance. Over the years, at her request, I have sold everything I could for your lady mother. Of your father's great fortune there is nothing disposable left, excepting your depleted castles and your sovereign lands of Provence and Anjou. Your territories of Maine and Guyenne are within the enemy's boundaries. The great gold bequest has been used, as have the wonderful treasures inherited and collected by your father and ancestors.'

Seeing on René's face a mixture of misery and guilt, Jacques Coeur, his voice strong with optimism, adds: 'And yet, Sire, do not forget that your salt mines in Provence still yield a worthy export from Marseilles, and the trading ships, including mine, pay well to use your port there. Then there is the income from your rich soil both in Provence and in Anjou. Believe me, all is not lost by any means.'

'Dear Jacques, forever positive, but that perfect dream I lived in Naples with my admirable wife has evaporated. We will never return,' and René breathes a pitiful sigh. 'We no longer have access to the huge sums needed to unseat Alfonso, and I know the king will not help, even if he could; he still has to contend with the English on his doorstep.

'The marriage of my mother, the only living child of the King of Aragon, to my father, Louis II d'Anjou, was arranged by *their* parents to bring about one great goal – an end to the fighting between our two royal houses. Yet in the end it achieved nothing; precious lives, our paradise and fortune – all lost.'

As René looks about him at his mighty seat of Angers, grown shabby with disuse and time, only now does Agnès notice how much this last year spent fighting in Naples, and his shame at defeat, has aged him.

Out of the corner of her eye she sees Jacques Coeur looking in her direction, and then he is standing beside her.

'My Lady Agnès,' he greets her with a slight bow, 'what a rare pleasure to see your delicate features again.'

Agnès smiles. She is used to flattery and generally ignores it, but his compliments are always sincere.

'I want you to know that it gave me much satisfaction to provide a wardrobe for you on the queen's behalf. I do hope our paths will cross again; perhaps in Lorraine,' he adds with a polite smile. Another little bow, and he is gone, before she has an opportunity to say a word.

Neither the king nor René's friend Pierre de Brézé, another of Queen Yolande's trusted protégés, is able to leave the fighting at this time to attend the funeral. 'But,' Isabelle tells Agnès, 'both have sent me messages and heart-warming letters – and the king insisted he fill the church with flowers.'

Agnès reads the note attached: '*To my beloved bonne mère, with respectful devotion, admiration and gratitude – your son-in-law, Charles.*' She knows the story of how the ten-year-old Charles de Ponthieu, as the king was then called, came to live with the Old Queen's family; and how the shy, awkward boy learned to put his trust in his *bonne mère*. And she *was* a good mother to him. It shocked Agnès to hear that his own mother, Queen Isabeau of France, had denounced her youngest son as illegitimate, solely to cement the Treaty of Troyes in 1420, which effectively gave France to the English in recompense for the French defeat at Agincourt! But Queen Yolande had spies everywhere, and she told Agnès: 'She lied, you know, about his birth.

I knew in my heart he was the late king's son, and that truth was confirmed by my agents. Queen Isabeau made her false claim solely to further the aims of the despicable Duke of Burgundy in exchange for his protection. Hers was a sorry life.'

Agnès often reflects on her interesting conversations with the Old Queen and remembers in particular Yolande's advice about how useful and important a clever, honest young woman could be to someone in a high position. 'Knowledge is power, my dear, never forget that, and even the strongest, most powerful of men can themselves be ruled by an astute woman.'

Following the formal and moving burial service in the cathedral of Saint-Meurice in Angers, truly a celebration of Queen Yolande's life, she is interred next to her husband, her beloved Louis II d'Anjou, as she stipulated in her testament. Her place within the imposing tomb she had erected for him in the choir has been waiting for her these past twenty-five years.

Together again at last, wrote René on the card he placed with a single autumn lily on her sepulchre. A year of conversation with Queen Yolande has left Agnès in no doubt how much this royal couple loved one another. It was their example – René tells everyone – that made him determined, even as a young boy, to share one day such a deep, enduring, passionate love in his own married life; and it was his mother who chose for him his 'peerless Isabelle' of Lorraine.

Chapter Three

Following Queen Yolande's funeral service, family and friends return to the castle to reminisce and spend more precious time together. War with the English is escalating, and far-flung family members cannot expect to meet again until there is peace.

Count Jean de Dunois, as dashing as Queen Yolande described him to her, joins Agnès. They sit together a little apart from the others, and he asks her how it came about that she spent the last year with that great lady he regarded as a mother.

'Yes, it still seems strange to me as well; an honour I shall never forget and will treasure always.'

'Would you tell me? I am so curious, forgive me.'

'My lord, after we landed at Marseilles, I spent some time at Saumur with Queen Isabelle and her party. As you know, Queen Isabelle's youngest, the Lady Marguerite, was only five years old when we left for Naples, and she remained with her grandmother. Naturally, our Lady Isabelle longed to see both her daughter and her revered mother-in-law.'

'Oh yes, of course, I can imagine,' he says, encouraging her to go on.

'Well, one day, we *demoiselles* were sitting stitching nearby when the two queens began discussing the Lady Marguerite's return with her mother and her court to Lorraine. We heard the Old Queen say with a sad tone: "My dear Isabelle, as you know, I am devoted to your Marguerite; it will be hard for me to part with her. She has been my comfort and delight these past six years, and I believe she has enjoyed her time with me as well. I want you to know that I have trained her as I did my own children, with love and care, to make of her the perfect consort for any king or nobleman."

'When she heard that, I remember how proud my Lady Isabelle looked, and grateful, because it was visibly true to us all.'

'Indeed it is; the Lady Marguerite is the perfect princess,' agrees Jean.

'Well, then Queen Yolande sighed and said to Queen Isabelle, her voice quite subdued: "How sad and empty my days will be without her light laughter, her gentle playing of the harp, her japes and jolly conversation about the trivia of her days."

'Then Queen Isabelle replied somewhat anxiously: "I know, my dearest Madame Mère, but I feel sure you understand that I want her to come home with us." Queen Yolande instantly reassured her – "But of course, of course, my dear" – and looked down at her embroidery, tears forming in her lovely eyes.

'Poor Lady Isabelle did not know quite what to do, and almost gasped: "My beloved Madame Mère, tell me how I can ease your suffering. You have done so much for us by having Marguerite with you, and helping our eldest, Jean, as well. Would you care to come to Nancy with us? But no, you cannot leave your beautiful home, and I know you are waiting – as we all are – for our beloved René. Is there any way I can comfort you?"

'Although we *demoiselles* were sitting embroidering a little further from the fire, we could hear every word and were wondering what would happen. I did not think Queen Yolande would come with us to Lorraine, but her sadness was very apparent.'

'Oh, do tell me more,' urges Jean.

'Well, then Queen Yolande said, almost as if she had just thought of it, "Dearest daughter, I have been thinking . . ."' – later, when she came to know her mistress better, Agnès would recognize that whenever Yolande began a sentence in that way, she was planning something! – '"is there a chance you might leave me one of your young ladies to keep me company for a while; to read to me, play the harp, ride a little or walk with me in my garden? Perhaps, with your court entertaining reduced during René's absence, you could spare one of them at least until he returns? It will be such an anxious time for me."'

Agnès pauses a moment, lost in her memories.

'At that, you can imagine, all our ears pricked up, hoping one of us might be the chosen one. Although of course we wanted to go home, but what an honour it would be to stay with her. Then the Old Queen added, looking directly at my Lady Isabelle: "I do enjoy the company of the young, you know."

'"Why, of course, dearest Maman," we heard Queen Isabelle say, "it would be a pleasure." We all held our breath again, looking down and pretending to stitch.

'"My dear, in your many letters, you have mentioned one or two of your *demoiselles* who I think might make ideal companions." I think at that point, we were all ready to faint.'

Jean Dunois laughs encouragingly.

'"And who was that, dearest Maman; do you remember any names?" asked Isabelle.

'"Well, yes, you may recall there was one I was quite curious about. I would never deprive you of a senior *demoiselle*, but she is the most junior, I believe, a modest maid. Perhaps you might not need her as much. I think her name is Agnès Sorel."

'Lord Jean, when I heard my name, I really thought I *would* expire!'

His handsome face is smiling broadly, urging her to continue with her story.

'"Perhaps you could spare her for a while? I have heard her sing prettily while playing the harp here. And she can recount stories of your life in Naples with René and the children. I am sure that will greatly comfort me while waiting for my son – to picture your life there as it was, and what I sadly missed sharing with you."'

'Aha,' says Jean, 'so that is how you came by the incredible privilege of sharing the great queen's last year.'

Agnès thinks his smile is almost a little too knowing,

but then, having been brought up by Queen Yolande himself, perhaps he would understand her thinking better than she could.

'Oh, believe me, my lord, I am aware of what an honour it was to be asked to offer some light distraction for the fabled Queen of Four Kingdoms. I tried to absorb the many subtleties of which she spoke as part of the art of becoming a worthy lady at the court of King René in Lorraine. Most of all, she could not stress to me enough the importance of my duty to my king and country.'

As Jean de Dunois studies the vision of beauty that is Agnès Sorel, he cannot help wondering what Queen Yolande had in mind. How well he knew the way her subtle mind worked; she did or said nothing without a reason. Was it not she who taught him how to manoeuvre in the snakepit of the royal court of France? Observing this astonishingly lovely young lady – guileless, innocent and unambitious – sets his Machiavellian mind working . . . Of one thing he is certain: he must keep a sharp eye out for her when the court of Lorraine joins with that of the king and try to prevent the wrong members – and there are many – from spoiling such innocent goodwill. Queen Yolande had something significant planned for her, of that he is sure.

'Yes, my dear Agnès, the importance of duty to king and country is exactly the lesson she taught us, the young group of children and cousins in her care. I was honoured to be among them and I will never forget that oft-repeated mantra, "*The importance of your duty to your king and country*". As you may know, King René is one of my closest and dearest friends. In fact, we met when he was just three years old and instantly formed a lifelong bond. For that reason, I am sure you and I shall meet often, and I look forward to that.' With those generous words, Count Jean de Dunois, as handsome they say as was his father, Prince Louis d'Orlèans, bows gracefully and, with a genuine and kind smile, he leaves her.

Agnès knows King René has always liked her. He told the others at his court that she was honest, modest and naturally beautiful. When they repeated to her what he said, Agnès had to laugh – she knew how he liked to tease – but later on, Queen Isabelle explained that she must not disregard or reject her God-given beauty.

'Agnès, my dear, do not shy away from your loveliness, nor be conceited about it. Accept it and give joy to others with what God has given you. Your face is a perfect oval, your skin as white as alabaster, and the sweet expression in your eyes, never far from kindly laughter, brings nothing but pleasure to those in your company.' Seeing the girl's confusion, she added, 'Dear child, believe me, I am not flattering you. It is as important to know one's assets as one's failings. You should use your beauty in the service of God, king and country – indeed, as I believe Queen Yolande would have taught you.' It was true – the Old Queen had said such things to Agnès and she remembered.

King René adds: 'Yes, I must paint you again, just as I have all the members of my court in Naples. Painting was one of my great joys there; most challenging of all was sketching the children playing with our pet cheetah, Vitesse. How patient she has always been; how could Jacques Coeur have known her gentle character? But then he knows everything, doesn't he . . .' René muses distractedly.

'My mother was right to choose you as her last companion. You always excelled among our young ladies: the best reader, the best voice at the harp, too; yes, you were the most learned and delightful member of our young court. I say that without any desire to compliment you, my dear. You know it is not my habit. I speak the simple truth. And I am sure there was much my mother was able to teach you that you will find useful for your future; you will benefit from her experience and knowledge of how to judge character, whether at court or among the people. Tell me: were you very disappointed not to return at once to Nancy with your friends?'

'No, my lord, truly I was not. I was honoured and happy to submit to any programme of my Lady Isabelle's choosing. When I looked at your royal mother to gauge her reaction, she reached out her hand to me and said in that marvellous voice of hers: "You will stay with me a while, won't you, Agnès my dear? It would give me much pleasure to walk in my gardens on your arm and hear your stories about life at my son's court in Naples. How I would have enjoyed visiting him, but I left it too late. You must fill in all the spaces between the letters I received, and describe to me in great detail your daily lives. Sometimes, weather permitting, we might ride out gently in the meadows; and in the evenings, you may read to me, or sing and play the harp. Would you do that to comfort an old lady?" she asked *me*, a lowly *demoiselle*, with her gentian blue eyes searching mine, all the while holding my hand.

'Sire, she was utterly, totally enchanting. There was I, a girl from Touraine in the Loire district, coming from no great family, without prospects or fortune, being asked if I would do a great favour to someone who could have anything she wanted! Believe me, I was deeply moved and grateful to have been chosen, and I vowed then to make sure she enjoyed every minute in my company.

'On the next day, my Lady Isabelle left for Lorraine with her entourage, and I found myself in attendance on your remarkable royal mother.'

'When you are ready, I will want you to tell me about your conversations – I need to know her thoughts in her last year dear Agnès, I am sure you understand?'

Agnès nods her bowed head. *How he suffers.*

'Sire, I am willing to tell you now. Your lady mother made my role clear. She told me that as one of Queen Isabelle's ladies, I must learn to help her by looking at your court and its members from the outside in – to see how their actions and decisions affected others. "I have noticed you have a sharp intelligence and your observances can be extremely helpful to my son and daughter-in-law," she said. And something else she repeated often: "It is vital always to put duty first – duty not only to your principals at the court of Lorraine, but to the King of France and your country." When I reached my room each evening, I would write down what she had told me so that I could remember all her wisdom.'

René sighs, but urges her on.

'Another day she said: "You must learn to understand the ways of ambitious courtiers, male and female. "Ambition," she told me, "is the path to excellence, but is justifiable only if the end result is laudable, a worthy task carried out to the best of your ability, and never at anyone else's expense." I will never forget that lesson, Sire. The way she said those words, I knew it was important for me to understand her message. That evening when I wrote down what she taught me, I underlined every word. I shall never forget what she said on that day.'

Agnès stops, anxious not to ramble on. But he says: 'Go on, my dear, you help to ease my conscience with your talk.'

'Modesty was another aspect of life which the Old Queen stressed: "Never forget we are all equal in the eyes of God, even if He chooses to raise some and not others. Most of all, be ready and willing to serve your king in any way he requires. That is the worthiest offering a subject can make."'

Visibly moved, René puts his hand on top of hers.

'My dear Agnès, these are the same lessons she taught me and my siblings and our cousins in the nursery. And it was our dear father who taught her – because her upbringing at her own father's court in Aragon had not been the same. Her inclination had been to put our father and us first, but he changed her thinking and she obeyed. My mother willingly put her life, her fortune and her children at the king's command. She would tell us: "I am proud to have inherited the Valois blood of my mother, and having married into France, I rejoice in being wholeheartedly French in my loyalties."'

Just then, Queen Isabelle approaches them.

'Ah, Isabelle! Come, do sit with us. Agnès is telling me of her time spent with my mother at Saumur.'

More relaxed in Lady Isabelle's company, Agnès continues willingly.

'Much of the time I just sat embroidering and listening while the Old Queen explained the intricacies of life at the royal court. "You see, my dear child," she would often begin, "a king has a great responsibility: he has to rule his country wisely, and his decisions are absolute, since he is the law. This is a heavy weight for any man to carry, even a great man, and the help and advice of prudent people whom he can trust, and are close to him, is what he needs most." She would pause, but I realised, of course, that she did not mean me – I would never be in a position to speak with the King of France or to influence him, and I wondered if I was to comment, or just quietly listen. I decided on the latter.

'"For many years I have advised the king on the best way to choose men and women of character and sound values. I have known him since he came to live with us as a boy . . ." and I remember how she turned and smiled at me as we walked our hacks slowly along a favourite path not far from the château. There were occasions when I felt she was simply voicing her own thoughts to herself – not really talking to me at all. "With time, the king has become a shrewd judge of character and has some excellent men around him to whom I drew his attention."

'Then she would tell me about the men she had placed by the king, and their qualities: your brother, Sire, Prince Charles d'Anjou, and Pierre de Brézé, your late father's equerry; Etienne Chevalier, "so loyal and generous"; Antoine de Chabannes, a great captain who she said was devoted to the late king and King Charles when dauphin. "There are others he can count on too," she told me, "like

André de Villequier and Guillaume Gouffier." And, of course, the merchant Jacques Coeur came in for high praise. Then she told me: "You see, my dear, I have had time to study the way your mind works, and I can sense you would recognize these courtiers I have told you about as the good men I know them to be." Indeed, she described these gentlemen to me so well that I felt I knew many of them already.

'Sire, your sister, Queen Marie, was a favourite subject, as was our king's early history, his many struggles and your lady mother's efforts to help him. Yet throughout our countless conversations she would often come back to the same theme: that the foremost role of a loyal and patriotic subject, especially one admitted to the inner circle at the court of a monarch, was to serve king and country as she had done since she arrived in France.

'"When you are in Lorraine with my son and his family," she told me, "his court will often mix with that of the King Charles, and this is where you can play your part: by helping my son and his wife to entertain the king with your gift of singing and playing the harp, for example; and by being attentive and encouraging this shy monarch to talk about his experiences, should he wish to."

'As you can imagine, Sire and Madame, this surprised me and I often wondered whether or not she was confusing me with your daughter. Forgive me – she had reached a certain age after all. "Of course," she would add, "he would not confide at once in a stranger, but in the company of my Isabelle, I know he will warm to a young, honest soul like yours and perhaps even unburden himself. He needs to. I know."

'Sire and Madame, when she spoke like this – and she did quite often – I admit I found these conversations somewhat perplexing, as I could think of no possible occasion when the king would even notice me, let alone wish to speak with me and tell me his innermost thoughts!

Agnès notices that Isabelle and René exchange frequent glances during her reminiscences. They are probably as perplexed as she was on hearing that Queen Yolande spoke to her of the king in this fashion. At times she feels that Isabelle seems to be listening even more closely than René; as if she is searching for something in particular she wants to know.

'Madame, Sire, I will never forget this instruction, one of her last: "Agnès, always be true to yourself and to the values you learned as a child from your Aunt Marie who sent you to the court of Lorraine, and during your time in attendance on Queen Isabelle; in this way, you will never take the wrong path like our king's mother, Queen Isabeau. She was an essentially good woman who turned into a harridan through a combination of disappointment, fear and a weak character."'

Agnès stops. René and Isabelle are silent, and she wonders if she has gone too far.

A knock at the door reminds them that a meal is being served and Agnès must leave them.

'Thank you, my dear,' says Isabelle. 'We will talk more soon. There will be time to hear your reminiscences during our journey home to Lorraine.'

The next day is spent with the myriad organizations involved in the departure of most of the guests and their servants, and it is not until the end of the day that Agnès receives a summons from Isabelle. When she arrives, Isabelle says with the warmest of smiles, 'Stay and sup with us, dear Agnès, and regale us with more of your stories. It relieves us greatly to hear how happy you made Queen Yolande during our absence.'

When the servants are gone, and they have done discussing the practicalities for their journey, René fills Agnès's goblet and signals for her to continue talking about his mother's conversations.

'I do admit, my lord, I was more than a little surprised at some of the things Queen Yolande told me,' she says almost in a whisper.

'What sort of things, my dear?' asks Isabelle as softly.

'Well' – a small sigh from Agnès – 'how she planned – no, contrived, yes, contrived and manoeuvred recalcitrant French nobles . . .' she pauses, 'to return to their duty. Their duty to support their rightful king, and not the English conqueror,' she adds almost forcefully.

'And do you know how she did that?' Isabelle asks guilelessly, not meeting her eyes.

'Well, yes,' and Agnès stumbles. 'She . . . she said the kingdom was so important that . . . that she had intelligent young women from Anjou . . . who had been recommended to her . . . brought to Angers to help her.'

'And how would these young women be able to help her?' asks Isabelle gently while examining the rings on her fingers. Agnès flushes but soon realises she must reply. She chooses her words carefully.

'I understand, Madame, Sire, that she taught them . . . with wise argument . . . how to persuade and influence those nobles who were leaning towards the side of the

English. Once she had placed them within the house-holds of these wavering dukes, she wanted them . . . to listen to the arguments of these young women and . . . and be gently persuaded to reconsider their position.' She is speaking more quickly now. 'Her goal was that such dukes and important nobles would swear alle-giance once again to their own lawful king – and not to the English usurper.'

An awkward pause follows, then Isabelle prompts in her sweetest tone, 'Dear girl, did she tell you what exactly was expected of these young women once they were accepted into the entourages of the noblemen in question? What their duties would be and how they were to succeed in their difficult task of persuasion?'

Agnès takes a deep breath. Queen Isabelle is pressing her hard, but answer she knows she must. 'Madame, I understand that they were fully persuaded by her that their only concern should be the good of their king and country.' Again she pauses, deeply embarrassed. 'To this end . . .' she continues slowly, 'they were to submit to any command or desire of their benefactors.' By now her face has become quite red and she turns to René, hesitating still, then says with an air of desperation, 'Sire, your lady mother assured me she would make herself financially responsible . . . for any children born to these fine young women from Anjou,' she whispers.

'She told you *that*?' René almost gasps with a wide-eyed look at his wife. Isabelle hushes him, putting her hand on his.

'Go on, dear child,' she says gently. 'This is important and most helpful to both us and your king.'

'My lord, my lady, in all honesty, I had a strong feeling that I too was being schooled in some way, but I am still not sure for what purpose. That she anticipated I would be of some kind of service to her was apparent to me within the first week of my stay in Saumur, but how, I still have no idea.' In her confusion, she knows she is talking too fast. 'The way she spoke to me of the tragic story of Jeanne d'Arc and her sacrifice had a powerful effect on me, but I was never under the impression that she planned for me to become a martyr and die for a cause.'

'No, no, my dear girl,' breaks in Isabelle firmly. 'Calm yourself, and do not be afraid. Queen Yolande would never have thought of such an extreme idea!'

Reassured, but slowly, Agnès continues. 'Each day, my admiration for her grew, and at the same time, all my instincts told me that she was preparing me for an important mission. I made a solemn vow in my heart that I would not fail her or the task I would be given, for I knew from the first day we met that I was in the presence of a great and noble lady whom it would be an honour to serve.'

She stumbles on, feeling their eyes fixed intently on her.

'Sire, throughout the time I remained with her at Saumur, I knew that your lady mother was living, waiting for news from Naples. Other ladies of her entourage told me she had sold her jewels, her gold dinner service, even some land – anything she could – to send funds to help you, but that in the end it was simply not enough, as you know . . .'

They have eaten, and as the three of them move to the fire, Agnès is invited to sit on a small stool; idly she caresses one of the pale grey levrettes lying about like cushions. Queen Yolande bred these lithe hunting dogs and sent them to Naples for her son, and they returned on the boat with Isabelle and her ladies.

Somehow Agnès senses René has still not heard from her what he wants to know: how his lady mother took the news of his defeat. As if reading her mind, he says, 'Go on, my child, tell us, no matter how much you think it might pain me to hear it.'

She inhales deeply and begins.

'It was at Christmas when we received the news King Alfonso had laid siege to the great fortress of Naples itself, although the walled city had held out courageously for the past seven months.'

René's sigh comes from his innermost being.

'We heard that you, Sire, had fought inside the city with the defenders until the very end.' He nods, but she can see he is struggling to compose himself. Still, he waves her on. 'We were informed that your own captains had forced you to leave the city so that you would not be captured and held to ransom. This news came to us through a courier of Jacques Coeur, sent ahead by the captain of one of his ships.'

'It is true,' whispers René, almost inaudibly. Again he waves his hand to make her continue with her story.

'We were told that two of your captains brought you to a secret tunnel that descended from the battlements inside the city's walls and which you slid down. When you reached the bottom, you were taken by rowing boat to a ship sent by Jacques Coeur. Please forgive me if I am wrong in any of these details.' She looks at René anxiously, but he nods, his eyes full of tears as he remembers.

'When Queen Yolande heard that to punish the people for resisting him, Alfonso d'Aragon, her own kinsman, had coldly ordered the city to be sacked, she cried out: "That must have broken my dear son's heart." She knew of the depth of the attachment and rapport you had with your citizens and soldiers who, we of your household knew, adored you to a man.' By now her own tears have welled up at the memory of that day when she and the Old Queen sat weeping in one another's arms, and she cannot continue.

René turns away to prevent his beloved wife and Agnès from seeing his distress.

'What did you all do then?' he asks, half choking, but Isabelle answers for her *demoiselle*.

'I wrote to Saumur that I was on my way south to Marseilles, to wait there in the hope that you, my darling husband, would soon arrive.'

Agnès smiles at Isabelle in gratitude for the respite.

'I will never forget Queen Yolande's sorrowful words to me, when she heard of your escape: "When he left for Naples, I knew in my heart that the outcome would be just as his brother's and his father's before him, the same for them all. That kingdom is a poisoned chalice, and it has ruined the House of Anjou. It was my duty to give the three of them my full support, and I have done that. Now there is nothing left." At that, I wanted to embrace her, to comfort her . . . but forgive me, I did not dare to presume.'

Agnès sees her mistress bite her bottom lip to stop herself from weeping, but she must go on to the end of the story – they want to hear it all, and she must tell them.

'Finally, in July, Queen Yolande had word from you, Madame, from Marseilles, that your dear husband had landed safely, though quite defeated in spirit as well as in fact. My Lady Isabelle, I saw the effect of your letter telling the Old Queen that you were obliged to hasten back to Nancy, and that her beloved son had neither the heart nor the energy to begin his journey to Anjou to be by her side at once. I was aware each day of your lady mother's longing for your arrival, Sire, but I could see as well that she understood yours was a sensible plan for the future survival of your House.'

After a pause, René answers the question in the minds of both his wife and her *demoiselle*.

'She was right – how well she knew me. I was physically drained, but also too ashamed to face the one person who had never failed me, who had supported five major expeditions for my father, my brother and myself; who had ruined herself and her descendants so that her husband and sons might conquer and rule that mirage of a kingdom we craved as our right. We all knew that my mother used her abilities to the maximum in our interests – her energy, her intelligence, her powers of persuasion, even her subtle threats – and spent all her revenues to finance our foolish dream. Now it is over.'

Isabelle takes his hand and brings the palm to her lips in sympathy.

'There is nothing left of my father's fabulous fortune. All used: for France's Charles VII, for my brother Louis, and for me. That is the true reason why I hesitated to leave the south. I remember thinking, "Here I am, why not examine my territory of Provence before flinging myself at the feet of my beloved mother and begging her forgiveness?"' And René hangs his head, his great body shaking with sobs.

'Sire, please calm yourself,' Agnès dares to whisper. 'Everyone in your lady mother's household was aware of her relief when she heard you had landed in Marseilles.' But he holds his arms across his chest, hands on elbows, rocking from side to side, eyes shut tight, his mouth a grimace of pain.

Slowly, with difficulty, it is Isabelle who takes up the story.

'You should know I blame myself for Queen Yolande's lonely end. I thought that with René on his way to be with her, you could return to help me prepare for his arrival in Nancy. How wrong I was. That was exactly the time she needed you the most. How I regret that decision. My dear, were you alarmed at my summons?'

'Madame, I admit I was torn in two – I longed to be back at your court with my friends in Lorraine again, but at the same time, I had become devoted to my astonishing patroness. Somehow I knew that once I left Saumur, I would not see her again. But her treasured son was on his way, so it was right to leave her to be with him.'

'How did you tell her?' asks her disconsolate lord.

'We had supped, just the two of us, and were sitting by the lit fire; despite the summer season, the evening had turned chill. I was holding my needlework and let it fall in my lap. Queen Yolande looked up, and I said: "Madame, now that King René is safely back in Provence and on his way to you, Queen Isabelle has asked if I might return to her service in Lorraine."

'Before I could say any more, she stopped me with a gesture and reached out to hold my hand. "I know, I know, and since he is on his way, it is right that you return to Nancy. I believe I have taught you all I can to see you safely on the path I believe your life will take. I am old and can foretell from my experience of the world what that path will be. You will do well, of that I am sure, because I can read deep into your mind and your heart. I ask you only to remember what I have said to you often: always follow that heart of yours, because it is pure and true and will never deceive you." Then she removed from her little finger this small ruby ring I am wearing and slipped it on mine, saying it had been good to her and would protect me also. She kissed my temple, lightly stroked my cheek, and with that special, slightly crooked smile, rose and left me.

'Sire and Madame, that is really the full story of my time by the side of this remarkable lady, your mother. At the end of September, after almost a year in her service, and with great reluctance, I left for Lorraine.'

Chapter Four

On her long and solitary journey back to Nancy, with only her guards for company, Agnès distracted herself by reflecting on her arrival into the service of the Duchess Isabelle from her home in Touraine in the Loire district. Isabelle was kind and warmed to her at once, but the rest of the young entourage never failed to remind her that since she was less well born than they, and as the youngest, she was of the least consequence among them and must keep her place.

Despite these handicaps, which she stoically accepted, her mistress would often single her out. When Agnès was not reading to her or playing the harp, Isabelle would caress her youngest maid's long golden curls and play at arranging her hair – even dress her in her own fine clothes as if she was a doll! Agnès was as tall as Isabelle, and being fair and slender, the same dresses and colours suited them both. Nor did Isabelle ever tire of teaching Agnès how to arrange her own hair. 'You have good hands, dear child, I like their touch – gentle but firm,' everything said with that kindest of smiles.

The *demoiselles* of Lorraine were taught by their duchess to be as gracious in their movements as she was; to lower their voices and their eyes when spoken to by a gentleman. 'It is most important,' she said, 'never to appear forward or indelicate in your speech or dress,' and yet at the same time, she would tell them how pretty they were. 'In my service as my maids of honour, you will all learn how to become great ladies, and I shall see you make dazzling unions – if I find you worthy!' How innocent were those early days at Nancy!

In 1431, their peaceful life at the court of Lorraine changed dramatically. It had always been known that the old duke's joint heirs would be his daughter, Lady Isabelle, and her husband, Lord René. When the duke died the previous year, his last testament was challenged by a male cousin. On the advice of Queen Yolande, Lord René fought the challenger, but was captured in a skirmish and handed over to another cousin, Duke Philip of Burgundy, who imprisoned him in the tower of his château near Dijon.

Not long afterwards, René's older brother, Louis III, died in Naples, and left René as his heir; still Philip of Burgundy refused Yolande's pleas to allow her to ransom her son. But due to her persistence, at last King Charles VII settled the disputed dukedom of Lorraine on Isabelle and René.

While her husband languished in Burgundy's tower prison, the ambassadors came from Naples and crowned

Isabelle Queen of Sicily in René's place. Determined to hold the kingdom for him until he could join her, Isabelle prepared carefully, choosing the most suitable of her young court for the journey to their new capital of Naples. When Agnès heard her own name read out, it seemed the most exciting moment of her life.

The court at Nancy was thrown into turmoil as the packing began – what to take, what to leave. Isabelle had to bid farewell to her beloved songbirds, always in her rooms in their huge cages and accompanying her on her travels within France. But she *would* take almost all her dogs – except the older ones – and her pet cheetah, Vitesse, a gift from the merchant of Bourges, Jacques Coeur. Among the court's young ladies, Agnès was the one least afraid of Vitesse, and the cheetah returned her affection. At two years old, the animal no longer had retracting claws and could not escape capture by climbing the trees in the park as she had as a cub, but if her claws no longer dug in, her teeth were sharp enough! Some of the girls had experienced little nips – more out of affection than aggression – and most of them kept a respectful distance. But Agnès and Vitesse could often be found curled up on cushions together by the fire. It pleased Isabelle that she could leave her *demoiselle* alone with the cheetah and not worry that the big cat would be teased or pushed about with long poles, as she had seen some of the servants do, and scolded them for it. 'Agnès' she said one day in front of the gathered staff, 'I want you to report to me anyone who you find mistreating Vitesse!' Thereafter, both the girl and the cheetah were left to enjoy one another. When they rode out in the countryside or with the hunt,

Vitesse would run alongside Agnès's mount, and soon the horses and even the hounds had become accustomed to her presence.

Early in 1435, Queen Isabelle of Sicily's huge baggage train set out from Nancy for the mighty fortress of Chinon in the Loire region, where King Charles VII had moved his court from Bourges. She needed his written and verbal approval for her mission, and the blessing of her mother-in-law, Queen Yolande, resident there with the court, before setting sail to represent her husband in his Italian kingdom. Isabelle was borne on a litter, with several of her ladies either riding or being carried alongside. Her *demoiselles*, many giggling with excitement, were on horseback; a solid guard of soldiers accompanied them in case of brigands on the road, and quite a number of courtiers. The servants followed with the baggage train. On the way, there was much merry banter. Although the *demoiselles* were not permitted any gallantries, flirtatious exchanges or glances with the young courtiers, that did not deter some of the older ones, while the thrill of the untold adventures that lay ahead made most of the younger ones quite as skittish as horses in fresh snow before a hunt.

After ten days' slow travel, they arrived at the great fortress complex of Chinon, its imposing stone towers rising from the river Vienne and great walls snaking around the headland as far as the eye could see. Once inside, the *demoiselles* were herded up to their rooms to wash and rest before descending to the audience room, where their lady, now officially styled Queen Isabelle of Sicily, was to be presented to the king, the queen and the court.

They were instructed by the Mistress-of-the-Maids to dress soberly: 'This is not a festive occasion; your lady requires His Majesty's blessing and that of the Old Queen of Sicily as well. You are to appear unassuming and keep your eyes lowered at all times.'

'Sounds more like a funeral,' said one of the *demoiselles*, which almost earned her a clip over the ear, while the rest hid their smirking faces.

They entered the Great Hall two by two behind Queen Isabelle; as usual, Agnès walking at the end of the line. They had been told to avoid the stares of the courtiers – 'They will only look at you in order to make you blush and disgrace yourselves' – and most of all, 'Do not catch the eye of the king.' In pairs, they curtseyed low before Queen Yolande, still a remarkably beautiful, proud lady sitting tall and straight on a throne to the left of the king, one step lower, and then to King Charles and Queen Marie. They then backed away to one side while making three further deep curtseys as they had been taught. 'I pray I do not trip over my train,' confided Agnès to one of the other young girls, both quite in awe of the occasion.

But something had happened. To judge from the many looks that were being directed towards Agnès by the courtiers, she was being talked about in hushed tones. Although she was still waiting to make her *révérence* before the monarchs, she became aware that she was being singled out in some way. Was it her dress? Her décolletage? Her hair or headdress? Then, as people fell back, she saw that the king was walking in her direction. She glanced to right and left, but no, he was coming towards *her*! Her heart beat so fast she thought it would jump right out of her tight bodice as she curtseyed very low. Then she felt his hand on her elbow, gently raising her up. Afterwards she thought she might well have remained there had he not!

'I welcome you to my court here, *demoiselle* Agnès, as I understand you are the youngest of your queen's ladies to travel with her to Naples.'

She stuttered some acknowledgement, but as she lifted her head, she could feel her fear melting at the sight of kind eyes looking into hers, and a sweet smile. She cannot now remember what else the king said – still too astonished that he had even noticed her – but she remembers the pleasantness of his expression, and that smile.

As soon as they were able, the *demoiselles* blended into the crowded court and ran up the stairs to their rooms, chattering excitedly.

'At last it's over; and did not our Queen Isabelle look and move with the grace of long practice?' said one girl.

'Her *révérences* to all three of the monarchs was so much lower and slower than any of ours,' said another. 'But why did she have to make a *révérence* to the Old Queen of Sicily as she is herself Queen of Sicily now?'

'Why does everyone feel sorry for you just because you are so young and they imagine you need encouragement?' and the gossip continued until, exhausted, the girls fell asleep.

The next day, they left Chinon for Marseilles, travelling by river where possible. In the boat or by road, Queen Isabelle often chose Agnès to be by her; she complained of headaches from travelling and wanted the girl to gently rub her temples. When they stopped under a tree for refreshments, she would ask Agnés to read to her, saying her voice soothed her.

In Marseilles, Queen Isabelle had many dignitaries to meet. There were merchants to see and other people of business; discussions to be held with her captains, representatives of the city and others from throughout her husband's newly inherited sovereign territory of Provence. Although her young ladies were there to attend to her, they were to keep to their rooms in her palace, packing and repacking all the extra purchases made daily by the queen and her courtiers, and desperately trying to stifle their excitement.

Chapter Five

It was not until 18 October 1435 that the new young Queen of Sicily, accompanied by her considerable entourage, animals, furniture, paintings, tapestries and courtly fittings, left Marseilles bound for Naples by way of Genoa. They sailed on ships sent by Jacques Coeur, and were accompanied by several of his galleons for their safety.

Standing on the deck of that great creaking vessel was the most exciting experience to date in the young life of Agnès Sorel: holding on to remain steady, bracing herself against the pitching, judging the waves. She would gaze up at the tall sails strained full, the wind in her face bringing tears to her eyes. She saw dolphins that seemed intent on racing the ship, and others that rode on the bow wave, their fixed smiles and eyes looking into hers. She could not imagine what Naples would be like, no matter how many questions she had asked, but she felt a deep sense of well-being and exhilaration.

When he had become the Duke of Burgundy's prisoner, Lord René had sent papers appointing Queen Isabelle the regent of his new kingdom, and she carried his seal. Although hers was a relatively small court, nevertheless quite a large number set out on this adventure. The new queen understood the importance of making a lasting first impression in her husband's kingdom.

Agnès was still overwhelmed by the honour of being asked to accompany her mistress, and had written to her much-loved Aunt Marie of her good fortune and this unforeseen change in her life. Her aunt wrote by return, counselling her: 'Dearest child, your future lies in your own hands. Be wise and do not allow your natural gaiety to exceed your position. To accompany your mistress is an enormous opportunity, and that you have been chosen is a sign of your good behaviour to date. Remain your modest self, say your prayers and obey your superiors. You know I wish you well, dearest child, and may God protect you in this strange land.' How dull she made her future sound, thought Agnès, but she kept this to herself and lived in her dreams of adventure.

Entering the bay of Naples was a breathtaking experience, and the courtiers and ladies were filled with awe at the sight. Agnès was as wide-eyed as the other *demoiselles*, astonished at the countless small craft sailing and rowing out to greet their new king's galleon, shouting welcoming messages and throwing flowers before their ship as it was towed to its moorings. Many hands lifted them down, then carried out belongings and placed them in a long line of buggies drawn by strong mules. The new arrivals were immediately surrounded by innumerable brown faces, gleaming teeth in broad smiles, happy laughter and the overwhelming euphoria of being welcome.

The climb to the great white turreted castle was thrilling: the bay on one side; the port active with trading vessels; whitewashed houses with pergolas of grapevines; children running everywhere, dogs barking, coloured birds flying and chirping. At last they arrived and were greeted by a large gathering of dignitaries, who fussed over them and replied to their hesitant questions posed in their newly acquired Italian. It did not take long before they were settled in. The young ladies were enchanted with their quarters: large shuttered windows overlooking the bay, a constant breeze lifting their spirits and cooling them from the unaccustomed heat.

'Agnès, Agnès, come and see the room I have been given – oh, but yours is equally as nice!' called Marie de Belleville, her best friend among the *demoiselles*, as she found Agnès leaning out from her balcony over the bay. 'And we each have our own terrace where we can sit and read or entertain one another in private,' she added excitedly. 'I think we shall be very happy here,' and with that, Marie took both her friend's hands and twirled her around until they fell laughing on to her bed.

Yes, reflected Agnès as she rode at a gentle pace from Saumur home to Lorraine, how good was their beginning in Naples.

During the heat of the summer months, life at the court of Naples was languid. The *demoiselles*, dressed in light cotton or muslin shifts, found shade under the many trees in the large terraced palace gardens, lazily picking grapes – if they could reach them from where they lounged

– while fanning one another in turn. To keep their arms white, their sleeves were long and wide. On outings into the countryside or to the sea, the girls wore large-brimmed hats of finely woven straw. Several of them cut out the crowns, pulling up their hair to lie on top of the wide brims to bleach it blonder in the sun, taking care not to tan their faces underneath. Luckily Agnès's hair was blonde enough and she had no need to suffer sitting like that. While the others remained in the sun fanning themselves under their hats – vanity winning over discomfort – she would lean motionless, dreamily, against the trunk of a tree, shaded by its many leaves, and watch the thin white plume of smoke curling, as lazy as the girls themselves, from the peak of Vesuvius.

Naples and the surrounding countryside seemed to be permanently in flower, even during the winter months, and the young ladies would sit painting in watercolours the blaze of creepers hanging over the castle walls. Many of Queen Isabelle's dogs had come with them, and soon news of her love of songbirds spread, and brightly coloured birds that chirped and sang merrily were sent to the palace in beautiful cages by well-wishers. The young cheetah, Vitesse, sitting motionless beside her mistress during audiences, was a source of amazement to the local people, the *demoiselles* giggling whenever they caught sight of a visitor's rolling eyes should the animal stretch or yawn and show her beautiful sharp teeth!

At court in Lorraine there was never a day without music, and Isabelle continued this tradition in Naples. The queen's minstrels played in the Great Hall of the royal palace, while local mummers and entertainers demonstrated their tricks with hoops and balls to amuse the courtiers. Dressmakers called almost daily, and the lengths of cloth they showed the young ladies were more beautiful than any they had seen in France. Almost all Isabelle's fine dress lengths arrived from the various Italian states; sometimes from the coffers of Jacques Coeur, or those of other merchants who arrived in Naples from the Levant or the Near East en route to Marseilles.

At times during the summer, the intense heat in the middle of the day and afternoon caused the *demoiselles* to remain indoors wearing only thin cotton slips sprayed with rose-scented water drawn chilled from a deep well in the garden, their windows shuttered against the sun. Daily lessons and religious instruction continued no matter how hot the season; they learned new card games, enjoyed drawing classes, wrote letters home. Each of them played a musical instrument, and in their own little theatre they performed short plays and concerts for Lady Isabelle and her guests.

One of the most popular of their visitors was the merchant Jacques Coeur, on whose ships they had sailed to Naples. When he heard from several of his sea captains who stopped there regularly of the welcome they received at the court, he dared to visit himself. Queen Isabelle received him most generously, recalling his various dealings with her mother-in-law, Queen Yolande. He proclaimed the court enchanting, full of charm and sophistication. All it lacked was the presence of its king.

Thereafter, the merchant would stop at Naples whenever he passed on his way to his trading sources. Queen Isabelle always received him graciously, and soon he became a familiar figure, as if a trusted friend of long standing which she knew he was of Queen Yolande's. Isabelle would invite him to recount stories of his travels and adventures to the gathered company, including her *demoiselles*.

How well Agnès recalled his every visit, and his warm smile whenever he saw her, always accompanied by Vitesse. He never spoke with her, only nodded and smiled, and Queen Isabelle told her how happy he was that his cheetah looked well and content. At his approach, Vitesse knew him at once and, as he smiled and stroked her, she purred as loudly as if Vesuvius was planning a small eruption!

The kingdom of Naples covered the lower half of the Italian peninsula, and although Queen Isabelle was taken to inspect her towns and citadels, her vineyards, orchards and arable land, her *demoiselles* usually remained behind with the children. Young, unmarried ladies in Naples were not encouraged to show their innocent faces outside their houses!

One thing they did manage, however, was to persuade their mistress it would do them all good to ride out into the countryside for fresh air and exercise. The kingdom was rich in land beyond the capital, and riding hacks were brought to meet their carriages once they left the outskirts of the city. There they would mount and gallop across the fields of long grass and wild flowers, always accompanied by the queen's personal guards. How they loved those lengthy rides when the heat of summer had subsided and the year slipped with slow elegance into autumn.

Such excursions were one of the highlights of their year

– and what magnificent horses they encountered there! Living with her Aunt Marie, Agnès had ridden since her earliest years; on horseback she knew no fear. Around Naples they visited stud farms stocked with superb high-stepping Arabian and Spanish breeds, and Agnès begged to be allowed to try them. Isabelle, an accomplished horsewoman herself, would often ride out on the more spirited animals with just Agnès to accompany her, her guards hardly able to keep up. 'How is it you ride so well?' she asked Agnès one day. 'You have such good hands, quite still, giving when needed, though firm. I notice your mounts obey you without showing stress of any kind.' Agnès told the queen of her childhood, and how her aunt's horses had been her real friends, much more so than her cousins.

Although she knew and kept her place, Agnès could not help becoming aware of the attention Queen Isabelle showed her, and her growing affection for her *demoiselle*. As for Agnès, she unashamedly adored her royal mistress, learning from her and her tutors as much as she could during the time spent without King René.

Then one day, they heard the servants shouting as they ran up the slope to the castle 'He's here! He's here!' At last King René had arrived in his kingdom. The court had known for the past week that he was on his way, and the preparations to welcome him had been hectic. More than three years had passed, and now the day for which they had prayed and waited patiently had come, filling them with joy – for their queen, for her friends and entourage, and for themselves. Queen Isabelle had her scouts looking out along the coast for his distinctive sails – white with the huge red cross of Lorraine stretching from top to bottom and side to side. He had written promising she would receive news of his approach down the coast from Genoa. Fast couriers had spotted his sails a week ago, and the court had been in a whirl ever since.

King René sailed into port on a great galleon accompanied by smaller vessels, all supplied by Jacques Coeur. As he was rowed ashore, surrounded by small boats full of local people shouting greetings and blessings and tossing flowers into his path, Isabelle was at the harbour to meet him. News of their tender greeting – he on one knee kissing her hand, before taking her in his arms – reached the palace even before they did.

No one was surprised to learn it had been his remarkable mother Yolande, the Old Queen of Sicily, who had finally managed to raise the enormous ransom demanded by the Duke of Burgundy for her son's release. At the time of René's capture, Agnès had not known much about the ongoing enmity between the royal houses of Anjou and Burgundy, and had assumed it was jealousy that prevented Duke Philip from granting René his freedom to enjoy his inheritance. In fact, the duke had wanted the Anjous to suffer for their rejection of his little sister Catherine as a bride for their eldest son, Louis III, and poor René had taken the blame. It had all happened long ago, but the scandal of this terrible slight for a crime committed by the little girl's father forced the Anjous to cancel the marriage. The resulting shame perpetrated by one royal cousin upon another, had never been forgotten by Catherine's quietly vengeful brother.

Finally, after two years of hard bargaining, it had been

settled. As well as the ransom – a small mountain of gold – René had had to promise his daughter Yolande in marriage to the son of Isabelle's cousin, Lord Vaudémont, his captor and the claimant to their throne of Lorraine. As part of his daughter's dowry, René had been forced to include a good part of his duchy as well. Vaudémont had won after all – if not the whole of Lorraine for himself – at least part of it for his heirs.

When the royal couple arrived at the castle gate, the *demoiselles* were waiting on either side in line, deep in their curtseys, their wide smiles matching René's own. To cheers and cries of 'Welcome to your home in Naples, Sire!' Isabelle led her husband through their ranks and into his own palace for the first time. During his long years in Burgundy's tower, René had learned to speak Italian and delighted in greeting his subjects and staff as he made his entrance. On that wonderful day, there were tears of joy in everyone's eyes. As she continued on her slow ride towards Nancy, Agnès found herself smiling at the memory.

King René was the epitome of a charming chevalier – he could be a troubadour, a story-teller, the best jouster in a tournament, a painter; he could dance and he could sing. In fact, he could do just about anything expected of a grand gentleman. He was also a brilliant mimic, imitating anyone's walk or way of talking – not in a mocking way, just to entertain. And his laugh! He could make the very walls shake. His adoration of his wife was utterly transparent, and Agnès prayed to her personal saint Mary Magdalene to be so loved one day. The joy they had in one another's company enriched the whole court.

His first days were spent with his wife touring his

territories and familiarizing himself with his kingdom. After a week they returned, and René set himself to finding out about the lives of the people of his lands. Visitors streamed into the palace to report on trade in the harbour, the harvests, livestock, timber for building ships, the steel works, and most important of all, the defences of the kingdom. But these serious matters did not distract him from enjoying being in his longed-for paradise at last. He joined the court on their rides, learned the local customs and songs, and met and entertained the many fascinating travellers who came to Naples.

Chapter Six

The court of Naples was a renowned delight but its king and queen were poor by comparison to the way in which they had lived at Nancy. René's captivity and the cost of his ransom had dramatically reduced the Angevin resources. And yet, during the next three years, King René and Queen Isabelle continued to receive their guests with their customary elegance and entertain them royally, gleaning information about the rest of the world, and especially eager to hear the news from France. But this period of perfect contentment and happiness in the most glorious part of the Mediterranean was too good to last.

King René's resources had been reduced to such a degree that his enemy Alfonso d'Aragon, his own cousin, supported by the untold wealth of Philip of Burgundy, was again making plans to advance further into René's kingdom.

Some years earlier, this Aragon cousin of Queen Yolande's

had been adopted by Queen Giovanna II of Naples as her heir. But he had disappointed her – even imprisoned her – and she changed her loyalty and her testament back to the Anjous, making Yolande's eldest son, her cousin Louis III d'Anjou, her successor instead. When Louis died suddenly and childless, Giovanna named his younger brother René as her heir. In his fury at being disinherited, Alfonso installed himself on the island of Sicily. His skirmishes on to the mainland continued and increased unabated until it seemed he was constantly at war with Naples.

The court of Lorraine had passed six joyous years in Naples when one spring day in 1441, King René called his household and his captains together. Standing several steps above them in the palace courtyard below, his dejected face spoke greater volumes even than his words.

'My dear friends – for I consider all here who have served us as our friends, whether from Lorraine, Anjou or from my citizens of Naples. As you know, our enemy Alfonso d'Aragon has been harassing our territory for some time. We – you – have resisted with courage and fortitude, but the situation has become desperate. I have used all the funds available to me – and more – to maintain my large army here to protect my kingdom from invasion. I cannot continue – there is nothing left. Nor can I risk putting any of you into more danger.

'It is with great sadness that Queen Isabelle and I realize we must accept the inevitable. I must send my wife, my children, my queen's ladies and any non-fighting personnel back to France while it is still safe to do so.'

Everyone stood stunned and silent. What could they

say? Some of the *demoiselles* began to cry, and Agnès too felt tears rolling down her cheeks.

René continued. 'I will remain here within the city walls of Naples and fight Alfonso for you and my kingdom to the bitter end, but I do not hold out much hope. My mother, the Old Queen, can no longer help me, nor can the King of France. We are on our own now and must do what we can.'

No one there was in any doubt. It was the end of René's dream, of Isabelle's, and the dream of their court as well. To leave this corner of paradise broke the hearts of all the French; life had been uncomplicated here, the courts of France, Burgundy, Anjou and their intrigues left far behind. News reached them from visitors, usually at third or fourth hand, and did not affect them much; the languor of the south had become embedded in their attitudes.

Riding towards Nancy, Agnes remembers the happiness of their life in Naples, their rides; learning the local customs and songs; their adventures climbing Vesuvius; meeting and entertaining many fascinating travellers. Oh, how perfect it all was! During the following days, with deep sadness, they began to gather their belongings. Arrangements were made for their mules, goats, sheep and other of the farm animals they had domesticated to remain. Their favourite horses, dogs and birds in cages, together with the cheetah Vitesse – less speedy now with age – were stowed carefully on the boats sent for them by the ever-dependable Jacques Coeur. A week later, and after taking tearful leave of their local friends and servants; a long look at their favourite sights of the bay, especially Vesuvius, the rooms of the palace and the gardens with their fountains and ornamental waterfalls, all those who had come from the courts of Lorraine and Anjou bade Naples and its loyal people a mournful farewell.

Finally, the ladies of the court, the children, the animals, and the non-fighting staff embarked on their sad voyage back to France, regretting their loss and grateful to leave the battle from which they were fortunate enough to have escaped. From among this merry band of friends almost no one talked or laughed any longer, everyone lost in prayer and memories as well as fear for those still fighting with René in Naples' fortress.

Six euphoric years had been spent in the paradise that was King René's and Queen Isabelle's court; but to universal sadness, the fairy-tale had come to an end. René knew he was losing the contest for his throne and, although loyally determined to make a last stand in the old city, he did not hesitate to send the others home.

The journey back to Marseilles was uneventful, the winds fair and the seas calm. Hardly a word was exchanged by the unhappy passengers throughout the voyage, their thoughts locked on to the friends and the life they had left behind. Some of Queen Isabelle's ladies and servants had husbands who had chosen to remain and fight to the end with René. How would they fare in the final battle? Would any of them return? Even the smiling-faced dolphins riding the bow wave of the ship could not lift their spirits on that unfortunate passage back to France.

Nor was there any news on their arrival in Marseilles as to the outcome of events in Naples. Queen Isabelle made her official greetings to the councillors of their port as brief as possible, and her party set out almost at once for Arles, the old capital of Provence, the new sovereign territory of King René. Despite the welcoming aromas of rosemary and lavender wafting from the many fields, of flowers and of sweet-smelling fruits, the travellers focused on their impending expedition across France to Anjou. After Arles, and a stop for important business at her city of Aix, Isabelle and her entourage began their long journey north to Saumur in Anjou. They went where possible by river, their purpose to call, with a heavy heart, on René's mother, Yolande, the Old Queen of Sicily. They travelled as if in a trance, an ongoing nightmare, their thoughts focused on Naples, on the fighting, on concern for their loved ones, for the dying, and, most of all, for their beloved King René.

It was some weeks before they saw at last the white turrets of Saumur. Waiting to receive the travellers was a beautiful girl of about twelve or thirteen years, who rushed to embrace Queen Isabelle before she had a chance to dismount. It was her daughter Marguerite, about whom she had talked endlessly to the *demoiselles*, read out to them her letters, but not seen these past six years. Too young for the journey, she had been left behind with her grandmother Queen Yolande, whom they had met briefly before their departure and whose redoubtable reputation they all knew. The Old Queen's welcome to Isabelle, her beloved daughter-in-law, was warm and all-embracing, and her famous smile included everyone.

'Welcome to Saumur, welcome home, welcome back to France,' she announced. 'Wash, eat, rest; tomorrow we will talk about everything that has happened in the years since we last met, and then we can discuss the future.'

Queen Isabelle curtseyed to her mother-in-law, and the

travellers were immediately struck by their mutual love and respect; most of all by their joint anxiety about King René. Then Isabelle and her daughter Marguerite, hand in hand, disappeared into their chambers and were not seen again until the next morning.

It was on that day when the sad exiles from the court of Naples arrived at Saumur, that a new chapter opened in the life of Agnès Sorel. Then began the fulfilling of the future that the Old Queen of Sicily had planned with such care. For the rest of her days, Agnès was never in any doubt how fortunate she was to have had the chance to remain with that great lady and learn all she had to teach her.

Chapter Seven

*A*gnès has been called to her mistress to tell her and René more of her reminiscences: 'Madame, my Lady Isabelle, as you know, I arrived back in Lorraine at your court at Nancy with mixed feelings. After spending a year by her side, I left the Old Queen with a heavy heart, and considerable confusion still as to my mission.

'As I unpacked in my old rooms pondering on this, I heard a courier arrive from Saumur, and rushed downstairs. "Bitter news, my lady," I heard him address you. "It is Queen Yolande, King René's esteemed royal mother. She is gone, Madame, died peacefully in her sleep." The great and fabled queen was dead! I slumped to my knees and prayed for her soul – and for all of ours.

'"And was my lord with her?" I heard you ask the courier, your voice trembling. "Madame, no," he replied. "It seems Queen Yolande had none of her family around her." My lady, I saw you cover your mouth with your hand as you withdrew hastily, and without a word, to your private suite, firmly closing the door behind you. There you remained alone for several days. A deep sadness descended on the court, and we too retired to our chambers.'

Agnès sees Isabelle and René take one another's hands as she ends her story, but there is one thing more she feels she must say to them.

'My lady, I was sincerely grateful you asked me to accompany you here to Angers to Queen Yolande's funeral. I know that my duty is to attend to *your* needs, and that the Old Queen has her children, family and friends to mourn her. But towards the end of her life, it was I who spent each day and evening in her company, and I feel something of her belongs to me too. Without a word, you understood that, and allowed me to come here to pay my own last respects to this great queen. I have kept to myself, taking care of your guests and the children, and believe me, I have not wished to intrude on your family's grief, but I want to thank you with all my heart for such kindness.'

Agnès can see that both her lord and lady are close to tears; with a sigh, Isabelle pats her hand and nods for her to continue.

'Sire, Madame, my memory of the Old Queen of Sicily is very recent, and I did not know her long; but please be assured that I mourn her passing deeply and sincerely. During my slow journey back to Nancy from Saumur, I wrote down whatever I remembered of our many conversations, as well as her inestimable advice, her tutoring of me; notes to add to those I had written every evening before bed while in her service in Anjou. In my sorrow during those first days back at Nancy following the news of her death, I reread my pages, and in my head I can still hear her beautiful voice speaking her last words to me as we parted: "My dear Agnès, never forget your duty to your king and country. That has been the guiding pattern of my life, and I trust it will also be yours."'

Agnès can see they are both tenderly moved by her recollections. With a silent embrace, and a cross made on her forehead by Isabelle, they leave her to go and greet René's brother, Charles of Maine, and his sister, Queen Marie of France.

The time has come to read the Old Queen's testament, and Agnès has been asked to stay and attend her mistress. The whole Anjou family has gathered in the Great Hall, as well as the many serving people and factors from the land surrounding Angers. There is a general sense that someone remarkable has been lost, and without Queen Yolande's presence the atmosphere is as if drained of life's vital essence. Agnès can see it in every face.

In her testament, Yolande declared her estate to be impoverished, having spent her fortune willingly in the service of the kings of France and Sicily. The faces of her remaining children show how much her death has affected them. She had dominated their lives, their decisions. The great queen's final testament is typical of her organized character: dividing her estate logically and fairly between her children and grandchildren.

Some days later, it is time for Lady Isabelle's suite to return to Nancy. It does not surprise her beautiful *demoiselle* Agnès Sorel that their cavalcade sets out with a marked slowness of step, as if even the horses are in mourning.

At Nancy, René and his court hear how sincerely and publicly Charles VII mourns his *bonne mère*, Queen Yolande. Some months later, the king pays a visit to the court of Lorraine and, in the presence of René and his brother Charles, announces that in recognition of the services to the country of 'the late Queen of Sicily', and in her honour, he has bestowed on her youngest son, his own court favourite Charles of Maine, some fine estates because 'he is Queen Yolande's second son with no prospects'. In the deed of gift, the king makes it known that 'this great lady' meant everything to him: supporting him in his early youth; always prepared to help him in any way, emotionally and financially; guiding him with her wisdom; offering him the security of her households; giving him moral support and advice. Everything she possessed was at all times put at his disposal; for this and more – namely, her love of him – he wishes to show his gratitude in this way.

That Charles VII has journeyed to the capital of the sovereign duchy of Lorraine in person to make such a sincere and public declaration of his devotion to his late mother-in-law greatly moves René. The King of France, Agnès thinks to herself, truly cared for Queen Yolande, and although she does not meet him on this visit, she studies him from the body of the court. Despite the many negative stories she has heard tell of his fecklessness and dissipation, she too is impressed by the sincerity she sees in his face while he makes his speech.

*

Agnès knows from experience that sadness never lingers around Lord René for any length of time. By February 1443, he is beginning to make plans and form ideas for the future. He lets his court know that his long absence abroad and his mother's death have brought him yet more titles and honours, but no increase in his revenues. Conquest, he declares, is no longer an option for him. Together with his brother Charles, also living at Nancy and dependent on him, he announces his decision to join the royal court of France. This, the brothers believe, is their only chance of preferment, and of finding opportunities to increase their income.

Isabelle calls for her *demoiselles* to assemble. When she can see they are all present, she announces with the air of someone about to say something exciting: 'Well, my dears, I have some news that will please you. I want you to pack and gather all your train; you are to set forth with us to meet with the court of France at Toulouse.' A spontaneous burst of applause and happy gasps meet her statement, and there is much chattering once she leaves them.

At last it is happening, just as Queen Yolande said, thinks Agnès as she runs to find Marie de Belleville. 'Marie? There you are! Please tell me exactly what this means.'

'Agnès, sweet one, it means a huge amount of preparation for everyone, the ladies of the court as well as for us *demoiselles*. The many maids, outriders, pages, grooms and more will all travel together with the court and be escorted by a large number of knights and soldiers from Lorraine.'

'And will the animals come along as well?'

'Oh yes, the hunting dogs, lap dogs, your tame old

cheetah – she hardly needs a lead any longer, does she? – and a number of birds in cages; you know how much Lady Isabelle adores her songbirds, and the talking parrots never cease to amuse Lord René.'

For so many travellers on horseback and on litters, there is an even longer baggage train of carts and carriages. For entertainment there are minstrels, court musicians, jugglers, and Isabelle's enchanting dwarves with their wicked sense of humour – what an amazing procession they make. Including overnight stops, their journey to Toulouse takes eighteen days, each one full of friendly chatter, laughter and anticipation.

When they finally arrive, the *demoiselles* in Lady Isabelle's suite are given lodgings on the west side of the city, in a series of rooms high up in one of the eight towers of the Château de Narbonnais.

'Marie, come quickly and look,' calls Agnès to her friend. The two girls lean out of her open window, made up of many small squares of glass framed in lead. 'See the river – it must be the Garonne – how it snakes around the city below?'

Near the château stands a tall, square clock tower, at least five storeys high and on a level with their turret. The town far below is a mass of towers and graduating rooftops of pinkish tiles, countless churches, convents and a number of bridges crossing the river busy with small boats. They stay there admiring the view until night falls, and the bells of the church steeples ring out the Angelus. Another of the *demoiselles*, Jeanne de Clary, joins them.

'I hear Toulouse has a reputation for being a joyous town, a city of minstrels and knights dedicated to acts of chivalry; I do hope we meet some and see a tournament soon.'

There is much to do, unpacking their lady's clothes and seeing to her many changes of costume for each day, and the château itself has a maze of corridors and chambers to find their way around and explore.

Ever curious, Agnés finds herself separated from the others. She turns a bend and almost collides with an elegant young courtier, who catches her by the shoulders and steadies her. 'Oh forgive me, kind sir, I was not paying attention,' she stutters, and looks up to see a handsome, smiling face.

'My dear *demoiselle*,' he says in a voice of liquid honey, 'it is I who must apologize,' and with that he bows to her unnecessarily deeply. 'My name is Pierre de Brézé, and I am attached to the court of the King of France. May I take the liberty of asking your name, dear young lady?'

Agnès curtseys, but no more than she feels necessary – after all, he cannot be aware that she knows all about him from Queen Yolande. Politely, and with a certain restraint, she replies: 'My name, good sir, is Agnès Sorel, the youngest *demoiselle* at the court of Duke René and Duchess Isabelle of Lorraine.' With that, she bobs again politely and makes to leave.

'No, please stay,' he says urgently, but Agnès just smiles and continues on her way. She is not quite sure where the passage will lead, but to her relief, she finds her rooms.

'Marie! Marie! I have just seen the most dashing and valiant gentleman I have ever encountered. His name is Pierre de Brézé. Queen Yolande told me all about him

– he is the *sénéchal* of Poitou and Anjou, and he said he was with the court of the King and Queen of France.' Of course she recalls Queen Yolande telling her: 'He is one of the most able and trusted courtiers I have placed with the king. Mark him well.' But she does not tell that to the others.

De Brézé certainly does not disappoint. Even in Naples they had heard of his gallantries and perfect features, and he is all and more than she expected. *So this is the gentleman Queen Yolande advised I should come to know and trust. I wonder why. Did she intend me to have some joint purpose with him? I will be patient . . .*

On another of her solitary walks around the castle, Agnès meets an equally dazzling young courtier – none other than Lord René's brother Charles of Maine, tall, elegant and with an all-embracing smile. She remembers him from the funeral in Angers, although they did not exchange any words there.

'Ah! I believe you must be one of the charming young ladies with my brother's court. Am I right?' This time Agnès curtseys properly – he is a royal prince after all. 'What a pleasure to have you join our company. May I ask your name?' When she gives it, he laughs. 'So you are the youngest of Lady Isabelle's *demoiselles*, the fabled lion-tamer – or is the ferocious predator that I hear lies constantly at your feet a leopard?'

'No, Sire, Vitesse is a cheetah, and she is tame, I can assure you.' Hearing conversation, several of the other *demoiselles* have joined Agnès as she reassures the gallant young courtier.

Charles of Maine sighs with feigned relief. 'Now I regret

even more that I did not visit my brother's court in Naples. If I had only known he had a circus with such beautiful young cheetah-tamers!' he banters as the *demoiselles* turn their heads aside in cheerful embarrassment.

Behind him arrive two more of Queen Yolande's favoured gentlemen – the captain Antoine de Chabannes, and Etienne Chevalier – and she notes them both carefully as they greet the group with more banter from Charles of Maine, who warns his friends that the *demoiselles* of Lorraine are all lion tamers! Agreeable faces, she thinks, Antoine's much more ebullient than that of the shy, gentle Etienne with his long-lashed grey eyes. Yes, they could both become friends, and allies.

'Agnès, dear child, come brush my hair before bed – I am tired at the end of our long journey, and your gentle hands soothe me.' Agnès remembers Isabelle telling her how Queen Yolande had advised her mistress to throw herself on the king's mercy when René had been captured defending her duchy from a male cousin, following her father's death.

'I recall her exact words: Do it Isabelle! He has a weakness for a pretty lady in distress!'" Agnès had packed her blonde mistress's black velvet court dress and those of her two fair children for maximum dramatic effect, clinging to her skirts before the king. And it worked. Charles VII forced the challenger to make a truce.

Nonetheless, poor Lord René was shut in the tower because his father had betrothed his older brother Louis when a boy, to Catherine of Burgundy for her dowry. Queen Yolande was always against the match, but her husband needed the money for another attempt to regain his throne of Naples. How that throne really was the *chimera* Queen Yolande always called it.

It was only after Louis d'Orlèans' brutal murder by 'Jean-sans-Peur' of Burgundy that Louis d'Anjou finally agreed with his wife and cancelled the betrothal. That was seen as a most shameful deed within a family of royal first cousins. But Louis and Yolande knew they could not ally their House with that of the murderer of the king's brother, cousin and their friend, even though the girl was adorable and loved by them all. One year later Catherine died of smallpox, though some said of a broken heart.

'That was the reason her brother, Philip of Burgundy, never forgot nor forgave the shame the Anjou family inflicted on his sister and family so many years ago, and punished my René for it,' said Isabelle with a sigh.

'I know you have not forgotten my next and third meeting with the king?' Isabelle turns to look at Agnès.

'Oh no, Madame, it was when we heard that King Alfonso d'Aragon, the challenger to Lord René's kingdom, had been captured by the Genoese!' exclaims Agnès. 'How brave you were when you seized the opportunity to go and claim your husband's throne. I will never forget coming with your court to Chinon on our way to Marseilles, to ask for the king and queen's blessing and that of the grand Old Queen of Sicily. What an honour to have been included among the *demoiselles* you chose to travel with you.'

Agnès wrote to the others left behind in Nancy about the meeting, and in particular, she described Queen Yolande:

'*She was extraordinarily beautiful, with the most intense blue eyes that seemed to pass right through me. But hers was not an unkind glance, more curious, and I was surprised at her interest.'* Still more surprising was hearing from Jeanne de Clary and Marie de Belleville afterwards: 'The whole room noticed the attention the king showed you, but you just kept your eyes firmly fixed on the ground as a maiden should,' and Marie hugged her and laughed kindly. The curiosity shown in her by the king, *and* the Old Queen of Sicily, was remarked upon by the others. When they mentioned it to Agnès, she was sure they were teasing and paid them no mind. Her own thoughts at the time were focused on the voyage to Naples. Now it seems as if a whole lifetime has passed.

Chapter Eight

This time, the meeting of the court of Lorraine with that of the King of France is to be a joyful sojourn, not the rushed farewell of seven years earlier when they were on their way to Naples. The *demoiselles* chatter excitedly: 'What clothes will our lady wear?' 'How long will the king speak with her?' 'How graceful she would look were she to wear her dress of delicate pale green silk and her emeralds.' Agnès will certainly suggest that ensemble if asked; it suits Isabelle admirably.

'Agnès, dear child, come help me arrange my hair – you do it so well,' she hears her lady calling, and on entering her lady's chamber, she glows with pride. Isabelle *is* wearing her suggestion – the pale green silk dress with her wonderful emeralds.

Since her brief visit to the royal court at Chinon all those years ago – when Agnès really only remembers the floor, since that was all she dared to look at – this will be her first meeting with the king and queen as an adult. Some of the other *demoiselles* remind her there had been a buzz about her at the time, but Agnès is sure, and says so, it was because she was the youngest and the last to leave the room.

Naturally, she wants to make a good impression – and the *demoiselles* want their mistress to be proud of them. One of the lessons Queen Isabelle has taught them: 'You will always make more of an impact by wearing something cut with great simplicity and elegance in a flattering colour, especially when surrounded by luxury and high estate. This way, you will stand out among the crowd of over-elaborate and fussy toilettes.' And they all bear this in mind.

'Marie, what do you think? Shall I wear my dress of mauve silk?' Agnès asks her friend, knowing with regret that Marie is perhaps the only one among Isabelle's *demoiselles* who does not secretly envy her beauty, and the way in which their mistress often favours her.

'Yes, do, its a shade that suits your fair colouring, and a cut that flatters you – quite tight down to your upper hips, and then the way it spreads out into a wide skirt and train at the back makes a lovely silhouette. Yes, wear the mauve – it really becomes you,' says Marie with her kind smile.

Like all the ladies of the court, as well as the other *demoiselles*, Agnès attaches a small bag of soft chicken feathers under the front of her skirt; it will give her stomach the slightly rounded look of the current fashion. Like the others, she has plucked her hairline high and shaped her eyebrows into a very fine line, then pinched her cheeks until they glow. All she needs now to complete her attire is her headdress. She sits so that her little maid can help her tie her hair on top of her head into a net, then cover it with a tall conical cap called a *henin*. To its tip she has attached a long veil of delicate pale pink chiffon, which will lift and play in the gentlest of breezes. A final touch: to the edge of her hairline she sticks a little rosette of black velvet to show off the whiteness of her skin, a very flattering and popular adornment.

'*Vanity!*' Agnès whispers to herself with a smile. *Yes, I am vain.* But before she has time to examine her conscience about this particular sin, she hears the bell of the Mistress-of-the-Maids summoning them. Quickly she wraps a cloak of pale blue velvet around her shoulders and makes for the stairs leading to the Great Hall with the others, all of them tittering with nervous apprehension.

With a show of immense aplomb and to a clarion blast of two dozen silver trumpets, the king makes his entrance, quite overwhelming Agnès and the other *demoiselles* as they watch, eyes open wide. He walks slowly, with dignity, and very straight – a fit, confident man, turning to left and right, smiling and greeting his courtiers and their ladies. He is surrounded by his musicians, some singing, some playing their instruments – lyres and tambourines, sackbuts, viols, trombones, and the slide trumpets, which Agnès likes the best. He is not tall enough for her to see him clearly in the throng, and she lets her focus drift to the music. The wind instruments are superb – a true *alta capella* like they had at their court in Naples, where King René followed the fashion of the great princely houses. Courts are judged on the quality of their music, and

Agnès has heard that the King of France's musicians are legendary.

Walking next to the king and holding on to his hand outstretched at shoulder height is Queen Marie, so unlike her famously beautiful mother Yolande. She is small, pale, wearing black which cannot disguise her roundness, the result of her many pregnancies. Just behind the queen, the twenty-year-old dauphin, Louis, makes his entrance, thin and sombre in black velvet, a large flashing brooch pinning a white ostrich feather on to his black velvet cap. Instinctively, Agnès recoils, and prays she does not meet him again after the way he insulted her at the funeral in Angers! With him, and not really keeping up, though just holding on to his high-held hand, trips his ethereal, delicate wife, the dauphine – Margaret of Scotland – to spontaneous applause from the company. She smiles enchantingly and turns to left and right, bowing, ravishing in blue satin and sapphires. Agnès sees the dauphin scowl in response, and she turns to whisper to Marie de Belleville and Jeanne de Clary, both beside her:

'I hear he dislikes his wife – do you know why? Her smile is so radiant, embracing everyone . . . I am determined to find out. Queen Yolande told me she is a delight. We must help her all we can, Marie.' Her friend smiles in agreement, her finger to her lips.

The Great Hall has filled with elegant courtiers, and their colours dazzle the little group of *demoiselles* from Lorraine as they try to absorb all they can while remaining out of direct sight of the king and queen. Thick, deep-coloured velvets, every shade of the rainbow; rich crimsons and cloth of gold; blues varying from deep lapis

85

to pale turquoise; shot silks shading from light green to pink, blue to mauve, yellow to orange and many more; ladies with the hems and sleeves of their dresses trimmed in various furs; and many wearing the fashionable pointed *henins* on their heads. From the tips of these float veils of pale chiffon, some shoulder length, some to the floor.

And the jewels! Every neck glitters with precious stones, pearls and gold chains – many draped from shoulder to shoulder across chests and attached to the join of sleeves; earrings hang on every ear and rings flash on every finger. The *demoiselles* cannot help their tiny gasps of admiration. Agnès hears a whisper among their group that almost all the beautiful fabrics, furs and jewels have come from the coffers of the king's bursar, Jacques Coeur, their favourite visitor to the court in Naples. While she is wondering whether he will be here in Toulouse, Marie de Belleville turns to her.

'Do not forget what Queen Isabelle told us – the king is not comfortable meeting new people. I wonder how he will receive her. After all, it is more than six years since they last met; she was not at Nancy when he came to bestow the estates on Count Charles of Maine.'

But how could it be otherwise than a joyful reunion between René and the king, whom he has known since early childhood? With an exclamation of 'Sire!' and an elegant bow from René, and 'My dearest cousin and oldest friend!' from the king, the two men embrace graciously, and then the *demoiselles* watch as he turns to greet their mistress:

'My Lady Isabelle, what is it about Naples that has made you even more beautiful to your king's eyes?' and she sweeps into a low court curtsey and tilts her lovely head. Marie and Agnès sigh simultaneously in admiration.

Over the next days, the three households – that of the King and Queen of France; the fabled court of Burgundy led by its duchess; and the court of Lorraine – merge together as easily as if they were one. There are many new faces for the *demoiselles* to note – when there is time, since they are kept fully occupied demonstrating how their Lady Isabelle and her entourage can be quite as alluring as any of the others. 'Allure,' she often told them in Naples, 'takes time and careful preparation.' Indeed it does!

To Agnès's growing discomfort, she is becoming aware that the king glances in her direction rather often.

'Marie, quickly, tell me true, for I fear the way the king looks at me may mean my demeanour or my dress is somehow inappropriate.'

But Marie assures the younger girl that she is not lacking in manners or comportment. 'Calm yourself, my dear Agnès. I am told he stares at everyone new at court. Only worry if our mistress says anything,' she tells her kindly.

Agnès does her best to remain out of the king's sight, but she cannot help studying him from afar, noting how worn and tired he looks. When she mentions this to Marie, her friend says: 'Well, he is forty years old! And he has fought and won many battles against the English in the past five years. That must have taxed him.' Agnès can see she is right, but she continues to observe him. He does not follow the current fashion of hose with short bloomers worn with tight-waisted jackets, but wears instead a long coat, beautifully cut of a superb dark red damascene, trimmed with marten around the neck and at the wrists.

'Do you see how he wears that fur *inside* his sleeves? Perhaps he suffers from the cold?' Agnès whispers to Marie. They both love fur and notice his with pleasure. On her minimal salary, Agnès can only admire such luxuries from afar, though Isabelle is generous and sometimes gives her one of her own dresses.

'Agnès, dear child, do come to my room – you are the only one among my young ladies slim enough for my clothes. Find one you like from that trunk over there,' she says, pointing. Then, when Agnès has chosen something, Isabelle insists she tries it on in front of her. 'Yes, that's a good choice – you will complement me when you wear this.' Isabelle likes her *demoiselles* to appear elegant as it reflects well on her court, and when she is especially kind to Agnès, the girl believes it is out of pity or to enhance her own image.

Curiosity has Marie and Agnès searching for another glimpse of the queen. 'How ill and old she seems,' Agnès says in surprise when they catch sight of her, 'but then she is with child for the thirteenth time, isn't she?'

'Yes, and she has been married for twenty-one years!' adds her friend.

Queen Marie's expression is as gentle and resigned as Agnès remembers from their last meeting at her mother's funeral, and she notes how attentive the queen is to the king. Her jewels are wonderful – one long string of huge pearls reaches down to her waist, worn with large pearl drop earrings. When in Naples, Lord René often spoke about his sister, but sadly, the girls hear it said that the Queen of France does not impress the assembled court in the same way as her famously beautiful mother, Queen Yolande.

Although the traditional bereavement attire for queens is white, Queen Marie chooses always to dress in black in memory of her many losses – the children she has buried; her beloved father, Louis II d'Anjou; and now her remarkable mother. Six dead children: what a sad burden, thinks Agnès; although the queen's first-born, the dauphin Louis, has grown well and strong. It is whispered by everyone that he is most unpleasant – as Agnès discovered at Angers, though she keeps this to herself.

Queen Marie knows something of the time Agnès spent with her mother at Saumur, so it had not surprised the girl when the queen sent for her after her mother's funeral, and spoke to her gently.

'Agnès, my dear, do sit with me and tell me about your time with my mother, and of your conversations. Of all her children, sadly, I knew her the least, since I was sent to Bourges to be with the king when I was still quite young. How we would have wished to be in your place during her last year.'

Unwilling to betray any of the Old Queen's confidences, Agnès replied: 'Madame, I passed most of the time in reading to your lady mother, or playing my harp and singing the ballads I learned in Naples, which she avowed she enjoyed.' Queen Marie seemed easier when she heard this and asked Agnès to continue. She told the queen what she had also told her mother – about their daily life in Naples, the flora and fauna, the great volcano and their small adventures. In essence, nothing of special interest, and somehow Queen Marie appeared almost relieved.

'I still wonder what she wanted to hear from me,' Agnès comments to Marie de Belleville. 'Believe me, Queen Yolande did not tell me any secrets.'

The handsome *sénéchal* of Poitou, Pierre de Brézé, continues to dazzle the gathering. This evening he wears emerald green velvet trimmed with dark sable, a wonderful brooch of precious stones at his neck that catches the candlelight and flashes with his eyes at the company. He sees their little group, advances and says with a bow and a smile: 'Greetings to all the lovely young ladies of Naples and Lorraine. Be welcome at our court of France. I hope we may continue some of our lively games and conversations during our sojourn here in Toulouse?' – and they all drop a curtsey, blushing demurely with eyes cast down.

When the Mistress-of-the-Maids appears, they know it is time to take their leave and retire, even though they would all like to stay longer. Supper will have been prepared in their rooms and they have an early start in the morning.

Later, as they prepare for bed, they agree with sincere approval that their Lady Isabelle was far more elegant than either Queen Marie or the famous Duchess of Burgundy – even though *she* was born a royal princess of Portugal!

As the days pass, Agnès has the opportunity to meet more of the courtiers described to her in detail by Queen Yolande. One of the gentlemen mentioned as being a positive and regular presence at the king's royal court is Etienne Chevalier, who the young ladies find striking for his gravitas and sombre appearance. He is the king's counsellor, private secretary and financial comptroller. Etienne is thirty-three, but looks older. Slender to the point of thin, and high of brow, he wears his hair short in a straight line to the lobes of his ears, like a monk's. His face is as serious as his clothes – cut in varying shades of dark grey cloth, though of excellent quality. They are told he has great wealth, but his choice of apparel appears modest. Though slow to smile, Agnès believes his stern look may be hiding a sensitive soul.

She decides to take pains to draw him out. Whenever they meet, she asks him as sweetly as she can if he might accompany her walking in the gardens, or perhaps be willing to sit by her outside under the trees, so that they can talk while she works on her embroidery.

'My dear *demoiselle* Agnès, I know of the time you spent in attendance on my esteemed patroness,' he says softly, with the hint of a smile. 'You may know that I visited her often at Saumur. How I miss that great lady – as I am sure you do.'

She returns his smile, and he seems eager to continue, telling her all about his life. In fact, she can hardly stop him!

'I am sad you did not know my wife – a remarkable lady, and I miss her dreadfully. Like you, she loved to embroider, and read. I often notice you with a book. Are you interested in flowers? The garden was one of our greatest pleasures. Which are your favourite flowers?'

'Oh, I am pleased you love flowers. I grew up in the country, in Touraine, and always enjoyed spending time in the flower borders, especially picking and drying lavender, though I love roses during their short season, and lilies. Yes, perhaps lilies are my favourites. Tell me about yours?'

And so they discuss gardens, and then animals – he loves dogs, and she tells him about Naples and their riding there, and the wonderful gardens of the castle. In this relaxed and easy way they begin their friendship, with Agnès always comfortable in his company.

Another gentleman Queen Yolande recommended is Antoine de Chabannes. Yolande described him as a brilliant captain and a loyal and honest courtier who came to the service of the king when he was still the dauphin. When Agnès sees the gruff captain in one of the passageways leading to the Great Hall, she curtseys and that stops him in his tracks. 'My dear *demoiselle*, you have no cause to curtsey to me, I assure you. I am merely a soldier in attendance upon the king.'

'Well then, that is reason enough, surely,' she replies sweetly. Seeing his confusion, she adds: 'You cannot be aware, kind sir, but I had the honour of spending the last year of Queen Yolande's life in her company, and she spoke often and most well of you.'

With that he relaxes, smiles at the compliment and accompanies Agnès on her way, talking all the time of his memories of Queen Yolande. When they reach the entrance, he says: 'I am aware your mistress the Lady Isabelle is waiting for you to attend her, but be assured, it would give me much pleasure to converse with you, my lady, whenever you have time and occasion.' Then, as if the idea has just occurred to him, he adds quickly, 'My lady, if you enjoy the chase, I will be happy to see to it that you are well mounted on a steady, gentle hack, should you wish.'

'Good sir, nothing would please me more than to be well mounted for the chase, but I prefer a fiery steed, since I have much experience and no fear on horseback.' At that Chabannes smiles broadly and bows, and Agnès feels she has made an ally if not a friend.

A week after their arrival, as the *demoiselles* of Lorraine gather as usual in the Great Hall of the château, Agnès catches sight of a familiar face from Naples and Saumur, a man she saw again briefly at Queen Yolande's funeral. It is none other than Jacques Coeur, who has recently been promoted to be the king's *argentier* – the provider of luxuries for the court's indulgence – and will therefore attend their company more often.

Whenever his ship docked in Naples, he would visit King René's court there and came to know each of Queen Isabelle's *demoiselles* by name, but Agnès did not see him at Saumur when he brought her warmer clothes. Before they met again at Angers, she had never really spoken to him more than in greeting. Here in Toulouse he smiles at her and gives her a shrewd look. There is something about him Agnès finds very appealing, and she sincerely hopes she will have an opportunity to know him better. From the way Queen Yolande spoke of him, this is a good man who, she suspects, carries many secrets in his wise head.

Housed in great comfort at Narbonnais, at first Agnès does not appreciate that it is Jacques Coeur who has provided every touch of luxury in the castle for the court's accommodation: the beautiful flowered tapestries covering the bedroom walls; the ravishing velvet hangings embroidered with the golden fleur-de-lys of France for the more formal rooms; and much else besides to help decorate the otherwise bare château. He has supplied the floor coverings, underlaid with rosemary and lavender, their scent rising with the press of many feet walking. Delicious-smelling wax candles are lit night and day, their scents of vetiver and bergamot, musk, oregano and – Agnès's favourite – jasmine drifting throughout the huge residence. Yes, Queen Yolande was right – she can learn a lot from this merchant, and hopes he will single her out and befriend her. She tries to stand near him whenever the court gathers, not only to hear his fascinating conversation but in anticipation of his addressing her as well.

The general talk of the gathering, to which the *demoiselles* are rarely asked to contribute, is usually about the king: how much he has improved in looks and stature since his military successes against the English; how well victory sits on his shoulders, bringing out the charm and subtlety of his wit. Maturity suits him, say the courtiers; he has grown into his features now that he has reached his fortieth year. Everyone agrees that he is the most courteous of all the gentlemen, and no matter what the circumstance, he always finds the appropriate words to fit any situation. Agnès also hears it whispered that of course the poor king is malformed, his legs too short, and his upper body too large, but she disagrees and confides to Marie de Belleville that she finds his physique and face rather pleasing. She recalls what Queen Yolande told her, something that means more than mere looks:

'You will find that the king is most cultured; he loves

books, and especially his own library. He often plays the harp – just as you do, and as well – in the quiet of his rooms, and takes great pains with the music in his chapels. I have come to know you, my dear child, and all that will delight you.'

'Madame,' replied Agnès, 'if I have the opportunity to know the king, then indeed it would.'

Whereupon her patroness added: 'Do not be surprised: the king may be a scholarly man devoted to learning, but he is also an excellent swordsman, sits a horse extremely well and plays a good game of tennis!'

Standing in the garden at Toulouse recalling this conversation, Agnès remembers how she laughed and asked: 'Madame, is there anything this king can *not* do?'

The great lady smiled, that special, mysterious smile Agnès had come to know and love: 'With the right guidance, I believe he could do anything he wanted.'

On one topic all members of the court agree: Charles VII's most important success has been to vanquish the *goddons,* as they call the English, and send them back to their land of Normandy!

Walking with Marie de Belleville, Agnès confides: 'Dear friend, may I confess to you that I am terrified of this paragon of a king, particularly when I catch him staring at me with a solemn face and I become certain that I am wanting in some way.'

Marie does not answer; she is not sure what to say, for she too has noticed the way he looks at her friend.

Another topic of animated conversation in the Great Hall at Narbonnais is the enchanting dauphine, Princess

Margaret of Scotland. The entire French court adores her – all except her husband the dauphin, who makes no secret of his loathing. One of the other *demoiselles* has befriended the dauphine's companion and confides to Agnès: 'The worst of it is that she seems unable to conceive, and her health is delicate.'

When Agnès is alone with her mistress, she asks her in confidence about the dauphine, and Isabelle explains: 'Margaret is loved by both the king and the queen; by the entire court, in fact, excepting the dauphin. I think it is mostly because she is the choice of his father, and they *really* dislike one another.'

'Then it is no wonder she spends all her time sitting quietly composing rhymes and poems with a small group of friends and admirers; at least they are kind to her.' But her lady makes a disapproving face, and Agnès realizes at once that she has said more than she ought.

The Duke of Anjou is often referred to as 'Good King René' and comes in for much praise from the court of France. Almost daily Agnès hears it said that 'The King of Sicily is quite the most refined and yet lavish of all the courtiers.' It is generally accepted that it is his darling Isabelle who has her way in most things concerning her husband, but without making it in the least obvious. Even her *demoiselles* are awarded a certain approval – at least in comparison with the style and appearance of the suite belonging to Queen Marie. The girls themselves chatter about all aspects of the royal court of France and agree, rather wickedly, and with muffled hilarity, that Queen Marie's ladies-in-waiting appear better suited to a convent.

As the prettiest of Queen Isabelle's *demoiselles*, Agnès

was warned by Queen Yolande, and is now reminded by Isabelle herself, the flirtatious ways of the young courtiers of King Charles VII and pays them no mind. She knows her waist is the smallest and her eyes are said to be the bluest, but so what? As she tells Marie de Belleville: 'Have we not all been taught by Queen Isabelle that beauty is fleeting, and that we should work on improving our minds and cleansing our souls?'

Marie is a kind girl and agrees wholeheartedly.

A week after their arrival at Narbonnais, Queen Isabelle summons her *demoiselles* in order to present them to the king. 'Marie, my knees feel full of water and I want to melt into the ground,' avows Agnès, but she is forced to join the others and stand in her place at the end of the line. Trembling slightly, she is pleasantly surprised to hear the king's gentle words to each of the girls standing ahead of her, to see that radiant smile reaching his eyes, a smile that reassures them, calming their nerves and trembling hands. She dares to look carefully at his face before he reaches her and recalls what Queen Yolande told her on their daily walks. Does she imagine she can see signs of the years of unhappiness, of insecurity, uncertainty and shame brought on by the many humiliations and indignities he suffered during his youth?

And then it is her turn at the end of the line. As she performs her deep *révérence*, lowering her eyes, she can feel his gaze burning down on her head, and without looking up, she rises and turns to pay her respects to the queen.

Chapter Nine

February in Toulouse, capital of the Languedoc, is cold, but the young ladies warm themselves by riding out with the courtiers to hunt with falcons. Charles of Maine and Pierre de Brézé look the most dashing – one in green, the other in purple velvet, their caps sporting beautiful long feathers. They make their horses prance and pirouette around three of the Angevin *demoiselles,* who laugh merrily at their genteel courtship. The hounds bark, the trumpets blow and the horses snort and jingle their harnesses, vapour rising from them in the cold air. It is a pretty sight. And then they are off, galloping as if to the ends of the earth. When they pull up, their horses steam so much their riders are hidden as if in the clouds, hardly able to see one another!

In the evenings, to everyone's delight, there is usually music – a famous minstrel with golden hair to his shoulders is a favourite, and at a sign from the king, he starts to play his theorbo and sing in a light, high, sweet voice.

There is often music played for dancing – especially the *carole*, a charming dance where everyone holds hands in a circle; the *balade* and the *rondeau*.

At High Mass on Sundays in the Cathedral of Saint-Etienne, the choir sings with a perfect harmony such as Agnès has never heard before – all in honour of God and their king. After the service, as Queen Marie and her ladies leave on their litters, the *demoiselles* of Lorraine curtsey and greet her with: 'Good morning, Madame, God bless you,' and she smiles and blesses them in return.

The younger ones walk on the light covering of snow, while most of the gentlemen ride, some boldly offering the *demoiselles* a lift behind them on their horses – 'Come, my lady Agnès, save your pretty shoes for dancing and ride on the back of my placid stallion'; or 'But my lady Anne, how will you be able to dance tonight with frozen toes' – and the girls look down, stifle a giggle and dare not reply.

The brilliant colours of the ladies' long robes and the courtiers' hats stand out in sharp contrast against the pale blue sky. Furs line cloaks or nestle around collars and cuffs; young cheeks are rosy, spirits are high, and everyone's breath comes in smoky billows. The riders and their horses are a multicoloured sight against the whiteness of the ground, and the *demoiselles* run and challenge one another as to who will be the first to arrive at the castle gates.

When the court is gathered in one of the great salons, to the anxious surprise of Agnès the king begins to single her out.

'My Lady Agnès, won't you sit by me awhile and tell

me more about your court's stay in Naples – it does interest me so.' When he turns, she can hardly believe that the king is speaking to her directly. 'Do tell me about the volcano, Vesuvius; did you climb to the top?'

She knows she must reply, but suddenly her throat is dry and she can hardly speak for nerves.

Over the days and weeks that follow, he asks many other such questions, as if genuinely interested in Naples and its surroundings. Some ten days or two weeks later, one evening following supper, he approaches her with a request.

'My Lady Agnès, would you be so kind as to help me? I have an aching head and your mistress Isabelle assures me you have the most soothing of voices.'

All she can think to do is whisper in reply: 'Sire, my Lady Isabelle is too generous. I really do not sing at all well. My lord, if you will please excuse me.'

'But I heard you singing the other day, and it sounded very well to me,' he says softly.

Is this an order? She dares a quick glance at his smiling face and returns her eyes to the ground. 'Not well enough for your ears, Sire,' she whispers again.

Her Lady Isabelle hears and quickly comes to her rescue, suggesting they all sing a roundel together with the other demoiselles; after that, she persuades Agnès to sing alone.

Later that evening, when they have gone to their rooms, Agnès confides in Marie de Belleville. 'Dearest friend, I admit I feel very intimidated by the king's presence and try to avoid seeing him, but he always knows where to find the "elegant demoiselles of Anjou", as he calls us. What shall I do?'

Marie answers simply with a smile, 'Obey, of course,' which leaves Agnès even more confused.

The weeks pass, and the king has to leave for business elsewhere. The *demoiselles* continue with their studies and enjoy exploring the surrounding area, both with the hunt and on visits to neighbouring castles. When their king returns, the court's entertainments begin again in earnest.

One day Agnès asks Isabelle in private: 'Madame, please enlighten me. What does the king want with me? He seems to be seeking my company, or do I imagine this?'

To her relief, Isabelle calms her. 'Why, dear child, the king is fond of young people, and curious about their lives. Do not disappoint him now; tell him more of your time in Naples and of the flowers and the animals and the birds you saw there. The butterflies especially would interest him, and the fish – yes, I know he would like to hear about the fish.'

Now and again during a banquet, Agnès becomes aware that the king is staring at her. If she meets his gaze, he raises his silver goblet to her with a little bow of his head. *Does he want to know about the wine too? I know nothing of that.* She can see his lips moving but she has no idea what he is saying.

The *demoiselles* of Anjou often find themselves in the company of René's friend, the gallant Pierre de Brézé, who makes a point of visiting them in their quarters, even joining them together with René for a game of cards. They both cheat! The *demoiselles* shout at them in amazement: 'Cheat! Cheat!' and René and Pierre laugh good-naturedly at being caught out. All the *demoiselles* are a little in love with Pierre de Brézé, but he never flirts with any one of them in particular. All his attentions are merely jolly banter. Sometimes Agnès wonders whether Queen Yolande intended *her* for Pierre de Brézé, since she spoke of him often, but he never gives her the slightest encouragement to think so.

At times Agnès catches sight of the merchant Jacques Coeur, who has come to Toulouse to install the king's *parlement*. All the *demoiselles* who met him in Naples hope he will tell them more about his travels to the East. It is his stories about the harems that particularly intrigue them, the eunuchs and anything to do with the Orient. His face interests Agnès; he is a fine-looking man, in his mid-thirties at a guess, features clean-cut and skin leathery from exposure to wind and sea air, with piercing eyes that – she swears to the others – can see through walls . . .

It is early April, and the court has been at Narbonnais for two months. Lady Isabelle has begun to entertain a small group of her friends in her apartments, chosen from among the two courts of France and Anjou. Sometimes she asks, 'Agnès, won't you sing to us tonight?' or at other times, 'Dear child, do bring your book of poems to supper this evening; the king will be among my guests and he has particularly asked for you.'

Agnès knows she must reply, and begs: 'Madame, won't you please forgive me. I feel shy in such august company and it makes me nervous to be so produced, almost like a performing dwarf.'

But Isabelle takes great pains to reassure her, and slowly she manages to overcome her terror of appearing before the king. He, for his part, invariably has a generous word to say after she has finished.

The regular guests at Isabelle's intimate evenings are the king, Lord René, the dauphine Margaret – without fail encouraging and sweet to Agnès – Pierre de Brézé and Etienne Chevalier; sometimes she adds Jacques Coeur, or the king's favourite chamberlain, André de Villequier, and another favourite, Antoine de Chabannes, as well as two or three of her other *demoiselles*, often Marie de Belleville and Jeanne de Clary. Queen Marie, well advanced in her pregnancy, always retires early to her quarters. The suppers are superb and the dishes presented are often laced with rare spices that come through the good offices of Jacques Coeur. When asked, he regales the company with tales of their origins, which captivate his listeners. A great story-teller and mimic, to the delight of the group he can imitate the accents of traders and tells stories of the strange travellers he has met on his foreign voyages.

Accompanying Lady Isabelle's parties there is music played by one or more minstrels; sometimes there are jugglers; the dauphine might start some roundels; or Agnès is asked to recite a poem. After supper, delicately flavoured wines are offered, and candied fruits or other sweetmeats. Laughter is the hallmark of these cheerful little gatherings of friends. The three or four young *demoiselles* know and keep their place, and yet they play their small parts.

Due to such pleasant, relaxed evenings, Agnès is becoming steadily more at ease in such elevated company, even with the king, who speaks to her kindly but no more than to the other *demoiselles*: 'Good evening, my Lady Agnès, will you be joining the dauphine in her roundels tonight?

I find them delightful,' and other such comments. It takes Agnès some time, but slowly she becomes less disturbed by the king's penetrating gaze, and bit by bit she even begins to expect and to quite enjoy his attentions.

Chapter Ten

The courts of France and Lorraine have been in Toulouse for more than three months and are nearing the end of their stay when Agnès begins to realize that something has changed. It is *she* who is looking out – albeit discreetly – for the king, and if she does not see him each morning, afternoon and evening, she feels oddly disappointed, almost as if she needs to feel him nearby, attentive to her, gazing at her with his wise, sad eyes. Could it be possible that he too needs to be near her? No, surely not. How foolish to imagine such a thing. Nothing has been said after all; it is just the way he looks at her – a softer expression, almost as if appealing for some sign of approval. Could this all-powerful man be trying to tell her he wants something more? From her, Agnès Sorel, the lowliest of Queen Isabelle's *demoiselles*? No. Impossible. And she firmly decides that she has allowed her fantasy to run away with her – which is not the sort of thing she normally does. Somewhat to her relief, she hears that the king must once again leave the court for duties elsewhere.

During his absence, Agnès seeks out her friend Marie de Belleville. She must know whether what she feels stirring in her heart is a figment of her imagination.

'Marie, dear friend, may I ask you something very personal?'

'Why, of course, Agnès, you can ask me anything you want,' says Marie with her sweet smile.

'I will understand if you would prefer not to answer me.'

Marie sees Agnès's beautiful face almost contort with apprehension. 'Ask me, my dear – I will help you if I can,' she says gently, laying a reassuring hand on the younger girl's arm.

'Well, I was just wondering . . .'

'Yes, what is it, dear one?'

'Marie, you are the kindest to me of all the ladies at the court . . . Can you tell me . . . Have you ever been in love? And if you have, what is it like? I mean, how would one know?'

Marie de Belleville is a little taken aback, but seeing her young friend is serious and in some distress, she thinks for a moment and then says gently: 'Agnès, my dear, are you asking me because you think *you* might be in love?'

'No, no, not at all.' Agnès quickly tries to cover her confusion with a little laugh. 'No, I was just wondering how it felt, that's all.' The two are walking down a long, wide corridor that was added at some time to the outside of the enormous castle in order to connect the rooms, rather like an enclosed balcony that completely encircles the huge edifice.

'Believe me, dearest Agnès, when it happens to you, you will know it. Your heart races whenever you hear your loved one's name mentioned; you search for him in a crowd and let your eyes meet; you want to spend all your time with him; you want to hold his hand, some physical contact – a stroke of your cheek – it need not be intimate, but it is, because it is he who is near you. If he is not there, you want to talk about him, say his name. You think of him all the time, and dream of him, and your heart beats so fast when he comes back from being away somewhere – even for a short time – you think it will jump out of your chest! Everything that interests or concerns him suddenly interests or concerns you. You want to know every tiny thing about him, and you never want him to leave your side. There are times when you think you could, and would, actually *die* for him. Now, my young friend, have you felt like this?' And Marie gives Agnès a searching look.

To the flushed girl's intense relief, just then they hear the urgent bell-ringing of the Mistress-of-the-Maids summoning them. Quickly they gather their skirts to one side and move as fast as they elegantly can towards the staircase at the other end of the long corridor.

Later that night, Agnès is lying in her bed and thinking about her friend's description of how it feels to be in love. *Yes, it's true I do feel all of the things Marie told me. I think I am in love with the king.* When she says it to herself, she almost cannot swallow.

But this is wrong, he is a married man, his wife is the Queen of France, the daughter of my mentor Queen Yolande! This cannot be. I am imagining that he cares for me. But I am not imagining that I care for him . . . I know I do. I believe I have fallen in love with this man, this mighty king who seems almost a child when he sits beside me with his eyes searching mine. What are these wild thoughts spinning in my head? What am I thinking of?

For the next few days, Agnès goes about her duties in some sort of trance, not really there at all, and she avoids Marie de Belleville in case she can read the guilty secret of her heart.

A few nights later, Isabelle joins her in the long corridor and takes her aside into a small alcove. 'Agnès, dear girl, I have decided to move your room to the other side of the courtyard – come with me and I will show you.'

Seeing her confusion, Isabelle gently puts her arm around her *demoiselle*.

'Dearest Agnès, you have been with me for more than eight years now, since you were quite young. During your time with us at Nancy, and then at our court in Naples, you must have learned a great deal about life in general, as well as at your studies. But especially during the year you spent with Queen Yolande at Saumur.'

'My Lady, oh yes, indeed,' agrees Agnès.

'I believe that these varied experiences have formed you into the young lady you are today.'

Yes, it is true, thinks Agnès. Isabelle has been her guide and mentor in almost all things. They are walking casually, talking easily, with no apparent tension between them.

'Since your mother died, and your Aunt Marie sent you to me, I trust you do know that I have looked on you as a daughter, much more so than my other *demoiselles*? I believe the time has come when I need to talk to you as I would my own daughter; and in a way that I know Queen Yolande would have wanted me to speak to you. Will you allow me that, dear girl?'

Agnès nods, wondering where this is heading.

'For a number of years, since Queen Yolande first saw you with me at the court in Chinon before we left for Naples, she and I have corresponded about your progress. At first I confess I did not understand her interest in you, but with time I began to realize her vision. You see, she and I are similar in many ways, and I believe I understood her.'

Yes, having spent those long months alone with the Old Queen, Agnès can see that the two women have much in common in their logic and reasoning.

'Once in France and married into the royal house, Queen Yolande worked all her life to improve the fortunes of our King Charles; for France – the country of her adoption – as well as for her own family. I know she told you this, did she not?'

Again Agnès nods. All her many conversations seem to come back to this theme.

'When I left for Naples with you and half the court of Lorraine, my dear husband was in Burgundy's prison tower. Queen Yolande knew, as I did, that once she died, there would be no one left to help the king remain focused on becoming a worthy monarch. When my husband was released, he would leave for Naples; Queen Yolande's younger son, Charles of Maine, did not yet share her focused dedication on the king's behalf; and her daughter, our beloved Queen Marie, has no real influence on him at all – sadly she is absent too often for her many confinements, and even when she is with him, he does not heed her wisdom.

'Queen Yolande's life's work could not be for nothing! She had to find someone to whom the king could become as attached as he was to her, someone to whom he would listen. She knew something important about Charles; that there is something he has lacked all his adult life, something he needs desperately, even without knowing it himself.' She pauses, and turns to look directly at Agnès. 'She knew that he has never been in love.'

Agnès feels her heart skip a beat, but Queen Isabelle continues walking, the girl's arm held firmly in hers.

'Could the power of love focus him on continuing with his mission of ridding France of the English, of ruling fairly and with wisdom, of denying himself the easy path back to his former, *unfortunate* way of life? It was a chance worth taking – and Queen Yolande,' she stops and says this slowly, 'in her wisdom,' even more slowly while looking into the girl's lovely face again, 'she believed that *you*, Agnès, you could be the one he might come to love deeply and totally; *you* could be the woman who can help him in the many ways he desperately needs.'

Queen Isabelle holds her arm firmly and sits Agnès down next to her on a bench. She must have turned white, for Isabelle quickly hands her a goblet of water and orders her: 'Drink'. When she has recovered and her breathing is steadier, the queen says:

'My beloved Agnès, now you know for what you have been so carefully prepared – and for such a long time. Throughout your years with me in Italy, I watched you and steered you as my mother-in-law instructed. And I have continued to observe you here over the past months. I can see quite plainly that you are in love with the king – just as he is with you.' Agnès gulps as Lady Isabelle pats her arm. 'Make him happy, make yourself happy, and God, who knows and sees everything, will understand your good intentions.'

'But, but . . . the king is married,' Agnès whispers.

'This plan for his happiness was the notion of Queen Marie's own mother, Agnès. Would she have devised such a proposal if it was not in the best interests of the king and the country? She knew what she was asking of her daughter, although she will not have said anything to her. But like all her children, Queen Marie was brought up to obey her mother and to live her life for the good of the king and the kingdom.

'I know you are a good girl; that you confess, and go to Mass and Communion. I have spoken to our chaplain, Father Denis, and he is ready to talk to you and reassure you. Do not forget the king was betrothed at the age of ten, without any choice, and has always done his duty by his queen. Now *you* have the choice to give – and receive – true love. I urge you, with Queen Yolande's blessing, to take it.'

Isabelle kisses the girl's forehead, takes her trembling hand, and leads her to the suite of new rooms prepared on the other side of the large tournament courtyard. There she leaves Agnès standing alone in the light of a single candle.

Chapter Eleven

Still trembling, and not quite sure how to absorb all Queen Isabelle has told her, Agnès washes herself and puts on the shift she finds on the bed. Then she lies down, quite exhausted, and is soon asleep.

A gentle caress on her cheek wakes her, and as she opens her eyes, she can see a pinkish sky through the window opposite her bed. Sitting beside her, one finger stroking her cheek is the king. Instinctively she reaches out her arms and he comes into them, covering her face and lips with many tender little kisses, like a butterfly anxious not to frighten her away. In her half-sleep she is relaxed and unresisting. Charles makes love to her with great care not to alarm her, nor disgust her, all the while whispering gentle words of reassurance, until he has her total confidence. They continue like this until the sun bursts through the windows and floods the room with its warm light.

Apart from his whispers, they did not speak during their

lovemaking, but now he begins to talk to her, sweet nothings – 'my darling angel', 'my delicate little one', 'how I have longed for this moment' – until she falls asleep again. When she wakes, he is gone and the sun is high.

I am the king's lover, and I find myself wanting to be near him at every moment of the day and night. He is gentle and kind, and because he does not force himself on me, I respond impulsively to his caresses. That first night, he was concerned I would feel pain, but in my mixture of emotions – love and terror, joy and pleasure – I found myself wanting his lovemaking more and more. Oh, that magical first night when we hardly slept and remained in one another's arms; but thereafter we talk and laugh and sigh with satisfied exhaustion.

At Queen Isabelle's court, her *demoiselles* have been taught to be modest at all times, and at first Agnès finds it difficult to undress and allow the king's eyes to cover her body, but his admiration and delight is so apparent that she finds herself relaxing, and doing all she can to please him in the ways he shows her.

Almost without saying, they both understand that discretion will be the most important aspect of their appearance in public. But Charles is so overwhelmed by his own happiness that it seems to burst out of him, and it is hard for him to leave her side, returning to cover her with kisses and promising he will come back quickly, and soon, and again and again. He is like a child who has opened a wondrous and unexpected gift. To see the light in his eyes and the softness of his expression fills her whole being with a happiness she never imagined possible.

I am loved by the King of France!

After that first, perfect, unforgettable time, her royal lover comes to her every night, and their exploration of one another continues with such passion and contentment that Agnès thinks she will dissolve like ice in sunshine with her secret happiness.

Who knows? she wonders. Queen Isabelle, of course – that was the reason for moving her to rooms away from all her other *demoiselles*. And those closest to the king must be aware that he does not sleep in his own chamber. Queen Marie is heavy with child and would not expect a visit from her husband, but Agnès is beginning to notice a certain deference in the way Pierre de Brézé speaks to her, and also Jacques Coeur, that most observant of men, said to have the shrewdest eyes in the kingdom. Lady Isabelle might not have told Lord René, but he is so close to the king that perhaps he has noticed; on the other hand, he never seems to be aware of anything the rest of his household sees, so Agnès cannot be sure about him. She is very mindful that she will have to behave with great caution so as not to anger any of these courtiers, and most especially Queen Marie.

But her lover does give her small gifts, and her fingers flash with several new rings. Naturally the other *demoiselles* notice these, but she assures them they have been sent by her father and passed on to her by the Queen of Sicily. 'But why has Lady Isabelle moved you away from us?' a number of them ask. 'Oh, she wants me to be nearer to her,' she lies. 'She often wakes with a headache during the night and sends for me to soothe her.' It is the best reason she can come up with.

Not only is she different, she *feels* different; no longer

one of her group of *demoiselles*. She has a secret, such a huge secret, and no one with whom to share it. Dare she talk to Marie de Belleville, or should she just hug it to herself a while longer?

The time has come to leave Toulouse and begin the long progress towards Poitiers, the next destination of the combined courts. The king, astride a white charger, rides with his closest gentlemen in front of the cortège, followed by the wagons of the queen, the dauphine and the House of Anjou. The carriages of the important ladies are hung with flat leather curtains to keep out the wind and the chill breezes of early spring, and pulled by pairs of gentle, sure-footed hacks. The insides are filled with fur covers and braziers with hot coals. The younger ladies, those like Agnès and her friends Marie de Belleville and Jeanne de Clary, who ride easily, do so, and the others take to less imposing wagons. These are followed by the clergy on their mules, the doctors and other officials.

The baggage train is enormous, as the king travels not only with his courtiers but with his furniture: his beds, tapestries, linen, gold and silver tableware. In fact, it is a parade of the whole court, for where the king is, there also is the government. Everything depends on him and is invested in him. For protection, the nobles are escorted by the king's personal bodyguard of one hundred Scottish archers, as well as other soldiers, extra horses and numerous hounds to hunt game on the way. Throughout their journeying, musicians play and minstrels sing, many of the travellers joining in along with them. And thus, in such merry company, the court leaves Languedoc.

During the journey, whenever possible, Agnès's lover contrives to bring his horse next to hers for a moment, their legs pressing together as their horses jostle – a caress of sorts – so that she is never unsure of his feelings for long, even if their spoken exchanges must be formal.

'How goes the ride this morning, my Lady Agnès? Is that sad, dull steed of yours not due for a change to a more mettlesome mount?'

'With your permission, Sire, I would indeed be grateful for something more spirited.'

'I will see what our stable master can find, my pretty lady,' he answers with a grin, and with that he is gone.

The following morning, a better mount is brought for Agnès to ride.

During the court's slow progress, many of the company join different groups, riding from one to another, chatting, gossiping and generally showing off on their horses. Agnès often rides among a group of the *demoiselles*, in particular with Marie de Belleville and Jeanne de Clary, but she is beginning to form a friendship with the young Scottish dauphine, Margaret, which would appear to be reciprocated. Often she finds herself riding beside Margaret's litter, and once the dauphine notices, she begins to converse with Agnès.

'What a fine young Arabian mare you ride, my Lady Agnès. I had not noticed her before.'

Agnès feels her colour rising, not daring to say how she came by the horse. 'Madame, yes, she is indeed mettlesome, and I have been asked to exercise her. Do you ride, my lady?' she asks, quickly changing the subject.

'Yes, oh yes, in Scotland I loved to ride on the hunt

with falcons. But I was stronger then, more like you, dear Agnès.'

To hear the princess speak with such warmth encourages her. 'My lady, would you like to ride gently with me when the weather is better?'

The dauphine makes to reply, but then she begins coughing and asks her companion in the litter for water. Agnès hears that cough often and wonders whether her new friend will be able to ride at all when just the motion of the litter disturbs her chest.

From that day on, Agnès makes a habit of riding up to the dauphine's litter. As the days go by, Margaret begins to tell her what she is reading or the poetry she is composing, which music and roundels she loves, and they discover they have much in common in their tastes.

This gentle, slight princess has conquered everyone with her delicate radiance. Whenever she enters a room it is with a happy step, looking around before choosing a group to sit with and then spreading her good humour at once.

'Ah, what a pleasure to see you this morning my dears,' she would say to the group of *demoiselles* in Toulouse, sitting working at their embroidery. 'It must be cold outside, but with the warmth of your smiles, all cold melts and we shall be merry! Will someone play for us?' And someone always did. Or she would tell everyone about her latest compositions, begging them to read her poems; or teach them her latest roundel and then ask them to perform with her. Wherever she is, the mood lifts, and her radiance surrounds every face like a beam of sunlight.

The only one Lady Margaret has visibly failed to charm

is her husband, the dauphin Louis. It is obvious to every-one what a deliberately unpleasant person he is. Although only twenty-one, he seems much older and gives a studied impression of world-weariness. His ambition to rule is as transparent as his loathing of his father the king. Forced into marriage at a young age with Margaret of Scotland for political reasons, he does everything he can to make her life a misery – which prompts the courtiers to do any-thing *they* can to compensate her.

'Won't you sit with us?' they beg her; or 'Please teach us your latest roundel and we will all practise and perform it tonight.' And Margaret beams with gratitude. Agnès, too, loves poetry and ballads, which may be one of the reasons why Margaret sees her as an ally. As for the beau-tiful *demoiselle* of Anjou and Lorraine, although she finds it even harder now to become close to anyone new at court, since she cannot share her secret, the dauphine makes it very easy to be her friend without either of them feeling obliged to divulge anything personal.

The one friend she *can* count on, however, is Marie de Belleville. One day, during conversation, someone mentions how much happier the king has seemed in the past month, and one of the group asks Agnès what she thinks. Agnès panics that someone has noticed something and leaves quickly, begging to be excused, saying she is not feeling well. In her concern for her friend, Marie follows and finds Agnès almost shaking in another room nearby.

'What is it, dearest girl?' she asks. 'Are you ill? A fever? Can I fetch you something, even the doctor? You are so pale.'

'No, no, it's really nothing,' Agnès replies, breathing deeply to calm herself.

'Did someone say something to upset you, my sweet friend? The talk was of the king, was it not?' Agnès says nothing, but Marie has been chosen to be at court for her wisdom and sensitive insight. She recalls the conversation she had with Agnès recently about being in love, and she takes Agnès into her arms and holds the sobbing girl.

After a little while, she dries Agnès's eyes and says, 'I understand: my dearest and gentlest *demoiselle* has fallen in love with the king. Am I not right?'

Agnès, like a volcano about to erupt, bursts into tears again, and turns away from her friend.

'Come, come, dear Agnès. What is more natural than falling in love? You are a modest girl – I know, I have watched you. You have never even pretended to the flirting young gallants that they might have a chance with you, although all make it clear that they are quite smitten with your beauty and enchanting ways.' Stroking the girl's hair away from her eyes, she continues, 'I am not surprised if you have fallen in love with the king. He has been admiring you for a long time, and has carefully wooed you. My role at court is to observe – and I have seen his growing adoration and your slow, hesitant warming to him.

'I saw Queen Isabelle take you to your new quarters and I understood why – I was just not certain for whom you were being isolated. But I should have guessed. Now,' says Marie, taking Agnès by the hand, 'let us retire to your room where no one will disturb us, and we can talk.'

The relief of having someone she trusts to confide in lifts

the great burden from Agnès's conscience; someone who will understand her nagging feeling of disloyalty towards the queen.

Chapter Twelve

ℐt is spring, and the almond and cherry trees are in flower as the king's cavalcade progresses towards Poitiers, the travelling minstrels serenading the court en route. As she rides, Agnès slips easily into a reverie about her royal lover, wondering whether she will ever come to believe what has happened. That the king should have singled her out seems totally unreal; and then there he is, his horse next to hers as he whispers: 'Good morrow, my love,' very quietly, with a smile that no one could read as anything but polite, then he is gone again to join another part of his convoy.

A confidante in whom Agnès has complete trust, is her mistress, the Lady Isabelle. She can see with one glance when her *demoiselle* is in distress, and always brings her hack alongside her with an easy smile, speaking in that pretty, light Lorraine accent. Gently she eases out anything that troubles the girl and puts it right with a word or two of advice or humour. What a comfort she is, especially during the king's short absences. Without her and Marie de Belleville, Agnès imagines she could not carry her enormous secret alone, and thanks them both constantly – not in so many words, but with her glances of unmistakable gratitude.

They stop at various châteaux and hostelries along the way, and somehow – with the help of Lady Isabelle or Marie de Belleville – when the king is with the convoy he contrives to pass most nights alone with Agnès.

'Do you know, my beauty, I spent nineteen years here in this region of Poitiers before I came into my kingdom,' he says one evening, lying on his back, half musing, Agnès content with his arm about her, her head on his shoulder. 'It was during the time that my cousin, known as Jean-sans-Peur, Duke of Burgundy, was my enemy.'

After a pause, she dares to reply softly, 'Sire, was he ever your friend?'

He turns his head and looks down at her – the beauty of that perfect alabaster face, those trusting blue eyes – and says thoughtfully: 'Well, at least I believe his son Philip, the present duke, is no longer my enemy.' And she wonders if she has not sensed a slight hesitation there.

The royal cavalcade remains a few days in Poitiers, where the king – radiating confidence and maturity, say the people – attends his *parlement*. Their next destination is Saumur in Anjou, home territory of Lord René. What mixed emotions Agnès is carrying back to this place where Queen Yolande painstakingly trained her to become the source of the king's well-being.

To her sadness, Charles cannot be with them. He who now fills her life each day and night will be gone, and she knows she will find that hard. 'Don't miss me too much, my darling,' he whispers. 'I will steal you away from good Queen Isabelle, and put you among the ladies of the Queen of France! Then we can be together always.' *That* Agnès finds even harder to imagine! 'Soon I will join you back in Saumur,' and with a gay smile and a wave, he rides away – and her nights are spent alone again.

Although the peace treaty with England is still in the process of negotiation, this is a time of great hope throughout the country. Letters patent are being drawn up for a definitive accord between France and England, to be sealed by a marriage union between the royal houses of the two countries.

The party of the Angevin court, including Agnès, reaches Saumur on 16 April 1443. René's brother Charles arrives soon afterwards. He brings the news that Queen Marie will not be joining the court and has moved on to Tours, the king's favourite château, to spend the summer there, quietly awaiting the birth of her child due in September.

On the day the Angevin party arrives at Saumur, the successful conclusion of the Truce of Tours, a peace treaty between France and England, is announced to universal joy. King Henry VI of England, son of the victor of Agincourt, whose mother Catherine is the elder sister of Charles VII of France, is to be joined to the French blood royal. He will marry King René and Queen Isabelle's youngest child, Princess Marguerite, the little girl they left for six years with her grandmother, Queen Yolande, during their absence in Naples. No one could have trained a future Queen of England better.

The Lady Marguerite impresses everyone who meets her. She has beauty, intelligence, elegance, and that particular graciousness that Yolande taught all those in her care. It is generally agreed that these qualities make her an ideal choice to become the bride of Henry VI of England. Queen Isabelle and King René are delighted and enthusiastically approve such a prestigious union between the two countries. No one doubts that it can only enhance this branch of the French royal family – which they sorely need after René's reversals in Naples. Interestingly, it seems there was never any question of Henry VI marrying one of the daughters of the French king and queen. Memories of his father claiming the French throne after he married Charles VII's sister are still raw!

Totally engrossed in her own happiness, Agnès has not really focused on this momentous event: the betrothal ceremony of the Lady Marguerite for a marriage that everyone believes will bring with it peace at last. The English king is eight years older than his bride, but they will make a handsome couple. The court learns that the marriage will be held at Angers and then again in England when the new Queen Marguerite arrives there.

For the wedding in Anjou, the English bridegroom will be represented by Lord Suffolk, who will stand in his king's place as the proxy groom.

The anticipation and excitement in the King of Sicily's household when they reach Saumur is contagious, with much merriment as great entertainments are planned. René himself, the most jovial of hosts, is in his element plotting the amusements, tournaments and feasts. During this time, the royal households of the King of France and those of Lorraine and Anjou mix easily. They have much to celebrate. In the first week of May, the entire court rejoices in the well-received union of René's brother Charles of Maine with Isabelle of Luxembourg. There are tourneys, fancy dress dances, picnics and hunts, and a delightful mixture of guests from Luxembourg and several of the German courts as well. The gentlemen of the various royal establishments are superbly attired and show off to one another – almost as much as the ladies, among whom there are plenty of beauties in their colourful silks and satins, glittering with jewels. As part of the festivities there is a thrilling competition between the French and English archers – and the winners? The Scots!

The court's activities keep Agnès too busy to reflect for long on her last stay at Saumur, but the Old Queen of Sicily's prophetic words come back to her when she finds herself in certain parts of the castle or the grounds where they often walked or rode together. She reminisces on how cleverly Queen Yolande instructed her – how wisely she prepared her for what she had planned; and all the while, Agnès was totally unaware of what she had in store.

June is remarkably hot, and the ladies of the court seek shade in the garden under the trees, the scent of lilies in the flower borders overwhelming as they stroll by them in the cool of the evenings. King René loves gardens and brought an abundance of flowering plants from Provence, especially the scented varieties. The general favourite is the heavily perfumed Damascene red rose given to him by Jacques Coeur through his agents in Damascus; René tells his guests proudly that the shrubs originally came all the way from Shiraz in Persia. From the petals of these deep red flowers their host has rose water made for the ladies' hands, rose jelly and even preserves. The rambling pink Eglantine and the white Alba climb energetically over many of the walls, and drying the petals is one of the occupations allocated to the *demoiselles*, to scatter on floors, tabletops, even pillows. They learn to dip the stronger red petals in egg white, then in fine sugar, another luxury brought to them by Jacques Coeur's agents in India. When coated in this precious sweet powder, the petals are left out to dry. What delicious, elegant sweets they make!

The gardens slope down to the riverbank, where the young ladies seek relief from the heat under the willows, picking varieties of artemisia. While one or two of the minstrels play and sing, the *demoiselles* sit making garlands from periwinkles, or collect sweet woodruff that they then tie in small flat bunches to pack with their clothes for travel, both for the scent and to discourage moths. There is always something on the river to distract the courtiers and the ladies – trading boats bringing their wares to the jetties, others with elegant people rowing, and jocular exchanges drifting across the water between the boatmen. Time and again Agnès finds herself looking up at the high, white stone Château of Saumur looming over the gleaming Loire, and happy memories flood back of her time here with Queen Yolande. The crenellations on the towers are in the shape of the fleur-de-lys – the folly of a previous royal duke – and the great drawbridge has been left lowered to allow the many guests to wander out and enjoy the surrounding countryside in the cool of the evening.

Whenever Agnès receives a letter from her darling lover the King, she tries not to look excited as she disappears into her room to savour every solicitous and reassuring word. She shows her letters to no one, reading his loving phrases until she knows each of them by heart and can repeat them silently to herself as if mouthing a prayer or poem. Just sometimes, she will select parts of the contents to tell Queen Isabelle, or her friend Marie de Belleville.

Chapter Thirteen

One day, to her surprise, Agnès receives a letter from her
cousin, the daughter of her Aunt Marie who brought
her up when her mother died. Antoinette de Maignelay,
companion of her childhood, writes begging Agnès to
invite her to join her at court – her life in the countryside,
she says, is so dull. Despite her trusting relationship with
the Lady Isabelle, and also with Marie de Belleville, Agnès
misses having an intimate friend near her, someone from
her youth with whom she can share memories and childhood secrets.

Since Lady Isabelle shows her such kindness, perhaps
she would not object to her asking her cousin to keep her
close company? After all, it was Antoinette's mother who
originally sent her to the court at Nancy.

To her joy, Isabelle agrees – Antoinette may come, and
should arrive in two to three weeks. During this time,
Agnès draws back the curtains she firmly closed when she

first arrived in Lorraine, and allows herself to contemplate her origins and early life.

Her father's family were country gentry, well established, and loyal to the crown. He was Lord of Coudun and Saint-Géraut and one of the advisers of the Duke of Claremont. Her mother was Catherine, the daughter of Raoul II de Maignelay and Marie de Jouy, owner of Verneuil in the Bourbonnais. Her mother's family circle served the cause of the young 'King of Bourges' – as Charles VII was known in his youth and before his coronation at Rheims in 1429. Her mother's coat of arms is an elder tree. That is all Agnès knows of her family background.

She remembers being told of her mother's death when she was quite young, and how she cried for her. Shortly afterwards, her father sent her to live with her mother's sister, Marie de Maignelay, who loved her as one of her own. In fact she loved her rather *more* than her own, which comforted the young girl but did not endear her to her cousins, Antoinette and Jeanne. Nonetheless, Agnès had a very happy childhood. The three girls were joined by two other cousins her Aunt Marie brought to live with them, and everyone told them they were the five prettiest girls in the county. They grew well, with long blonde curls and blue eyes, and were full of easy laughter.

Agnès's early life was much like that of most children of her class, and she was given a thorough education. The girls all learned to read, and were also read to from the classics; taught to write an elegant hand and to study Aunt Marie's Book of Hours. They learned to sing, to dance the graceful and quite complicated movements to music of the day, and to sew a fine stitch. They had to master at least one musical instrument, and Agnès's was the harp; she was informed quite frankly that she possessed a sweet voice and some talent at her chosen instrument. All the girls were given drawing and painting lessons as well.

Inevitably, the summer months were the most enjoyable of her youth. Then the girls would run about playing in the garden or jump astride their ponies and race one another across the meadows; or they would row in their little boats on the river and try to fish, none too successfully. During harvest time they would collect the wild flowers at the edge of the fields, make daisy chains, and chat to the village children helping their parents to bring in the loads. Theirs was a country childhood, free and easy, filled with sunshine, rivers for bathing and nature to observe and enjoy. The Maignelay girls learned the names of the flowers of Touraine and observed the wild-life in their forests and fields, especially the birds, which fascinated Agnès in particular. She was acknowledged as the most fearless but also the most sensitive rider of their group. Horses and dogs adored her – a little less so her cousins, but with this she was not really concerned; her aunt was pleased with her studies and her contribution to the daily chores, and that, she felt, was sufficient reward.

Then came the day that Agnès will never forget. She had not long celebrated her eleventh birthday when her aunt called her to come to her room, and to come alone. All reprimands were usually given to them as a group, or at least to Agnès and Antoinette at the same time, so this was unusual and made her a little anxious. Had she done something terrible? She searched her memory in vain.

'Agnès, precious niece, come and sit with me by the fire,' Aunt Marie began. When they had settled, she continued: 'I have something I want to tell you that has troubled me ever since I brought you here to live with us following the sadness of your mother's death.'

There followed a long pause while Agnès looked at her feet, conscious that Aunt Marie was having difficulty choosing her words.

'You see, my darling girl, I loved and admired your mother tremendously. She was the person who meant the most to me during my young life. No one could mistake her goodness of heart – and the total unselfishness and generosity of spirit that shone out of her. It was what made her loved by everyone who knew her – and also what caused her death,' she whispered.

'As the elder sister, it was my position and duty to nurse our mother when she fell ill. However, I dearly wanted to attend a great ball at the court of Lorraine and show off to my husband. It was the first time one of our family had been invited there, and for me it was a dream come true – my first court ball, and to dance in the arms of my dearest love! Typically generous, your mother agreed at once that we should go – she would gladly take my place nursing our mother – and sent me off with her blessing to enjoy myself. I did feel a little guilty, but my happiness overcame my family obligation.

'At the time, we had no idea that our mother was suffering from the plague, and after she died, my sister – your dear mother – was not long in following her. When I returned with my husband from our happy sojourn in Lorraine, we learned to our shock that both my mother and yours had already been buried.

'I suffered terribly from guilt and did everything I could to make your childhood happy within our family, and I hope you felt my love for you.' When she saw Agnès nod, she continued. 'And now an opportunity has arisen whereby I hope to redeem a little of my fault in causing your mother's death, ever praying for her forgiveness from above. Since you came to us, I have remained in contact with the young Duchess Isabelle of Lorraine. One day not long ago, I received a letter saying that she had an opening for a *demoiselle* at her court at Nancy, and would I like to send one of my girls? Agnès, my darling, I put your name forward, and you have been accepted.'

How well Agnès remembers that moment, and how her head began spinning.

'What does that mean, dearest aunt? Are you sending me away to a strange world I know nothing about, without friends or protection?'

Aunt Marie took her hand, and with the other stroked her cheek in such a sweet, kind way. 'Agnès, dearest child, how like your mother you are, and you will be just as beautiful. For that reason alone I would like to keep you near me, but this is a wonderful chance for you to advance into a different world; into the circles of the powerful and important people who shape the destiny of our country. You could learn much more than we can teach you here. I have long been aware of your thirst for knowledge, your curiosity to learn about everything; and I have always been conscious of your superior intelligence. My greatest prayer is that you will meet someone worthy of your rare gifts and marry him. Go, my dearest child, and with my blessing. You will always be welcome under my roof and I will come to you whenever you should need me. My responsibility for your mother's death sits heavily on my shoulders. I am asking you to lift that weight by accepting this great opportunity. Will you do it for my sake, and for your mother's?'

Agnès kissed her aunt and left her room without a word. Marie's confession had left her with much to reflect upon. *My mother died from nursing her own mother?* She had never been told that their deaths were due to the plague – just 'an illness'. All these years, overcome with her feelings of guilt and remorse, Aunt Marie had been waiting for a way to compensate her. Now Agnès would have the privilege of entering into the household of Duchess Isabelle, wife of Duke René of Anjou, who had recently become joint ruling sovereigns of Lorraine on the death of her father. Such a position for a daughter was the goal of every family, especially one from the minor nobility.

A few weeks later, Agnès left Touraine full of nerves at the thought of her thrilling future and deeply regretting the parting from her dear aunt and cousin. Naturally Antoinette could not understand why it was Agnès who had been chosen to join the royal court of Lorraine, nor could Agnès tell her.

And now, a lifetime later, here she is back in Anjou with René and Isabelle, this time carrying a wonderful secret which her heart is bursting to share, and waiting to be reunited with her cousin, with whom she can relive her nostalgia for their childhood.

Chapter Fourteen

When Antoinette de Maignelay arrives at Saumur, the cousins fall into one another's arms, overwhelmed and overjoyed to be together again. It has been more than seven years since they last saw each other, and how they have changed! Agnès is awestruck by Antoinette. Before her stands a *woman*, not a girl at all; a mature young woman with flaming red hair and blue eyes open wide, feigning innocence. She has filled out and is quite curvaceous, considerably more so than Agnès, though with a small waist. The cousins are the same height, but Agnès can see at once that Antoinette has experienced more of the world than she has. Her own life during the past seven years has been joyful, yet completely innocent in the virtual convent of Queen Isabelle's court.

Before he left, the king put his treasured Agnès under the protection of two men in whom he has complete trust: Pierre de Brézé and Jacques Coeur. Now Agnès can share with Antoinette the careful attentions of these companions charged by her lover to take special care of her.

'My Lord de Brézé, may I present my dear cousin in whose family I spent my childhood – Antoinette de Maignelay,' and the dashing Pierre bows low and sweeps his hat almost to the ground in mock appreciation of her voluptuous beauty.

'It is I who am honoured and delighted to make your acquaintance,' he says, and Antoinette flushes and wriggles with pleasure. Not yet accustomed to the way of courtiers and their little charades, naturally she assumes he means it. Agnès will soon put her cousin in the picture about that one! Pierre never gives any other impression than genuine admiration – it is one of his more studied tricks, she discovered some time ago. Ladies are invariably swayed when they meet him – until they come to know him and his habits.

But it does not take Agnès long to notice that Antoinette has her own little ways of flirtation too. Already in the first week of her cousin's arrival she finds herself wondering: *have I made a mistake by inviting her to court?* And then she chides herself: *how selfish of me – she is only having a little fun after a life in the country with almost no entertainment.*

It is quite a different matter when Agnès introduces her cousin to her other *chevalier servant*, the serious, thoughtful Jacques Coeur. Antoinette was always clever as a child – and sly – and she realizes at once that Jacques is quite a different style of courtier. There is no possible merit or gain to be had from flirting with him. But she is adept at being utterly captivating, and both Agnès's friends give the impression that they enjoy her company as much as she does theirs.

When Agnès studies her two guardians, she notes how dissimilar they are, and yet how alike. Pierre and Jacques may come from completely different backgrounds, but they both possess naked ambition, although – and she stresses this to Antoinette – it is primarily intended for the benefit of their king and country. 'Pierre de Brézé is a gentleman of noble blood from Normandy, whereas Jacques Coeur is the son of a furrier from Bourges, who, through his own talent and hard work has become a most impressive and successful merchant. He has earned the king's confidence with justification.'

Jacques is always dressed in the most exquisite fabrics, his pockets full of little treasures that he produces now and then for the amusement of the *demoiselles*.

'See this smooth ruby, red as blood: it was once set in the forehead of a great stone statue in faraway India, until a robber gouged it out with a knife and then met a slow and tortuous death for his crime . . .' They sit with parted lips, begging to hear more. 'But how did *you* come by it?' one of the *demoiselles* asks him, and he replies, his smile inscrutable, 'Ah, my dear young ladies – beautiful things come to those who seek them . . .'

Or he might produce a pearl as big as a crab apple, or some little figurine cast in gold. Each piece has a story with which he regales his rapt young audience, and none are more captivated than Antoinette and Agnès. But even more than his stories, it is his eyes that fascinate the king's lady love – they never stop moving, as if looking inside the heads of those around him, searching for secrets hidden there. Sometimes Agnès notices him exchanging guarded looks with Pierre and wonders what they are plotting.

Agnès has allowed herself to become better acquainted with Jacques Coeur, visiting him once a week, because she knows her lord the king trusts him completely with many of his own secrets. Does Jacques know hers? she wonders. It troubles her a little that when they are talking, he always arranges to distance her from the presence of Antoinette, or sends her cousin on a contrived errand. He says nothing, but Agnès has begun to realize that his apparent approval of her cousin is merely due to his good manners – or guile. No, he does not like Antoinette, and whoever he does not like, as she knows, he does not trust.

Despite this tiny, nagging misgiving, Agnès feels she *should* take Antoinette into her confidence about her royal lover, since she will need both Marie de Belleville and her cousin to help keep her relationship with the king from the court – and especially from the queen. She consults Marie, who looks thoughtful.

'Agnès, I must be honest with you. I am not convinced your cousin has primarily your interests at heart. She has asked you to bring her to court on the pretext of keeping you company. But she is never with you! In my opinion, she has come only to better herself; and if you are her stepping stone to that goal, then she will take good care of you – but only for as long as it suits her purpose. Forgive me, please, if what I say hurts you, but one look at her was enough for me to read her scheming character. If you were to ask me, I would send her home at once!'

This is the first time Agnès has heard Marie de Belleville,

the most perfectly mannered young lady of the court of Lorraine, speak with such a passionate opinion about anyone – and it alarms her.

'Dearest Marie, I know you only have my well-being at heart, but please try to get to know her a little better. I believe you may not have had sufficient time to understand her. She is shy, and perhaps seeing you as my closest friend here has made her a little envious and unsure of her place in my life. Will you not give her another chance?' And Marie puts her arm around her younger friend and with a tender kiss on her cheek promises she will try to keep an open mind about Antoinette for a little longer.

Privately, however, Marie de Belleville has no doubt whatsoever that Antoinette de Maignelay is a scheming, brazen hussy, and she vows to keep a very sharp eye on her to help protect Agnès, someone whose purity of heart she recognizes and admires.

Chapter Fifteen

In September 1443, Queen Marie gives birth to her eighth daughter and names her Madeleine. Educated by her formidable mother to obey and do her duty, the queen has produced children regularly, which is what her husband expects of her. Her problem has been to bear a *healthy* child, let alone another son. Never once did she question her parents about their decision; nor has she ever disobeyed her husband, whom she adores despite being fully aware of his faults since their shared childhood.

When the king arrives at Saumur, he finds the court intent on the treaty with England – the union of friendship between their countries and the royal Anjou marriage that will seal it. At last he can believe in a peace that will bring prosperity to the whole of France, *his* France.

Charles surprises the court by travelling straight to Saumur without stopping first at Tours to call on the queen and see their latest child. After all, Tours is no distance from Saumur . . . But Agnès is not surprised; she knows why and is elated. Her patience during the long, lonely weeks is rewarded: the king – her first and only love – has returned to her without stopping to greet his new daughter. And all is as it was before he left: their love as tender; their passion as unrestrained.

Agnès has woken to see the pink dawn through her windows, and she studies her lover's sleeping face in its light on the pillow. How this man has changed from the stiff, reserved *seigneur* she first glimpsed at Chinon on her way to Naples. More than six years later, at Toulouse, she found a more relaxed, successful king, secure in his role yet still formal and royal. Today, she has a gentle, tender, passionate man sleeping beside her, his arm resting across her stomach as she lies on her back, her head turned, watching him. How can she stop this perfect moment of her life, this enchanted morning, from melting like snow in spring? How can she keep his love, his trust, his confidence? Will he ever feel the need to confide in her? That was what Queen Yolande was training her for, after all: to advise the king; to keep him on the right track.

When she asks Marie, to her surprise, her friend is still very much against Agnès confiding in her cousin.

'My dear child – and you are still a child in your lack of worldliness – you will come to regret this decision.'

'But why? Marie, she is only here because I asked for her, and should she displease me, I shall have her sent home. I do feel quite safe, I assure you.'

'Agnès, I promised you I would take a little longer to decide about Antoinette, and I have. Now I trust her even less than before. It is no wonder to me that the king loves you – your heart is pure and true, and he can see your love for him shining out of it. But not so Antoinette's! She is not here for you. *Because* of you, yes, since there was no other way she would be admitted to the court. But her intention is not to help you, unless whatever you ask helps her too. There will be many times when your interests coincide, so that she will do your bidding with pleasure. But I beg you to believe me: you are harbouring a dangerous snake in your bosom! I am convinced of it!' and she leaves the room quickly, almost in tears.

What can Agnès do? Send Antoinette home? All night she thinks about her past life, about Aunt Marie's guilt over her mother, and how she gave Agnès the chance of a future by sending her to the court of Lorraine. No; she cannot reject the daughter of the woman who did so much for her. Agnès owes her dearest aunt everything she has – even the great love she has found with the king.

By morning, she has decided to tell Antoinette her secret.

'Dear cousin, I have something I must say to you, because I need your friendship and your help more than ever.'

Antoinette gives her a strange sideways look. 'But of course, my dear Agnès, I am yours to command, as you know!' and she laughs.

Agnès continues undeterred. 'I want you to know, and with his permission, that the king is my lover, and that we shall need you and Marie de Belleville to help guard our secret.'

At first Antoinette looks at her in total amazement, almost incredulous; but then she embraces her cousin. Holding her at arm's length, a hand on each shoulder, and gazing into her eyes, she says sincerely: 'My dear Agnès, but this is wonderful news! I am pleased and honoured that you share your secret with me – and I take it with Marie de Belleville as well?' Yes, she can see from Agnès's face that she has told her also. 'We shall be your guardian angels and keep you safe from the wicked tongues of the court. You can count on me, dear cousin. Your secret is safe with me – and I am sure also with Marie. Now I must rush, I am on duty with the queen,' and quickly she leaves the room.

It takes a moment for that last remark to sink in. *On duty with the queen* – she must mean the Queen of France, since Antoinette has nothing whatever to do with Isabelle, who does not like her, and is certainly not attached to her court. How is it possible that Antoinette has *duties* with the Queen of France? She is only at court as Agnès's guest after all. She ponders this question as she heads towards Queen Isabelle's quarters for her instructions.

Agnès knows very well that of all the ladies in service with her, Marie de Belleville is still her only real friend. Both Marie and Antoinette keep her informed of whatever gossip they hear from courtiers, their ladies and the staff of any of the three courts. Confident that they will defend her whenever they can, Agnès keeps her own focus entirely on the king's happiness.

Chapter Sixteen

King René and his brother Charles of Maine have both been newly installed as members of the Royal Council – a singular honour – and as Companions of the King at festivals and tournaments. Among the inner circle of Charles VII's court, the brothers freely admit they are seeking opportunities for preferment, chances to improve their own situation and that of Anjou. René's debts are common knowledge within the Angevin court, and with his brother's lack of income from his occupied county of Maine, the courtiers are aware that the royal brothers are aiming for high positions in the king's household.

René has been involving himself energetically in his family's interests, so much so that he seems totally unaware of what has been happening between the two royal courts, the king's and his own. When he returns home from attending to matters in Lorraine, he is delighted to find that the king is at Saumur, especially when he hears that Charles intends to stay longer than his usual sojourn. Agnès can read René's face: naturally the king would enjoy being back here and reliving his youth; what other reason could there possibly be for coming to stay at Saumur? René is such a good, honest soul; how could he ever imagine his king falling in love with one of his wife's *demoiselles*?

Marie de Belleville tells her that when Lord René heard the king did not divert to Tours to view his newborn daughter, he thought nothing of it: 'I find it quite understandable that he made directly for Saumur! It's a place he has loved since coming to join us here as a boy; not odd at all.' Marie adds with a smile: 'Queen Isabelle gave him one of her looks,' which the *demoiselles* recognize as meaning *he is an idiot*, but with his customary shrug, her husband kept his peace! *So he still does not know . . .*

René has built a magnificent manor house opposite his imposing château at Saumur and has filled the flower borders with a profusion and variety of plants: gillyflowers in pink, crimson and white; sweet woodruff; pink, red and white peonies; marigolds; periwinkle and scented violets. Daisies are another of his favourites, especially the big ox-eye ones, and primroses that flower throughout the spring. Every shelf and tabletop in the castle and the manor holds vases filled with sweet-smelling flowers – arranging them is one of the duties of the *demoiselles*. René, who loves instructing the young of his court, gathers them about him in a circle on the grass, where they sit making daisy chains to decorate the tables.

'I am sure you have recognized that the fleur-de-lys, the royal symbol of the kings of France, is more likely to be a stylized iris than a lily,' he tells them, and in the heat they murmur dreamily: 'Really?'

'Yes, it's true, and the blue iris has always been the most popular.' With that he slaps his thigh and gives a great laugh. They are never sure if he means what he says – with that twinkle in his eyes to confuse!

The time spent building up to the treaty with England and preparing the wedding arrangements is full of elegant distractions. With Pierre de Brézé's inventiveness and Jacques Coeur's talent for providing the costumes and decorative elements required, the festivities will be a delight. But the master of ceremonies is always Lord René, the recognized genius of entertainments.

For Agnès, these summer months are the happiest she has known in her young life, spent in loving complicity with the king. Throughout the dinners, dances, feasts, hunts, picnics, parties and musical entertainments, the lovers exchange glances, whisper assignations, meet secretly in bowers and gardens. They ride out side by side with company or almost alone. They watch sunrises from her bedroom window and sunsets from rooftop balustrades. If ever he is called from her side by day, at night she regales him with fanciful stories that she invents in his absence. She makes him laugh and never sees him cry. She knows he is happy – as is she.

Agnès is not so naïve as to imagine that her lover's elevated position does not affect her – how could it be otherwise? And yet her love for him is so bound up with his need for her, a need she recognizes and to which she can and does respond. *Is it not like this for every woman in love? To be desired not only for her body but also for her heart and mind, as I know I am?* Her entire being is dedicated to his happiness; it is the essence of the love they share. Yes, she knows she sins in the eyes of God and the world, and she suffers for it. Her lord and lover is married, and she was brought up to believe that marriage was an institution ordained by God. But then again, she tells herself, he did not choose his wife and was not consulted. Then reason whispers: *What prince ever is?* Queen Yolande herself told Agnès that she had arranged their union when Charles was ten and Marie only eight years old. Each day Agnès continues to argue with her inner self: *Is a king with so many responsibilities not entitled to love?*

She spends long hours in prayer trying to reason with her conscience, and from childhood habit she turns to Mary Magdalene, patron saint of sinners of the flesh, of which she is surely one of the worst. *If I pray sincerely, Mary Magdalene might intercede for me with the Lord above, and perhaps He will understand.*

While she struggles with her conscience on the moral issue, she has no difficulty with the gifts her lover showers on her, which she unashamedly accepts and enjoys. Many she passes on to the Church in the hope of buying some remission for her sins, sins she cannot and *will not* stop committing. Her passion for the king is all-consuming – even if it means she is destined to burn in hell for ever. . . .

'My love,' she whispers one night as he comes to her, 'I have a wonderful secret to share with you.'

As he clasps her in his arms, he asks: 'And what might that be, my darling?'

She frees herself and stands back to watch his face. 'I am expecting our child.'

How he embraces her! How could she have doubted – no, *feared* – his reaction?

'Oh, most precious love of my heart, this is wonderful news indeed,' he says as he holds her to his own heart. *He who has had so many children, yet seems pleased about another!*

Agnès cannot help wondering: will he still hide me from the world? Surely his joy will surmount his caution? There is no doubt Charles is overjoyed at this seal to their love, which daily brings out the best in this strange man.

In the seventh month of her pregnancy, Agnès stops wearing the little sack of feathers under the front of her dresses – now she has her own bump to fill the usual place. Since she is so slender, her pregnancy has not shown until now, and tomorrow she will take her cousin and leave the court until after her confinement. They have no need to go far – Charles has arranged for a charming lodge to be prepared on the other side of Saumur's forest and Agnès finds her Aunt Marie there waiting. She has come to be with her for the birth, and has brought Agnès's own former nurse to help. What a fuss they make. 'Well now, my little one,' says Nanny – which always makes Agnès laugh, since she has grown much taller than her – 'we must be sure you are eating correctly and resting, as well as doing some walking to make the coming of the baby easier . . .' and on she prattles, but Agnès's immediate concerns are somewhat different.

'Dearest Aunt, I have been charged to tell you that the birth must be kept a secret within our family, even though

I know how overjoyed my lord the king feels about this symbol of our love.' Of course, the good woman understands and agrees.

After celebrating the treaty and the betrothal of the Lady Marguerite d'Anjou at Saumur, the court has left for René's capital of Nancy in Lorraine to prepare for the actual wedding ceremony. At the same time, the king and the dauphin have returned to the fighting and advanced with their troops to quell a revolt in the city of Metz.

At this important and intimate moment of her life, Agnès is cosseted, surrounded by people who love and care for her – and even though she knows Antoinette would have much preferred to move to Nancy, it is for just such an occasion as this that Agnès needs her cousin to remain by her side.

'I thank you for staying with me, dear cousin, since I realize how much you would prefer to be with the court, enjoying the preparations for the royal wedding.'

'Hush,' says Antoinette, 'you know you are my first concern, and what would the king say if he heard I had abandoned you in your time of need?'

And just then it occurs to Agnès: what an odd thing for Antoinette to say. The king would not know or presumably care where she was, if he had even noticed her . . . *Had* he noticed her? She has not yet presented her cousin to Charles, and this little comment of Antoinette's keeps popping back into her mind as she lies in her shady room, thinking.

October 1444 is unusually warm, although Agnès is comfortably installed behind shuttered windows, waiting calmly for her great moment. She looks at the beautiful tapestries on the walls, gently lit by candlelight. Her room is deliciously scented with herbs, and she is reassured by two good birthing women thoughtfully sent by Lady Isabelle, surely at the king's suggestion. They will join with her aunt and Antoinette, as well as the old family nurse. She feels secure, confident in the love of her king, who sends messages almost daily – and she has no fear of what is to come.

In the next room, her birthing bed is draped with clean sheets and many pillows; the cradle stands prepared, and nearby is her parade bed. After the birth, when she has been washed and dressed, she will be moved into this and made ready to receive her baby into her arms. Her room, hung with long green velvet curtains, has been beautifully decorated for her and her child. She is content and happy.

When her time comes, Agnès is ready and all goes well. She pushes when told, and even rejoices in the pain as penance for her sin, and again, and again. Then she hears: 'It's a girl, a beautiful little girl,' and a great peace floods over her; she feels complete and utterly fulfilled. Her aunt and her own nanny wash her gently, scent her slightly with a fresh flower mist, dress her in a long clean shift, and settle her among the great down pillows of the parade bed.

'Here is your daughter, my darling girl,' says her aunt, handing her the clean and swaddled baby. As she looks into eyes as blue as her own, Agnès knows that all is well within her world.

'We shall call her Marie – that is the king's wish,' she announces proudly to everyone around her.

There is a frown on her aunt's brow. 'But that is the

queen's name; don't you think it would perhaps be inappropriate?'

'No, it is the king's wish to call her after the mother of Jesus,' she insists, and so it is done. Her girl dwarf turns some joyful cartwheels, which makes them all laugh; Antoinette is solicitous; and Agnès is completely gratified holding little Marie to her breast. Nothing else matters.

Lying in her cocoon of contentment, Agnès reflects how it vexed Charles to have to leave her to give birth without him beside her, but she has assured him in her replies to his many notes that she is in good hands. How right she was – there were no complications. As soon as she can sit, she composes a letter for her lover that will be ready for his next courier. His tender concern for her comfort and well-being has touched her and, if possible, made her love him more.

'Dearest Aunt, tell me – everything will change now, will it not? The king will want to let the court – and the world – know of his association with me, the mother of his child. Is that not how it will be?' But her aunt just shakes her head and says quietly, 'Do not push him, my dearest one, let him take his own time to recognize his child and acknowledge you as his daughter's mother and his dearest love. I am confident it will happen.' Agnès is not troubled, sure of the king's love and that her aunt knows best.

Fit from constant travels on horseback, and young, Agnès recovers quickly from the birth. She is encouraged – indeed, *urged* – by his loving letters that she begins to plan her return to be with him at court. The winter is over, snow thaws all around. Yes, it is time. Like her contemporaries,

Agnès is content to leave her infant with her wet nurse and in the care of her aunt. No children are brought to court – their place is with their minders, not their mothers, who are expected to glitter again mere days following a confinement. With her figure restored to its former slender silhouette, Agnès feels assured of her welcome by the appreciative eyes and loving arms of her darling king. He has sent a suitable escort and comfortable litters for her and Antoinette to proceed towards Lorraine and join the royal court at Nancy.

Chapter Seventeen

$\mathcal{I}$t is the second spring Agnès will spend with her royal lover, shielded by good friends who will guard their secret. Charles has decided whom he can trust to protect her, and his choices do not surprise her: Pierre de Brézé; Charles of Maine; Jacques Coeur; Etienne Chevalier; Marie de Belleville and of course, her cousin Antoinette. These six members of the court are designated by the king to be her constant companions.

The royal court is well installed already at Nancy, and to her joy, the king rents a beautiful manor house for Agnès not far from René and Isabelle's ducal palace. Here they can meet and spend time alone together. The owner of the house admired the lifestyle of the Romans and installed a steam bath fitted with underground pipes that is a marvel to experience, especially alone together.

It is the king's wish that Agnès leave the royal household of her protectress, Lady Isabelle, and join that of

Queen Marie. The idea horrifies Agnès. How can she, the king's lover, be in service to the queen? Charles reassures her: he will ask his wife in his gentlest manner; what can the poor queen say? Agnès begs him to leave her where she is, but the two royal courts are due to separate soon and they cannot bear to be apart.

Once the king removed Agnès from her service to Isabelle and installed her among the *demoiselles* of Queen Marie, Agnès's official accommodation is with her new mistress's other ladies in the main palace, but at the king's insistence at least she has her own private room. When not on duty with Queen Marie, she slips away to the manor house to meet her lover, or just to relax and enjoy a steam bath with Marie de Belleville or Antoinette. Naturally there is a lot of talk and jealousy of Agnès at court, and she does all she can to share what she feels privileged to have received. In fact, she spends some of her free time with the queen's ladies for just that reason, dressing modestly and wearing few jewels.

When Agnès arrived at Nancy, how tenderly her lover welcomed her: 'My dearest love, my greatest treasure!' he whispered while embracing her. And then, a rush of questions: 'Are you well and healed? Tell me about our little Marie: is she as pretty as you? Has she your blue eyes? Does she have hair already?' and Agnès, moved by his caring curiosity, assured him laughingly: 'All is well, my dearest, yes, with us both.' He shows such interest in the baby that she almost forgets how many children he has already – another can hardly be a novelty, yet the way he talks of little Marie it is as if she is his first!

Since her arrival at the court of Lorraine, Agnès has hardly found a moment to think about herself. Totally involved with the many entertainments organized by King René, she lives in a carnival of wonders that never stops, all designed to celebrate the strategically important marriage of his daughter Marguerite and the peace that it will seal. If it seems that the preparations for this wedding have been going on endlessly, then that is indeed a fact. But for now there are balls – sometimes masked; banquets with entertainment by minstrels and jugglers; tournaments enlivened by the many visitors arriving with their colourful entourages, attendants leading high-stepping horses in every direction; and the daily hunts to hounds or with falcons. The king offers Agnès the choice of the royal stables, and she glories in her mastery of his most challenging mounts. This, she can see from the look in his eyes, pleases him greatly. There are many official engagements for Charles VII to attend, and Agnès understands she cannot be by his side at those times, but somehow, and often, he manages to steal away to spend a moment with her, and many a night as well. She is secure, assured of his love – and happy.

The union of France and England to be sealed by the marriage of Henry VI and Marguerite d'Anjou is the historic occasion the realm has long waited to celebrate; the confirmation of peace between their endlessly warring countries. The event has created the opportunity for René's court of Lorraine, together with that of Charles VII, to show the assembled grandees of his country, as well as those from England, that France can rival the splendour of the most fabled court in Europe, that of Burgundy! With great ingenuity Lord René has laid careful plans to produce several novel musical entertainments and surprising theatricals for the delight of the numerous guests.

Gallant knights have journeyed to Nancy from Europe's illustrious courts to partake of the festivities, the tournaments and the jousts, and all freely admit that the French are worthy contenders in splendour. Even that legendary chevalier Jacques de Lalaing, the most noble and successful tournament knight in all France, does his best to impress. His extravagant train of attendants includes pages dressed head to foot in white riding white palfreys, each caparisoned to the ground in cloth of gold scattered with little bells attached that tinkle with every movement. No one has ever seen anything like it! 'My lady,' Agnès calls to Lady Isabelle, never far when possible from her protégé, 'with such a splendid show, at last my Lord René can have his revenge after the sad years he spent imprisoned by the Duke of Burgundy!'

'Yes,' Isabelle laughs contentedly, 'he has invited the world and set out to dazzle it – and I believe he has succeeded.'

'Brilliantly!' agrees Agnès with all her heart.

But in view of the extravagance of the entertainments, the whispers from the inner circle of the Anjous hint that their Good King René, as they still often call him, will ruin himself. Agnès listens and recalls the advice Queen Yolande gave her. Summoning all her courage, she decides to approach the king with her fears. When the moment seems right, she dares to whisper her concerns.

'My dearest love, please forgive my impertinence,' she says, looking down, and immediately he raises her lovely head.

'What is it, my darling?'

'It's just that my Lord René's family is most anxious he is ruining himself – and them – with this dazzling series of entertainments. He believes – as we all do – there is no worthier cause to celebrate than the peace the union of France and England will bring us through his daughter's marriage.' Having said it all in one breath, she lowers her eyes again and bites her lip, fearing a reprisal. But the king gently puts his finger to her lip and smiles. Agnès sighs, for that smile tells her he will indeed recompense his impoverished Angevin cousin. How love has changed this notoriously fractious and capricious man!

The thought of reconciliation between France and England fills everyone with hope for the future. As well as bringing peace, the marriage of Marguerite d'Anjou and Henry VI will enable the kingdom's depleted revenues to recover. Later, at night, Agnès will whisper in the king's ear again, just to make sure. She thinks of her time with Queen Yolande and all that she told her, and realizes how well that great lady foresaw her future and the ways in which she could be of use to the boy the wise queen had painstakingly trained to become a true king.

Throughout the preparations for the important event, Isabelle is the perfect hostess: presenting her guests to one another, a kind word here, a warm smile there, consistently radiant. How she inspires the admiration of Agnès and the *demoiselles,* all bursting with pride for her and for the Anjous. The fact that such a large number of august visitors have arrived at her court in Lorraine for this significant union, and that they remain for such a long stay, is a triumph in itself for the King and Queen of Sicily. Isabelle is still quite young – in her mid-thirties – and with the help of Jacques Coeur, she wears the most magnificent court dresses – velvets, brocades, crackling taffetas – for every occasion. Louis' dauphine Margaret, more slender than ever with her strange diet of vinegar and green apples – which even Agnès, who never criticizes her, doubts can be healthy – appears ravishing in her tight dark velvet bodices, with matching shaded chiffons floating from her arms and waist and trailing from her tall *henins*. Seeing the sadness in her eyes, Agnès does her best to cheer her.

'My lady, please be joyful. Even if our Anjou princess and her kingly husband do not find perfect love, their union will ensure peace – and surely that alone brings happiness to your anxious heart?'

The dauphine smiles at Agnès and her hand reaches up to her neck. Her jewels are spectacular – many of them wedding gifts from various rulers and potentates, and today she dazzles in diamonds and pearls. 'Such magnificence is worth nothing, my sweet Agnès, without a fond understanding between husband and wife. I pray they will have at least that between them.'

The bride of Lorraine, the 'peace dove' as many are calling Marguerite, is at her most radiant and delightful, rightly enjoying her first leading role as she begins to appreciate the status she is acquiring. Marguerite's charm is as celebrated as her beauty, elegance and ability. What a Queen of England she will be, and how proud she makes everyone; the older members of the court say how she resembles her grandmother Yolande when she arrived from Aragon as a bride. All Agnès thinks is how proud Queen Yolande would be to know what a significant role this child she nurtured for more than six years has before her.

But there is still work to be carried out on behalf of the king. Pierre de Brézé is actively engaged in diplomacy, doing his utmost to regulate the affairs of France with Philip of Burgundy; settling with the Holy Roman Emperor; and completing the terms of surrender of the city of Metz.

The devoted Etienne Chevalier is never far from Agnès's side, acquiescing to her every wish – a true *chevalier servant*, despite his long face, totally loyal to his king and always ready to do his bidding – and hers. 'We all know that Etienne is madly in love with you, my Lady Agnès,' Pierre teases, 'hence the sad face he carries about with him like a shield.' She replies that it is wicked of Pierre to mock him.

Then there is Antoine de Chabannes, the epitome of a crafty old soldier but with a sound, good heart and always ready to help. Invariably he greets Agnès with some merry soldier's joke, which often she does not understand; when she does, she finds herself flushing bright red. But he means well, and she knows his is a sterling character. Pierre claims he has learned almost everything he knows of soldiering from Chabannes, and the king wants him to teach the dauphin survival techniques. Not so Louis! He makes it clear he wants no help from a rough soldier like Chabannes.

The ladies of Queen Marie's suite, as well as those in attendance on Lady Isabelle, discuss without cease the splendour of the knights who will attend the wedding;

what the bride, the royal family and they themselves will wear; who will sit where, and of whom they dream already. With peace in the air, everyone's thoughts have drifted to pleasant pastimes again after an age of living in fear.

The day of the marriage, 24 May, is one of glorious sunshine with a gentle breeze. The ladies attached to Queen Isabelle rise early to be ready before entering her chamber to help her to prepare for the ceremony. The *demoiselles* are to wear long dresses of white silk, with the bodice cut to fit tightly under a short bolero jacket of crimson velvet edged with gold lace. When Agnès saw Jacques Coeur a few days earlier, he told her: 'Do not be surprised, Lady Agnès, I beg you, at the jackets I have added to the dresses of all the *demoiselles*. I know you feel warm now, standing in the spring sunshine, but you will find it quite cool in the cathedral.'

All the dresses have trains, which Agnès thinks are a little short for true elegance, but then she is not in a position to say much – as yet. Somehow she knows that the time will come when *she* will dictate the fashions of the court! Around her waist she wears a gift from her beloved: a gold chain studded with pearls. It is lovely but not ostentatious, and despite being admired it will not be thought too remarkable; although she catches a sly smile from Antoinette as she fingers it.

I was always a little vain, thinks Agnès, *but now I have become worse. I know it. I enjoy dressing in the luxurious silks and velvets I have always admired, and my king allows me more and more trinkets. I must confess sins of vanity to Father Denis.* But she is also grateful to God for the beauty He has given her, and that she may use it to please her cherished king, whom she loves with all her heart.

The procession is to be led out by the king's heralds, their chests emblazoned with the royal arms of France and Anjou, the same on the pennants hanging from their silver trumpets. What a triumphant clarion call they will make – this is truly a proud moment for the House of Anjou!

Following behind the heralds is the King of France, leading King René. *How elegant my lover looks.* Charles wears a long sky-blue coat covered in small fleur-de-lys embroidered in gold thread; his sleeves, which almost trail the ground, are lined in ermine like his coat. As he draws level with Agnès, she catches his eye; his expression softens into a half-smile as she drops her head and performs a low court *révérence.* Just behind him walks the dauphin Louis. How proudly he advances, as if confident of receiving a new and major role in the kingdom. Charles has told Agnès of his satisfaction with his son of late, but she doubts he will grant him the honour he craves. How unalike they are, this father and son. Pierre de Brézé believes the dauphin is in love with Agnès and that is the reason for his hatred of his father. Agnès is not so sure.

Lord René is striking in emerald and gold silk damask, while his son and heir, Jean of Calabria, wears a most beautiful damask tunic, the sleeves appliquéd with multi-coloured precious stones. Only Jacques Coeur could provide such splendour – young Jean could never afford it – but this is his family's great day and perhaps the good merchant has lent it to him. Next in the procession, sitting tall on a splendid prancing black charger, is Pierre de Brézé, the favourite of all the court ladies. His black velvet outfit is densely over-stitched in a trellis pattern of tiny pearls; his horse caparisoned in black velvet quilted using gold thread, glinting in the sunshine. Aware of his allure, Pierre bows and smiles, and a combined sigh rises from the ladies! Behind him follow the great lords of the king's court: the Duke of Brittany, the Count of Clermont, Count Louis of Luxembourg, the Count of Saint-Pol and many more, all splendidly attired in the colours of the rainbow and sparkling with precious jewels. For this historic occasion, each does their best to outdo the other and to appear as spectacular as they can – a feast for the eyes and the senses.

The more intrepid grand ladies of the court who ride, follow behind them, their high headdresses and veils fluttering gently in the breeze. As usual, it is their horses that Agnès notices – well-bred and caparisoned to the ground in various shades of velvet, damask and other elaborate fabrics, each stitched all over with gold or silver thread, which is also used to plait the horses' manes and tails. The king has given Agnès the beautiful grey Arabian mare the dauphine noticed earlier during their journey, and she encourages her to pirouette to left and right, enjoying the admiring observations she can hear. The mare's neck arches, and she works her lips as she tosses her long dark mane threaded with little bells on golden strings. How her nostrils flare with every roar and salvo of the crowd as her experienced rider lets her dance and show off her high spirits! It is such a happy day, full of promise, and Agnès is not ashamed to glory in its every aspect.

Suddenly, as if to add to the joyful confusion, all the great bells of the city begin to toll, and the horses pirouette even more as countless marguerites cut from gold and silver cloth rain gently down on the procession from the windows and balconies above. These are draped in tapestries and brightly coloured embroidered fabrics hanging over balustrades and window ledges. Wherever one looks there are marguerites made out of every material imaginable and stuck onto every surface. Garlands of the flowers cut from coloured paper hang above the riders' heads, stretched between the houses on either side of the road. Banners stamped in gold letters spelling out *Vivre le roi*, *Vivre la princesse* or *Vivre la reine d'Angleterre* hang between the daisy chains. Agnès turns to her fellow *demoiselles* and smiles. They are all entranced with the same feeling of wonder – as if the city has erupted in a great wave of jubilation in anticipation of this marriage that will bring their tired, bruised spirits peace at last.

All forty of the *demoiselles* follow in procession behind the King and Queen of Sicily. Behind them, a little distance back, appears the bride, advancing in solitary splendour, seated on a litter draped with a golden cloth and carried by four elegant young knights also dressed in gold.

Before the procession enters the church of Saint-Martin, everyone gathers outside to be placed in their correct order, and Agnès has time to quietly observe the scene unfolding before her eyes. It is an occasion she will write down in her book of memoirs, the day peace was formalized between France and England through the marriage of a princess of Anjou, and she wants to take note of every detail of the magnificent company. Inside, William de la Pole, Earl of Suffolk, waits to act as proxy bridegroom, but in the meantime, Agnès takes a close look at the bride.

Isabelle told her that when Henry VI of England received Marguerite's portrait, he fell in love at once – and no wonder. Today she is a vision of beauty in silver gauze embroidered all over with tiny pearls in the shape of daisies. Her waist is worn high and Agnès knows she has added a little bag of feathers over her stomach underneath in the current fashion. Her sleeves are long and wide, hanging well below her hands – slit open down from her elbow to show a lining of ermine to emphasise her new status. To complement her golden collar studded with rubies, the neckline of her dress is heart-shaped. On her head she wears a little golden coronet edged around the base with pearls. From the back of this hangs a double layer of silver gauze, which joins with the long train of her wide skirt. Marguerite, the bride of Anjou, is a sight that has Agnès gasping in admiration, together with the other *demoiselles* and all who see her.

To judge from the cheering and exclamations, it is not hard to appreciate how much the elegance of the ladies of the court – and of the courtiers – astounds and thrills the crowds. The colours they wear seem like a multiplication of the rainbow, with floating silk veils, trims of exotic furs, gold chains glinting in the sun, precious stones flashing – even leather bridles, reins and spurs are gilded. Many of the horses' manes and tails are plaited with ribbons in colours to match their riders' outfits, and little silver and gold marguerites are dotted wherever possible. People throng the streets, children perch high on shoulders, but they leave a goodly path for the royal procession to pass between them.

Everyone is waving and calling, *'Montjoie! Montjoie!'*

and *'Noel! Noel!'* and *'Vivre le roi!'*, *'Vivre le bon roi René!'*, and there are many calls for the bride, who blushes each time she hears herself addressed as *'la reine Marguerite'* or *'la reine d'Angleterre'*.

As the courtiers and ladies ride ahead to dismount and await the arrival of the procession, Queen Marie, Queen Isabelle and the bride lead the grand line of litters, each draped in cloth of gold or silver, or in shades of silk and satin to complement the dresses of their occupants. Red and gold ribbons, the colours of Lorraine, float from every balcony along the route as the guests ride past; golden standards bear three silver birds flying across the horizontal red band of Lorraine's flag, and the same adorn each doorway, while children excitedly scatter still more daisy heads. Agnès turns to Antoinette riding beside her and laughs: 'I think I will have to shield my eyes from the orgy of colour and glitter before me!' And Antoinette smiles in complicity as she concurs. Many of the courtiers have added ostrich and other feathers to their hats, and they flutter and bob about in the light breeze which lifts and plays with the delicate gauze veils of the ladies.

There is a sense of exhilaration and expectation in the air, added to the delicious aromas of the strewing herbs. The scent rises and disperses among the crowd – rosemary, lavender, sweet woodruff and hyssop – as the approaching horses pirouette and stamp on them with their shod hooves. The procession is deliberately slow, flavoured with regular wafts of the delicate scent of garden flowers drifting over the crowd. For their part, people exclaim with a loud 'Ah!' of delight as yet another gorgeously attired lady or courtier passes them slowly on the way to the church, waving and bowing graciously.

There is no doubt in the mind of anyone attached to King Renè's court that this astonishing display of luxury and wealth could only be due to the genius of one man – Jacques Coeur. Who else could understand as well as he that a nation long deprived of a show of splendour needs to see glamour and brilliance, especially in their hour of triumph? Jacques Coeur rides near King René, and Agnès edges her horse close to his. 'You are to be congratulated, my good friend,' she tells him conspiratorially with her slow smile.

'And for what, pray, my Lady Agnès?' he replies matching her expression with his own secretive smile. 'Are you referring to your fine little Arabian mare? I see you handle her with expertise.'

'No, my good sir, but to all the magnificence you have arranged to be displayed on this historic day, for no one but you could do that!'

The grand merchant of Bourges never replies quickly. He has a way of pursing his lips before he speaks. At last he says, still smiling with pleasure: 'You are correct, my fine lady, I cannot deny it. I felt that the occasion warranted a great show, and I hope I have provided it – for the glory of Anjou and my late patroness, Queen Yolande.'

'Yes, I believe I can feel her smiling down in appreciation from above. But tell me, dear sir, how did you bring us all this magnificence?'

'Why, I used my fleet of caravels to convey to France the most luminous fabrics from the Orient, materials embroidered in every colour as well as with thread of silver and gold, and even decorated with precious stones;

I brought fans made from the feathers of birds unknown in Europe. I brought gold ornaments with emeralds and rubies, so that the courtiers could attach exotic plumes to their hats and even to their horses' headbands.'

'Tell me more,' she urges him. 'What else shall I see?'

'Colours, my fine Lady Agnès, in combinations even you could not imagine: purples mixed with reds; greens with blues; yellows with oranges – every shade imaginable will be on display,' he answers her, 'adorning the horses as much as their riders.'

He is right: it is indeed an unforgettable kaleidoscope of brilliance.

'My dear Jacquet, as I will henceforth call you, everything I see before me is as breathtakingly beautiful as you describe – and all in honour of this important occasion. Won't you tell me: where do you find so many and such splendid things with which to glorify our combined court of Anjou and Lorraine on this most historic of days?'

Again he gives her his enigmatic smile as he tells her. 'Ah, my dear lady, you should know that money can buy almost anything.'

But it still puzzles her why *he* should be the one able to provide the most beautiful of everything to be found available in the country and beyond.

'Please, dear friend, satisfy my curious mind – won't you tell me how you became the greatest merchant in France, because it is to you the nobility go to find and acquire the most exquisite clothes, furs, precious jewels and furnishings for their castles. Even our horses come through your good offices!'

He laughs and shows his perfect teeth – and she begins to wonder how he came by those as well!

'As I have told you before, my lady, everyone owes me money. They do repay *some* of their debts, but rarely all, and then, soon after, they or their ladies buy again. The more they owe me, the greater the hold I have over them. Since there are many who pay me a little, there is always money coming in, and it adds up, believe me!'

At that moment Agnès feels a slight tremor of fear for this man who has so many powerful lords in his debt; it is like holding a fistful of vipers, and she cannot stop herself from wondering if he might not find *himself* bitten one day. Fie! Surely not, he is far too clever for that!

Chapter Eighteen

$\mathcal{T}$he wedding celebrations last for eight days; superb sunny days of feasting, jousting, tournaments, parades, dances and every kind of music and entertainment. René is famous for arranging tournaments, and for this glorious occasion, he outdoes even himself! When he can, her lover the king spends the nights with Agnès, and never fails to find a moment during the day to whisper sweet words in her ear. On the eve of the last day of the wedding tournament he comes to her room, this time wearing a strange, almost anxious expression.

'My dearest love, my beloved Agnès, I want you to do something for me.' He has never before been a supplicant, and without hesitation she replies:

'But of course, my lord, anything!'

'Tomorrow is the last day of the tournament celebrating the most important moment of my reign to date.'

He stops, almost hesitating. She holds his hand and plays with his fingers to reassure him.

'Tell me, my lord, what is it?' Something is troubling him.

He takes a deep breath. 'I want you to ride by my side into the tourney ground tomorrow.' Then the words burst out of him in a great rush: 'I want to show my people the woman who has taught me to love.'

For a moment, Agnès is unable to speak. Such a declaration of love would be a joy beyond compare – and yet it would be made in the presence of the queen his wife. 'My lord – forgive me, but the queen will be present and this would surely shame her.'

Gently, he takes her face in his hands. 'My dearest darling, I can assure you that the queen will not be there on the morrow.'

'But the court, my lord, the court will know and someone will tell her, and that too would shame her.' Surely he can feel her despair – wanting to please him but not insult the queen his wife? He looks pensive for a moment. Then he turns her to face him and, with both hands on her shoulders, looks deep into her eyes.

'My love, in great secrecy I have had made for you the most beautiful suit of armour of silver interlaced with gold, in which you will look more lovely than any lady who has ever worn armour before.' He can tell she is wavering, and goes on: 'My beloved Agnès, I must ask you to hear me. Some years ago, I sinned grievously in betraying an honest young woman sent to me by my *bonne mére*, Queen Yolande. This girl from Lorraine declared adamantly that she wanted to save France. Yes, as you know, it was Jeanne d'Arc.

'France was in crisis. Orléans was besieged and the people were starving. If our second greatest city fell to the English, then they had won our country completely. I was lacklustre and despondent, and could see no way out of our inevitable defeat. I had no army, but unbeknown to me, Queen Yolande, at vast expense, recalled her Angevin army from their march to Marseilles, from where they were to sail to Naples to fight for her eldest son. She herself renamed her troops "the Army of Jeanne d'Arc"! She dressed Jeanne in a suit of white armour and put her on a great white charger with instructions to remain on a hill out of arrow range overlooking Orléans, holding a huge silk banner of Lorraine, white with a red cross. Yolande's plan was to present Jeanne d'Arc as an icon for the French, a dazzling, almost mystical image that would inspire both the Angevin army outside Orléans and the wretched starving people inside to defeat the English. She was the symbol that assured them "God is with you".

'And they battled like never before, the skeletons within and the newly named Army of Jeanne d'Arc from outside. After nine days of fierce fighting, the city was relieved. By her example, the "Maid of Orléans", as they called her thereafter, gave back to my oppressed people the courage they had lost, and they rose up for her because she also gave them faith. Everywhere she went, men, women and children flocked to her. She was the country's heroine, this fragile young woman of seventeen years, so simple and pure.

'It is my tragedy that when I was given the opportunity to save her, *I did not*. I allowed myself to be swayed by envious courtiers and prelates who felt she had stolen their glory, since it was they who had done the fighting while all she did was sit on her great white horse facing the city. They resented her claim to have a direct line to God – which the prelates clearly did not, or He would have helped them sooner.

'When she was captured the following spring, I should have paid her ransom; I should have paraded with her beside me before the people, for them to see and acclaim the Maid of Orléans, who had given them their freedom and inspiration. Instead, I abandoned her to a terrible death.' As he says this, his pitiful expression wrenches her heart.

'You, my beloved Agnès, in your honest, sweet way, have done for me what she did for my country; with your simple, genuine love and faith in me, you have lifted me out of my recurring despondency, just as she did my country; you have given me joy and hope in the future, just as she gave my country. Do not disappoint me, my love: ride with me on the morrow onto the tourney ground. Let me show you to my people just as I should have shown *her* to them. They know I have changed in the past year – everyone comments on it. They see my self-confidence, my good humour, my successes in battle. Now I want them to know why.'

Like all France, Agnès is aware that Jeanne d'Arc, wearing the white armour made for her by Queen Yolande, rode beside the king in his youth, but that she herself should do the same? What right does she have? And yet it seems to mean so much to him that finally she agrees.

When the armour is brought in and she sees what he wants her to wear, she understands. It has been formed of the most delicately chased silver and set with precious stones, a remarkable work of craftsmanship. *It is due to his love for me, and his pride, that he wants me to be by his side when he enters the lists to the acclaim of the crowd.* Agnès is overwhelmed with the force of his love, and of course she is grateful, but still she cannot help thinking that such an act on her part must shame the queen, present or not. With this demonstration on the tourney ground, she will know that Agnès is the one her husband truly loves.

Agnès has too kind a heart not to be mindful of the queen's suffering. Does Marie resent her? Even secretly hate her? She runs to her confessor, Father Denis, to beg forgiveness and reassurance. Whenever she sees Queen Marie at her court, she genuinely tries to humble herself and keep the lowest profile possible.

Despite her reluctance to attract attention, however, Agnès does use her influence with the king. Although she has had almost no contact with her brothers during their separate childhoods, her father and Aunt Marie have corresponded regularly about them and Agnès is confident of their quality. To please her, Charles places two of her brothers within his domestic employ, and two others are installed among his personal guard. Charles has learned to trust her and knows she would not propose them unless confident they will be useful and loyal. Agnès is well aware how it looks to the gossiping courtiers, but she believes her judgement to be sound. This is what the Old Queen trained her to do – to help the king by suggesting suitable candidates, even if they come from her own family. And there are others of her choices he promotes to his Council Table. It is commonly accepted that Charles VII is a shrewd judge of character, no longer easily fooled and it is becoming clear to the court that he appreciates the opinions of his young mistress.

As to her own protection, from among the royal ladies she knows the dauphine will speak for her to Queen Marie, as would Lady Isabelle, who understands what her mother-in-law planned for the sake of the kingdom. Isabelle knows her *demoiselle* thoroughly; she has tested her loyalty, her sensitivity and her ability to handle the most delicate situations. And she appreciates that Agnès holds in her hand the future of the House of Anjou and its domains. This the girl knows and is grateful to have such a stalwart champion.

Chapter Nineteen

*I*s Jacques Coeur an angel or a devil, Agnès asks herself. Surely a protégé of Queen Yolande cannot be a devil – or can he? He tempts her so! She admits to the sin of vanity, but now she must add extravagance to her list of faults. And the king, to please her, urges her on; when he has commitments elsewhere and little time for his darling love, he almost pushes her towards Jacques Coeur's warehouses: 'Find yourself something to amuse you, my darling', or 'Isn't there something you might like to give your dear aunt, or a friend? Now run along and search for a beautiful toy' – as if she is a child. She tells herself she goes just to listen to Jacques' stories, and that is also true, but invariably she spots some incredible treasure. She knows, just as does her dear Jacquet, that whatever she takes away, the king will allow her to keep. Agnès is not greedy – she always thinks of others to whom to give gifts she believes they would enjoy – but having unlimited credit must inevitably lead to indulgence.

It is true what the courtiers are saying behind her back – and her good friend Marie de Belleville would not lie to her even when the truth is unpleasant: she has become extravagant, wickedly so. She loves seeing the treasures within Jacques' warehouses, those caves of dreams, temptation and delight, and he knows her potential value as his best client, for once her relationship with the king is universally known, Agnès will become the natural leader of fashion. Every lady will want to buy what she wears or decorate their houses in similar luxury. And that great merchant of Bourges will be waiting, ready, the doors of his wonderful warehouses wide open and ready to supply anything and everything. So what if the courtiers overspend – and he knows everyone's limits – that is their decision, and to his advantage after all. No, Jacques is no devil, just a merchant like any other, in pursuit of his living. . . .

It has not taken Agnès long to see how cleverly Yolande wove her web of influence to train those she trusted to surround Charles VII for the good of France. But that astute Old Queen is no more; and her protégés, like Agnès, and Jacques, and Pierre de Brézé, are intent on making their own careers as well as safeguarding the kingdom. She reminds herself that the day might come when the king could abandon her – she has seen enough of his capricious nature to prepare her heart even for that. As for guarantees for her future – so far, she has none, and she has a child. Like all illegitimate children, her little Marie belongs to her father, not to her.

Yes, she reasons, we three friends are in a position to help glorify the king, the country – and ourselves, but in that order.

The Mistress of Beauty spends the next four months in the glow of the king's love. Not surprisingly, their relationship has become scandalous common knowledge, but she does whatever she can to appease everyone, smiling sweetly and remaining as modest in her behaviour as possible, if not in her attire.

Finally, the day has arrived when Agnès is to be presented to the Queen of France as one of her court ladies. Mindful of her situation, she makes a deliberate effort to appear as lacklustre as possible, wearing a light grey dress with a little coral necklace, her *henin* floating a grey chiffon veil. When she enters the audience chamber, she makes as deep a *révérence* as she can without sitting on the floor – one of her greatest dreads – and keeps her gaze lowered. There will be no brazen eye-to-eye contact between her and the Queen of France, whom Agnès genuinely admires. Naturally she expects to be scrutinized by Queen Marie's entire court; all know she is the king's mistress – who does not? She will never have a chance of making a friend amongst them, and rightly so. If any one of them approaches her making overtures, then that lady could not be loyal to Queen Marie. Agnès would never trust anyone who left the queen's side thinking her friendship might be more advantageous.

But she is grateful to have one good friend among them; Marie de Belleville has also been moved to Queen Marie's court from Nancy. It would not surprise Agnès if this was at the initiative of Queen Isabelle, sensitive to her need of an ally in an unwelcome environment. Something on which she can count is that Marie de Belleville will be fair and tell her honestly whenever she may have erred.

On one of her first nights in her new surroundings, Agnès, who has her own separate suite of rooms, is lying contentedly in the king's arms as he strokes her cheek with the back of his forefinger in the way she loves.

'My love,' she begins, 'I have a great boon to ask. Would you arrange for my cousin Antoinette to be transferred to general duties nearby, so I can at least have her to confide in when not in waiting to your lady queen?'

She is surprised how readily he promises he will do so. Once again that little worm begins to wriggle in her subconscious and sets her thinking. Was this wise? She has Marie de Belleville, even though she is often on duty with the queen . . . Why did she ask for Antoinette when Marie de Belleville distrusts her so . . . *Why am I so sentimental?*

Agnès has never questioned the genuine friendship between the king and the queen. Marie was trained by her formidable mother to do her duty and accept her fate with grace and fortitude. As to her true feelings, Agnès doubts she will ever know them, but if she was in the queen's place, she would be hard pressed to display similar grace and fortitude – and she admires Queen Marie the more for it.

In the same way that Agnès has come to accept her good fortune, equally she must accept her destiny. After all, should anything happen to the king, what would become of her? This has been a worry at the back of her mind since the birth of her daughter. One night, her motherly instinct gives her the courage to unburden her fears to Charles.

After making love, when both are in that wonderful relaxed frame of mind, she says, almost in a whisper: 'My lord, I am afraid.'

'Of what could you possibly be afraid when you know you hold my love in the palm of your little hand?' he says, pressing it to his lips.

'My lord, what if something should happen to you? What would become of me and my child?' In reply, he covers her with sweet kisses of reassurance.

Not long after this conversation, the king makes Agnès Sorel a wondrous gift. He bestows on her both a home of her own and security – namely, the royal Château of Beauté-sur-Marne and its estates, because, he says: 'Its name becomes you.' Thereafter she is to be known as La Dame de Beauté, the Mistress of Beauty.

Her lover's understanding touches her as much as his magnificent gift, and at the first opportunity Agnès goes with him to visit her new domain.

'Come, my darling, let me tell you a little about your new home. Beauté is famous as the best positioned and loveliest of all the royal châteaux within the Ile de France. It is known for its good air – most important at a time when there has been, and still is, such danger from plague in our country. There is a mill nearby, and the lapping sound of water enters the rooms facing the river Marne, where I suggest you choose your personal suite.'

The château was a favourite of Charles V, her lover's grandfather, who kept a library there and often stayed when he wanted some rest. It is situated at the end of the forest of Vincennes and Charles tells her she will have access to excellent sport, with large herds of deer, adding: 'I know how much you love to ride to the chase.'

Then he holds her hands in his. 'You, my darling, who loves gardens, will be delighted with the flower beds that surround the park and the château; then beyond the gardens there are windmills and pools for keeping an abundance of fish: pike, bream, perch, carp and eels for the table.'

As they come nearer her gift house and first own home, Agnès sees several high towers and an imposing watch-tower guarding the moat. Approaching through the park, she comes upon a magnificent fountain, and rides past a number of the domain's other buildings, including a pretty manor house. How glad she is that he has come with her – how she had to beg him to show her his gift himself.

By the time they dismount, he has caught her eagerness and interest, leading her up to each of the castle's three floors. There is just one very large room on every level, beautifully furnished with the best of everything.

'The library was my grandfather's most precious possession, and it houses as many as five thousand books,' he tells her enthusiastically looking around the room. Then, 'See out there – the four-sided tower is dedicated to the four Evangelists and is exquisitely painted inside. I will show you when we go down.'

Wide-eyed with delight, and breathless with appreciation, Agnès can barely speak. 'My darling,' she whispers, 'I am completely overwhelmed. Everything is perfect, magnificent, yet nothing dwarfs me – I feel I belong here,' and she throws her arms around his neck.

Once disentangled, Charles smiles with the pleasure gained from giving, and warming to her joy, he tells her: 'You know, my grandfather entertained his most important guests at Beauté when they, too, wanted a little peace. So you see, my darling, the whole was aptly named, and is a fitting gift for you. You and I will retire here whenever possible, and I believe you will even be happy here without me. Think of this citadel as your refuge, your place of safety, hidden from the world and its barbs.'

Agnès finds it hard to believe that such a wondrous place is now hers – and is very moved, almost tearful. This place of beauty, truly well named, is her first home, and one of such grace and charm. The king wipes her eyes and kisses them, and she asks him to tell her more of its story.

'My parents, King Charles VI and Queen Isabeau, used Beauté for the hunt and to appreciate the remarkable countryside of this area. Now, my darling Agnès, you have another reason to be fond of my Constable Richemont, since it was he who recaptured your château from the English five years ago.'

When it becomes known that Agnès Sorel has received this wondrous gift, no one at court is any longer in doubt as to her position in the king's life. She admits to Marie de Belleville that this pleases her, 'Because hiding a great love is so difficult – it shines out of our eyes, doesn't it!' As the châtelaine of Beauté-sur-Marne, Agnès now has her own title and estate, and the king assures her that she and she alone will receive its revenues. A man in love, he wants her to have her own income and not be wholly dependent on his gifts, although he gives and she receives with pleasure.

Despite such an overwhelming endowment, which establishes without doubt her status, Agnès feels she must broach another troubling aspect of their relationship. It will be difficult for her, and several times she hesitates, but finally she gathers up courage.

'My lord, there is something I must ask,' and at once he takes her in his arms and carefully probes the question out of her. 'Sire, I am at a disadvantage – you have always been most kind to me, and gracious . . .'

Again he strokes her cheek and urges her on. 'Yes, my darling, my precious love, tell me what concerns you – you know there is nothing I would not do for you.'

Encouraged a little, she begins hesitantly: 'I have been told it is the custom for . . . an agreeable gentleman to be found . . . as a husband for a royal mistress . . . so that any children born to her and the king would have a father and a name.' Charles looks serious, yet he says nothing. But she *must* know, and the words come out in a rush: 'Have you chosen such a gentleman for me, my lord?'

She feels herself trembling, awaiting his reply. Her lover's reaction is one she will never forget. He takes both her hands in his and kisses her fingertips one by one, then her palms. Is this a build-up to bad news? Still she trembles awaiting his decree.

'My beloved Agnès,' he says, gazing into her eyes, 'I have never known real love before you, and I will not share you with any other man. I want you for myself alone and for ever.'

She collapses into his arms, and for these words she loves him even more. The idea of having to divide herself between an official husband and her royal lover is something she could not have borne. Her relief is so apparent that he holds her tightly in his arms to stop her shaking, and strokes her as he would a child.

Guilt? Yes, she does feel guilty. She is sinning against the laws of God and the Church – and against the sacrament of marriage. When the king comes to her apartments, she knows his wife must be suffering. Each morning when he visits the queen, she is surrounded by her ladies, including Agnès, as he greets her with a friendly, 'Good morrow, my dear.' He kisses her hand and her brow, but even as he does so, his eyes search the room for his mistress. 'Are you well?' he asks. 'And what news of the children?'

The queen bravely lifts her head and always gives the same answer: 'Well, my lord, well,' and knows he is not looking at her.

Agnès is the opposite of brazen, staring at the ground whenever the king is in the queen's quarters, but when she does look up, she can see with what goodness Queen Marie answers him, how warmly she smiles when she tells him of her day and the news of her court.

'And you, Sire, are you sleeping well these days; we see so little of you?' *Is this a barb?* Then with a merry laugh, 'But I know you are preparing for the visit of the ambassadors from the emperor, and they can be so vexing!'

Agnès manages to convince herself that in her dutiful devotion to her husband, the queen is even pleased for his happiness. Surely she must have noticed how transformed he is through his newfound contentment – and hers?

Chapter Twenty

Some weeks after Agnès is given her magnificent estate, she is with the king and the court at the royal Château of Loches. Absorbed in her happiness, she is inspired to make a gift to the cathedral, to thank God for her good fortune in being loved by such a remarkable man. After considerable thought, she presents the collegiate church with a golden statue of Mary Magdalene, enclosing a relic of the saint's hair, 'Hair that would have touched the feet of Christ our Lord,' she tells the king.

In her honesty, Agnès admits that her reverence for the saint does not preclude her acceptance of her lover's wondrous gifts – invariably sourced by Jacques Coeur from his vast array of treasures. Her château is steadily filling with luxurious and comfortable furnishings – tapestries and Araby carpets, exquisitely worked gold and silver vessels, furniture, paintings, the finest bedlinen and much else. How can she resist whatever Jacques Coeur offers her? He has a way of presenting rare furs and jewels, *objets d'art*, paintings, precious golden dinner services, and she knows – just as does her clever Jacquet – that her king will deny her nothing.

Agnès knows that by wearing the latest fashions in the most beautiful fabrics brought to France by her friend the merchant, she will help to augment his business, since the court's ladies rush to imitate whatever she wears. The trains of her dresses are now the longest, and her jewels rival those of the queen herself. Yes, she is aware how much comment this causes, and she does her best to make it clear that she is in no way in competition with Queen Marie.

The king continues to visit his wife some nights and always treats her with the greatest respect in public; and, Agnès hears through Marie de Belleville, in private as well. But even when he is in the queen's company, his eyes regularly find those of his mistress, although otherwise he pays her no more attention than any other lady from his wife's entourage. Watching the elegant way in which he behaves towards Marie, Agnès feels even more respect for her lover.

As for the courtiers, their attitude to her and her position in relation to the king is mixed. Some are outraged; others pretend to be; many accept her in the same way as the queen appears to do, with an outward show of respect but no sign of encouragement to come closer. Inevitably there are those who try to ingratiate themselves in the hope of preferment, and these she recognizes at once. Well schooled in the ways of courtiers by Yolande d'Anjou, Agnès is not easily fooled by anyone.

Her dearest confidante, apart from Lady Isabelle when she visits the king's court, remains Marie de Belleville. Having known Agnès since she was the youngest and the least important of the *demoiselles* at the court of Lorraine and Naples, Marie has never changed towards her, and for that honest kindness the Mistress of Beauty is grateful.

She also has her cousin Antoinette to lend her companionship – although occasionally that nagging little doubt about her loyalty seeps into Agnès's head. There is something about the way Antoinette looks at her . . . But generous as she is, Agnès does her best to push away these thoughts. It is just that Antoinette has changed so much. When Agnès sees her cousin making up to a number of the courtiers and flirting with them in a way that would have shocked her mother, she is aware how much her cousin's behaviour is contrary to all their early training to make of them young ladies. She even catches her looking at the king at times, though he never returns her glances. Besides, Agnès feels totally secure in his love, and decides not to let it bother her. *It's just Antoinette's way . . .*

The king has asked Agnès to sit in on the meetings of his Council. It is a great honour, and although she always holds her tongue, afterwards he asks for her opinions and she gives them freely. Charles is aware of her many conversations with Queen Yolande, and knows that his *bonne mère* judged Agnès to be a sensible young woman. Sometimes he accepts her suggestions, but she is never under any illusion that she has any real influence on his decisions. Perhaps he enjoys hearing a totally disinterested point of view, as hers surely is. There are some members of the court, and even of the Council, who believe the king heeds Agnès's guidance, but they err – Charles VII is his own master and merely listens to his Dame de Beauté on occasion to test her judgement. The Constable Richemont likes to praise Agnès by calling her the kingdom's 'guardian angel', but she knows this is no more than generous flattery. She recognizes that he is a dear soul, even if he tries not to let it show.

The Constable and Agnès have understood one another from the first, both having been advanced into the king's service by Queen Yolande, and they identify with one another's total loyalty to the monarch. Nor is the Constable alone – there are a number of other sound and loyal men around the king, first noticed and then promoted by Yolande. How well Agnès recalls the Old Queen telling her at Saumur that each one of her chosen few would willingly die for their king, and she has taken note of who they are.

Chapter Twenty-one

In April, the entire procession of the king's court and that of the queen departs for Châlons in the west. On this journey, the dauphin accompanies them. Louis has returned to his father's court with glory as well as the gratitude of the Emperor Frederick III for bringing his Swiss subjects under control. When a number of foreign courts request his services, the dauphin chooses to remain in France, waiting to be rewarded with a place on the King's Council. Instead, his father sends him on quite a minor assignment on behalf of the grand old Duchess of Burgundy. The duchess herself is remarkably able and subtle in the art of negotiation, a skill taught her by her husband – it is said – to compensate for his many infidelities. It is she who managed, with her delicate diplomacy, to have her brother-in-law, Duke Charles d'Orléans finally released from the Tower of London. The Duchess of Burgundy happens also to be a great-granddaughter of a former King of England, John of Gaunt, and far too majestic and proud to allow herself to be placed under the command of Charles VII's gauche and haughty son. The dauphin's bitterness, intensified by his father's lack of trust, has made him rude and intolerable, and it is not long before he finds himself dismissed by the duchess and sent back to his father. This is just the beginning.

It is June, and the days are long and humid. In order to receive the acclamation of a number of towns nearby, the king has chosen to hold his assembly meetings in the delightful country manor of the Archbishop of Châlons at Scarry nearby. It is perfectly situated in a pleasant valley and on the banks of the river Marne, a most agreeable location for passing a hot summer. The senior ladies of the kingdom – Queen Marie; her sister-in-law Lady Isabelle; the Duchess of Burgundy; even the dauphine Margaret – gather under the cool of the trees to chatter and lament their lives, while their young attendants make merry with the junior gentlemen of the court.

Everyone is aware that the dauphin Louis is the cause of his lovely Scottish wife's misery, but what can one do to cheer her? The older ladies too are burdened by their own difficulties. The Duchess of Burgundy, who is nearing fifty, is constantly deceived by her husband with younger women and longs to return to her native Portugal; Lady Isabelle is having to console her husband, 'Good King' René, who knows he will never regain his many thrones and sees himself as a drain on her; and Queen Marie is having to tolerate her husband's undisguised love for her beautiful *demoiselle*.

*

The dauphin does not need spies to ascertain the true nature of his father's relationship with Agnès Sorel – it is totally undisguised. There was a moment, when she first came to court, that Louis thought he might take Agnès from the king just to spite him. That he failed gives him another reason to hate his father, especially as he continues to resent his enforced marriage to Margaret of Scotland. Perhaps there may be some truth in Pierre de Brézé's belief that in the eyes of the dauphin, the ravishing Agnès, Louis' contemporary after all, is more suited to be *his* mistress than his father's. In the early days of her arrival at the royal court, Louis tried to impress her – or at least to win her regard – with a gift of some wonderful tapestries. Agnès felt repelled by him already at their first meeting in Angers, and certainly did not want to be beholden to him, but nor could she afford to affront him, especially in public. 'Gracious sir,' she said at the time, 'I accept your most generous gift of these tapestries with pleasure,' and she bowed low, turning away quickly so that his loathsome lips could not kiss her hand. No sooner did she accept the tapestries, which really were very beautiful, than she gave them to the abbey of Loches.

'My Lady Agnès, I hear that you have passed my gift of rare and precious tapestries to the abbey at Loches,' hissed the dauphin in her ear on his return, and for the whole court to hear. How he hated her for that!

Agnès bowed low and replied: 'My lord, they were indeed exquisite and too fine for me, so that I felt them more suited to adorn one of God's houses,' and promptly withdrew.

Louis has never understood that the man she loves, his

father, is a hundred times his worth. With that thought, Agnès can comfort herself against the wrath of her lover's son. Nor does it help her relationship with the dauphin that she is close to his wife. In recent months the Lady Margaret has become Agnès's closest confidante and is generous enough to understand her joy at being in love, something she herself has never known.

The dauphine has developed into a most learned young lady, and continues to indulge her passion for composing rhymes and rondos. Her health has always been frail, and such a sedentary occupation suits her. But the dauphin, like many of the young military men of the court, scorns literary and musical talents in a woman, complaining bitterly to anyone within earshot: 'My lady wife sits up night after night with her little group composing – or dancing – because music means more to her, it would seem, than producing children.'

In fact Agnès believes the dauphine is afraid of her husband – and not without reason. Although Princess Margaret never divulges anything to anyone about her conjugal experiences, Agnès's female intuition tells her that the poor dauphine can never have experienced the gentle, charming ways of love that she herself shares with the king, nor the excitement and ecstasy. On account of this sadness, Agnès feels even more affection for her. True, Margaret is spoilt – who can deny her anything? Certainly not the king and queen, and in Margaret's frustration and unhappiness her occasional capriciousness is overlooked. Anything she asks for is granted, and at times, some of her demands may well seem frivolous or whimsical.

Meanwhile, the king's cherished mistress is becoming aware that her own extravagance is causing much negative gossip at court. In her position, naturally she is the victim of envy, but Agnès reasons that through her extravagance she can help to return the court of France to the great and glorious spectacle it used to be. It is her ambition to have the court of Charles VII admired and imitated all over Europe, something she knows has been for long his dream. *Surely that is my role in this perplexing world?*

Complaints have reached her that a number of the courtiers criticize her profligacy; that she appears over-dressed and grand; her trains longer than any princess's; her immodest décolletage worn deeper than at any other court; her *henins* taller than anyone else's; her jewels, furs, furniture, silver, linen and gowns all better – no, the best. Yes, she knows it is time, but, she reasons, why not? It pleases her lord and lover to spoil her; he can afford it, and she is warmed by the way he delights in her genuine appreciation of each gift. She *wants* him to admire her, which is the stimulus for her to make great efforts to appear radiant before him at all times.

Agnès often wears black, which suits her pale skin and blonde hair and brings out the blue of her eyes. Black velvet looks best, or black brocade with a little silver thread – sometimes damask intricately embroidered with red roses. What beautiful lengths Jacquet has brought for her from Damascus! Yes, she definitely looks her best wearing black – especially with the superb pearls, large as cherries, that her lover has given her. She herself asks him for nothing, except that he helps her charitable causes or her friends in need. The rest comes from him spontaneously.

When Charles VII realizes how much Agnès delights in her Château of Beauté, he begins to give her other wonderful, great houses. His next gift is the Romanesque manor of Roberdeau, situated at the foot of the fortress of Chinon. Beneath it there is an underground passage that enables the king to join her without anyone knowing; no doubt it must have been used for similar purposes for many years! Another gift, five leagues from Bourges, is the Château of Menetou-Salon, though they spend very little time there. These magnificent houses come so fast, she rarely has time to even visit them, like the Château of La Croysette close by Issoudun.

And yet the king seems to feel most comfortable in relatively small and secluded manor houses, almost secret, which surprises his mistress. Nor did he inherit the building mania of most of his family. She comes to the conclusion that her lover is something of a nomad, never really feeling safe anywhere for long enough to allow himself to settle in. No sooner have they arrived somewhere than he is eager to move on, but since Agnès is happy wherever he is, she does not mind.

Another cause of gossip against her, of which Agnès has slowly become aware, concerns the handsome Pierre de Brézé, but as the king himself knows, this friendship is completely innocent. Pierre is an outrageous flirt, but the entire court recognizes that he means nothing by it and certainly never follows up on any of the inviting glances he receives.

'Why, my Mistress of Beauty, how your name suits you this morning,' he will say, or, 'Never have I seen such blue eyes, bluer than a periwinkle, bluer than a forget-me-not

– and what man, once he has seen our Lady of Beauty, could ever forget her.' Many similar comments flow from his flattering lips in those famous honeyed tones, which make the younger ladies of the court giggle and the older ones smile and shake their heads. Pierre is patently ambitious and would never risk his own career even to imagine a relationship with the king's lady! Moreover, he knows very well that her heart belongs entirely to Charles. And yet the general gossip is disturbing, although known by the king to be totally untrue.

Chapter Twenty-two

$\mathcal{E}$very member of the court spending this summer at Châlons seems to feel an enchanted atmosphere, their sense of relaxed contentment resulting in almost juvenile behaviour. In the cool of the evenings, groups of court-iers and ladies, sometimes including the king, wander into the cut-grass fields around the château and play blind man's buff or hide-and-seek, and chatter like excited chil-dren. They lie on their backs in the grass and watch the moon, note its quarters, and rejoice in its light when full. Silly wishes are made that could never come true, and they confide them, of course – which destroys any hope they might ever have had! They take buckets of water to catch the moon's reflection and then make another wish.

One night after dinner, when the courtiers are engaged in such nonsensical games, a plot emerges from that genius of entertainment Charles of Maine, as talented in this way as his brother Lord René. Together with the Count of

Saint-Pol, the king and some others, they put their heads together away from the ladies and come up with a plan. Their appointed spokesman is René, who announces:

'We have decided we should hold a tournament!' Gasps of delight and clapping of hands. 'But not just any tournament, no: it must be the best and the greatest of all . . . one that will rival even the legendary tournaments of the court of Burgundy!'

'Ah well,' his audience is heard to mutter, 'Burgundy is the standard all Europe strives to emulate.'

The king shouts, 'Hurrah!' with enthusiasm and is as light-headed as the younger courtiers about him. That settles it, and off they set for the queen's chambers to gain her consent.

'Madame,' says Lord René, bowing low, 'we have devised a splendid plan to hold a tournament of such magnificence that Burgundy will pale into chivalrous insignificance! We trust you will give us your blessing?'

The queen laughs and agrees – what else can she do? – as do the other ladies of her court. With René d'Anjou at the helm, this will be the best, the most dazzling tournament of all time!

There is nothing the King of Sicily does not know about tournaments, a subject he has studied all his life: how they used to be run, and how they should be run. The preparations take two weeks to perfect – fifteen days filled with careful planning to implement every aspect of the ceremonial for this complicated sport. Each combatant has an entourage whose details have to be carefully choreographed: their clothes; their horses' tackle; their equipment. Then there are the various clarion calls used by the heralds to denote each stage in the competition; the dimensions of the lists; the colours of the tents and the flags on them signifying the identity of the knight-competitor within.

Invitations are sent and the excitement generates a tremendous response.

On the first day of the tournament, not a breath of air stirs and the multicoloured flags hang limp on their poles. Beautifully decorated stands are draped with tapestries, and carpets cover the ground. At this time of year there are summer flowers everywhere, and garlands of lilies, white roses, sweet violets mixed with lavender, heady scented stocks and marigolds are hung against the walls of the pavilions. Countless vases filled with peonies, irises and more lilies, with lady's mantle and wallflowers, stand on every available surface. Everyone wears their best and most colourful. The *demoiselles* of the court are dressed in silks and satins of all shades; circlets of carnations, daisies or poppies serve as little crowns on their heads. They gasp at the courage of the combatants; they applaud; they laugh and call out to their favourites. The ground shakes with the pounding of hooves; the loud crack of a wooden lance snapping; and the audible intake of breath when a favourite knight crashes to the ground.

For seven days they watch in awe as the most glamorous, noble young knight in France, Jacques de Lalaing, who is attached to the court of Burgundy, wins again and again, taking on all comers in his elegant, courteous fashion. Tall, blond and handsome, Lalaing is just twenty-two years old and as chaste as he is able – a true knight of the school of chivalry as described in the twelfth century by Chrétien de Troyes in his stories of the quest for the Holy Grail. King René often regaled the *demoiselles* in Naples with tales of chivalry from this writer. Not only is Lalaing the handsomest knight in Christendom, whose mere glance can cause ladies to melt and blush with delight; even his horses are beautifully turned out, each day in a different caparison, gold or silver cloth, or velvet in rainbow colours, stitched or quilted using gold thread. His jousting armour, inlaid with intricate patterns of silver and gold, is as elegant as if made to be worn only on parade, since it has never been damaged, nor dented from the force of a fall from his horse. Long ostrich feathers, white and red, play in the breeze from the top of his ornate helmet. This is a knight who is truly a sight to see and admire; and the ladies of the court most certainly do, and sigh.

But there are others who take part valiantly, even if unhorsed by the hero: the counts of Foix and Clermont, the brave Bueil, and the Count of Saint-Pol, who wins the ladies' trophy several times. Then there are Agnès's favourites, Pierre de Brézé and Charles of Maine among them, who survive the challenge.

After all the action during the day, in the evening there are balls and banquets, concerts, singers, mummers, jugglers, and acrobatic performers on the trapeze or making human towers. The king is entertaining and no expense is to be spared. The country is revived and rejuvenated in the person of this transformed monarch! In recent months, France has won her battles, and the king is seen as strong and content. Agnès joyfully admits to herself that she has something to do with his mood of contentment, his *joie de vivre*, and, yes, excitement. Only they know that she is once again with child, and their happiness shows. Agnès is fortunate not to experience any difficulties with this second pregnancy either, no illness or pains. Marie de Belleville is always by her side, and her cousin Antoinette comes to relieve her, attending to her according to both the king's wish and her own.

On the last day of the tournament, when the audience thinks all is over, suddenly the heralds blow their trumpets to announce an undeclared bout and two unidentified knights enter the lists with their escorts. With their visors closed, the mystery knights begin their first run down the length of the lists on chargers in padded wraps to the ground and feathers on their forelocks matching their riders' colours. Four times they charge at one another, with their lances hitting each other's shield with full force in the middle, but neither is unseated. Twice their lances break, yet their efforts are elegant, their moves clearly practised. It is obvious to the spectators in the stands that they must be known combatants, visitors from somewhere within France. At each run, the crowd roars with delight, and finally the two knights approach the tribune where Agnès sits with the queen and her other ladies.

As they make their bows to thunderous applause, at the queen's request they raise their visors – and to universal amazement the faces of Pierre de Brézé and the king are revealed! This king, who has never joined in battle for love of his queen, who never wears armour and will not ride over a bridge for fear of assassination, this lover of Agnès took all those risks today on the tourney ground with the court's best challenger, Pierre de Brézé! In her heart Agnès knows why he did this, and she hugs the sweet knowledge to herself and to their child within her.

That evening, to signal the end of the tournament, the king holds a banquet followed by a ball at the Château de Scarry, where Agnès has lodged throughout their time at Châlons. What an atmosphere: relief from those afraid for the competitors; the joyful exhaustion of those who were successful at the lists; and the delight of all who took part. The tournament has succeeded in establishing Charles VII as a king in peacetime as well as at war; a king who can be an admired host as well as a leader of men. It has added the final touches to his regal persona in which it has taken him such a long time to believe.

Charles, who normally never dances, invites Agnès to join him on the floor and twirls her with uncharacteristic exuberance. Even the dauphine Margaret appears joyful and laughing, although Agnès knows her unloved heart is heavy. Lord René rightfully radiates a triumphant glow – his plans have worked to perfection, his king is recognized as the host of a tournament to rival those of Burgundy. How surprised their grand duchess seems that Charles VII's court of France can do as well as the renowned one of her husband! Queen Marie, as always, retires to her nest of mourning, while those who remain dance joyfully till dawn.

Only then does the king take Agnès to her chamber and into his arms. From somewhere comes renewed energy to love – and they do, most tenderly, until both sleep from fulfilled exhaustion.

Chapter Twenty-three

*T*hroughout the summer, Agnès has remained close to the dauphine, Margaret of Scotland. One day she notices a lady of the dauphine's suite being rather flirtatious with the king, which makes her somewhat capricious herself. She calls for Pierre de Brézé and whispers: 'Who is that brazen hussy throwing herself at my lord? Get rid of her at once!' And it is done. Pierre has the girl escorted to her room, arranges for her belongings to be packed and has her removed from the court into lodgings in the town. She is told not to return. *How dare anyone even dream of taking my place by the king's side! I am his lady and no one is going to share that position!* This is a new Agnès, who is beginning to exert her undoubted power . . .

The replacement *demoiselle* she suggests to the dauphine is called Pregente de Villequier, a protégé of Pierre de Brézé who is adept at writing roundels as well as composing poetry. She will suit the dauphine very well.

A short time later, Agnès has another reason to call on Pierre de Brézé, but this time to help him. The king recently promoted Pierre as Count d'Évreux and *grand sénéchal* of Poitou, but she has cause to believe that his position is being threatened.

'Pierre, my friend, do you see that young courtier over there? He is André de Villequier, brother of the charming Pregente who you recommended for the dauphine's suite. I suggest you watch him carefully as I have reason to suspect he is trying to manoeuvre himself into your place with the king.'

It was Queen Yolande who subtly suggested that Agnès should look out for potentially useful people as her own attendants or to place within households in which she had an interest. In this way Agnès learned that André de Villequier, who is another of the Old Queen's protégés, cares only for his own advancement and enrichment. She and Pierre see themselves as the king's guardians, and Villequier soon confirms their suspicions of him.

Through their friend and ally Jacques Coeur, who has agents everywhere, they discover that Villequier asked Jamet de Tillay, the master of the dauphin's household, to find someone to spy on the dauphine under the pretext of concern for her health. It was not long before the chosen spy reported to Tillay that Lady Margaret was alone in her room in the dark with a man! When Tillay and two others burst in on the dauphine in the gathering twilight and sitting by the light of a fire, they found her harmlessly composing rhymes with a young courtier from her group called Blosseville. 'Madame,' cried Tillay, 'what is going on here?'

The poor princess burst into tears – most probably of fright, though Tillay implied to the court that this was proof of her guilt. Blosseville, a most correct and respected individual, a talented composer of roundels and poetry, was obviously innocent, but this foolish encounter causes a great scandal.

'Have you heard – the dauphine was alone in her rooms in the dark with a man not her husband!' one shocked courtier tells Agnès. Another maintains: 'No, it was the dauphin himself who burst in on them, sitting alone in complete darkness.' When Agnès hears the story directly from Jacques Coeur's inside man and ascertains the truth, she relays it to the king.

'My dearest lord, you know me to be honest and not a fool. Please trust me when I say that the dauphine is completely innocent of any wrongdoing. Night fell and she and her friend, that most respectable courtier Blosseville, continued their enthusiastic composing by the bright light of the fire. There was no impropriety; I beg you to believe me.'

Her lover strokes her cheek and tells her to run along – just as he would a child! 'Now my dear, do not concern yourself with the business of others in my family.' His dismissal is quite firm and she withdraws at once, but she is troubled by the king's reaction. As much as the court enjoys the gossip, no one familiar with the dauphine could believe in such a silly tale.

Already ailing for some time with consumption, Princess Margaret sinks into a deep depression. And no wonder! She, a foreigner at the court of the King of France, the wife of the heir to the throne, has, albeit inadvertently and innocently, embarrassed her parents-in-law and brought shame on her husband.

Agnès is almost the only one the dauphine allows into her chamber, and she tries hard to cheer her. 'Madame, believe me, this is just foolish talk. No one who knows you could ever believe such a story.' But the sad little dauphine will not be consoled. Agnès's dear, delightful friend retires from the court, seeing no one, wrapped in her guiltless shame.

The following spring, the dauphine sends for Agnès. 'Dearest friend – and you have indeed proven yourself a true friend to me here, where I sense that even the king has no time for me any longer . . .' Agnès demurs, but it is true. The most important role of a dauphine is to produce an heir, and this Margaret has not done. 'I have decided to go on a pilgrimage to Nôtre-Dame-de-l'Épine. I am sure Our Lady will give me grace to overcome this sadness.'

As Margaret leaves in her litter, Agnès watches her frail figure, wrapped in furs. During the dauphine's pilgrimage, absorbed in prayer, no doubt kneeling on the chilled floor of the church, Margaret catches a cold that quickly develops into pleurisy. On her return to Châlons, she takes to her bed and never rises from it again.

When the doctors ask the master of the dauphin's household how this illness began, Jamet de Tillay insinuates that it is her topsy-turvy routine that has harmed her health, sleeping by day and sitting up through the night writing poems. Typically, neither the dauphin nor the king has much patience with an illness brought on by poetry!

Whenever Agnès tries to speak to Charles, he brushes the subject away.

Throughout her suffering, the dauphine continues to maintain, not only to Agnès but to all her visitors, that she has never wronged her husband: 'Jamet de Tillay is the one responsible for my misery, with his false accusations and insinuations. His lies will be the cause of my death. How deeply I regret ever having come to France.' Nothing Agnès can say will persuade her that she will get better with a little patience.

Pierre de Brézé calls to tell Agnès that he has visited the dauphine's sickbed. 'My lady, you can imagine how deeply I was moved to pity – you saw her yourself only yesterday. As I walked into her antechamber, I could not help myself exclaiming loudly to the gathered company there: "This poor innocent lady is suffering, and probably dying, on account of another's slander. We have all been blessed by her delightful company and now we do nothing to avenge her."'

As he left the dauphine's apartment, he saw the slanderer, Tillay, and recounts to Agnès how he turned on him: '"Jamet de Tillay! I accuse you of being responsible for the imminent death of the dauphine Margaret. She is dying of pleurisy and the shame brought on by your lies and false accusations!" My lady, if he had been an honest man, he would have challenged me to a duel for insulting him, but I am by far the better swordsman, and Tillay knows he bears the burden of guilt.'

There is no doubt the dauphine Margaret is dying; all the court knows it. In order that she can receive the last sacraments without hatred in her heart, Agnès tries to persuade her to forgive her slanderer. But she refuses adamantly. It is only on her deathbed that she agrees to pardon him. To everyone's consternation and sadness, she dies regretting – indeed, *cursing* – her way of life and most of the people in it.

Because he knows Agnès is one of the few who genuinely loved her, the chaplain reports to her the dauphine's dying words. 'Thank you, Father,' she tells him. 'Now they are engraved forever on my heart.'

The entire court appears moved and strangely disturbed by the death of the tragically wronged dauphine, most particularly Queen Marie, who loved her as her own. For his part, the dauphin makes it plain that his wife meant very little to him. And yet this devious prince, ever conscious of his appearance to the court and the country, feels it necessary to be seen to defend her memory, and lays a charge for slander before Jamet de Tillay. Agnès dares to whisper to her lord that perhaps the person responsible for the dear dauphine's death will now be held accountable. From the look he gives her, she knows she should have held her tongue.

Somehow Jamet de Tillay's trial comes to nothing, and the matter simply melts away. Yet Agnès cannot forget that the whole sorry tale began with the king's favourite, André de Villequier . . .

Not long after the death of the dauphine, several unexplained events occur that trouble Agnès. Lord René has left the court, it is said, due to some mischief invented by the dauphin, and has retreated with Lady Isabelle to his capital of Angers. Why does Agnès feel the manipulations of the dauphin everywhere? Then she hears talk, and others whisper it, that Pierre de Brézé has been in league with Lord René for the same unspoken misdemeanour. Yet others say, no, actually they are both engaged in secret talks with the dauphin. That Agnès cannot believe –neither Pierre nor René can have any interest in associating with the dauphin, of that she is certain. She dare not say a word to her darling king for fear of another of his searing looks, but she ponders over this muddled story.

Ever since her arrival at court, Pierre de Brézé has shown himself to be her disinterested friend as well as her strongest supporter. She knows from his own lips that he drew Queen Yolande's attention to her in Toulouse, and together they alerted the king to her presence. But is this really true? Queen Yolande never said so. And who was Pierre at that time that he would have had the ear of the king? Yet who does not occasionally add a little harmless lustre to their own name? Hardly a reason to distrust him, even if many of the court do. Who knows better than Agnès that success invariably breeds jealousy? Has she not seen for herself how many of those she believed to be her friends in truth hate her for her beauty, success and influence with the king?

But why should Pierre have any private contact with the dauphin when Louis is still in disfavour? Or has the king asked him to be a middleman between them and heal their rift? Louis should be learning how to rule, but with Agnès feeling threatened by him, and rightly, there is no place for him at his father's court. No one doubts that the dauphin is tomorrow's man, but Charles VII has many good years still left, and Pierre's future looks safe where he is.

As for her good friend Jacques Coeur, it is whispered that he too has been seeing the dauphin privately. Well, that makes more sense – a merchant is a merchant and sells wherever he can, surely? But if true, say the gossips, why not do it openly? Or would the king no longer trade with him if he did? Agnès will try some pillow talk to find out. She needs a cool head to deal with so much treason-ous hearsay floating about the court.

Often she asks herself: what would Queen Yolande do in similar circumstances? No, she will not allow the animosity she feels around her to affect her judgement. She will rise above it – just as Queen Yolande would; and for reassurance she will rely on the sound sense and good friendship of Marie de Belleville. Daily she thanks God and Mary Magdalene that she never has the slight-est reason to doubt the king's sincerity. His love for her is utterly constant, transparently true, his attentions over-whelming; and with such consolation, she believes there is nothing she cannot bear.

Chapter Twenty-four

The time has come for the court to move on from the place of the dauphine Margaret's tragic death. The king is constantly in a hurry, and with a small group of close friends and advisers he leaves Châlons ahead of the queen and the main court. Agnès is honoured to be included among his advance party as they head into Touraine. There they stay at the queen's favourite palace of Montils, and then on to Agnès's beloved Loches. But even here the lovers find that the court and the petitioners surrounding the king are too numerous, leaving them no private time at all.

In November, Charles decides to break with tradition and move to the charming mansion of one of his chamberlains, Jean de Razilly, not far from Chinon. Nestling in a wooded valley, this large country house, with its tiled and pointed towers, sits in the middle of an idyllic park with the river Vienne, a tributary of the Loire, running through it. Here the king's chosen group install themselves with their attendants, leaving the queen and the court not far distant in the royal Château of Chinon. Charles visits Marie regularly, never failing in his duties to his wife, but by moving to Razilly, he is away from the pressures of the main court, its intrigues, jealousies and potential enemies. The moment he leaves Chinon and returns to the agreeable manor house in the forest, he is in another world, a world shared with Agnès and a few loyal and trusted friends. The house is made warm and comfortable, log fires blazing, and by strewing lavender and thyme, meadowsweet and marjoram liberally on the floors, Agnès rids their rooms of the damp, musty smell of most buildings at this time of year.

Even for some of his closest courtiers, Charles is a king difficult to fathom. Since childhood, growing up with the Anjou family, he has been known as sincerely religious. He attends three Masses daily in the chapel and sees no anomaly in his love of Agnès with regard to his marriage and his God. The queen is a loyal and long-standing friend as well as a duty willingly undertaken; Agnès is his pleasure, and he feels he has a right to both.

Following his last Mass of the day, he and Agnès ride through the woods and fields of the valley, always keeping a good distance from the curious and often hostile local people. Charles has never learned to be comfortable among the public at large, and despite Agnès's best efforts, the fears of his youth have never left him. At Razilly they lead the life of landed squires, indulging in country pursuits, especially in riding to hounds. They chatter excitedly with their companions about the hunt, their horses, the countryside, the birds, the harvests – all the practical topics that interest country people. They picnic, exchange tales of experiences, tell merry stories and laugh a lot. It is a charmed time for them both.

The nights are theirs alone. Outside it is cold, but they have fires at either end of their room, and soft furs on the floor and on their huge bed. In low candlelight, Agnès dances for her lover with a slow, weaving movement, all the while humming a little tune. Jacquet has told her stories of how the women of the harems danced for him in Egypt and elsewhere in the East, gently swaying, semi-naked, with downcast eyes. Agnès does the same, entwining the fine shawls the merchant has provided around and between her naked limbs. The king plays a wistful tune on the lute as she dances for him; sometimes he sings with his wonderful voice while she sways idly to the rhythm of the music, her long blonde hair hanging loose around her shoulders. When she slowly lets fall her shawls, one by one, he carries her to the bed by the fire or to lie with him on the furs placed on top of the deep rugs on the floor. Sometimes she is a slave girl, escaped from his harem, and when he catches her, playfully her lover ties her hands behind her back with a silken scarf and covers her eyes with another before putting her over his shoulder and carrying her off to their bed. He is so strong, and yet tender. Oh, what nights they pass at Razilly . . .

When they are alone, their existence is spellbound. And yet Charles must receive his ministers, attend to his duties, and hold grand receptions in the main château so that no one feels excluded by his absences from the body of the court.

Christmas comes and passes; still they remain in their Razilly love nest, never at a loss for words or ways of entertaining themselves, with or without their small group of intimates. The great fires in the hall blaze with whole trunks of oak and walnut, and the herbs and orange peel thrown on top add to the festive atmosphere. Music – there is always music – plays from another room: tambourines and lutes, viols and slide trumpets. Agnès likes the soothing, mysterious sound of the wind instruments best of all.

At the end of January, with the snow lying deep, she gives birth to her second daughter, whom they name Charlotte, the feminine for Charles. This time the king is with her throughout, and she is sure this child will lead a charmed life. Her Aunt Marie and the same team attend the young mother, just as they did for the birth of her first daughter. All goes as smoothly as before, and Agnès and Charles together give thanks to God for another healthy child.

It seems there is nothing too good for the king's beloved – her slightest wishes are fulfilled. She virtually holds her own court, with ladies to attend her as if she were a royal princess, and Charles has given her a most generous pension to keep her in this high estate. Officially, Agnès Sorel is still a part of the queen's household, but in fact her own has become larger and grander than that of her royal mistress.

Greed has never been part of her character, but it cannot be denied that Agnès has come to appreciate and love luxury. How not, when Jacquet continues to make her presentations of new irresistible wonders as they arrive with his galleys from the East, offering her the first choice of the best of everything: furniture, tapestries, carpets, gold and silver vessels the most luxurious fabrics from China, Syria, Egypt, who knows . . . And the jewels he shows her! Huge, perfectly round pearls brought up from the shallow waters of the Persian Gulf; rubies, emeralds, sapphires, loose or beautifully fashioned into brooches, necklaces, rings. Dear Jacquet is her inspiration and her downfall, since she cannot refuse to accept the wonders he lays before her. And he knows it!

'My Lady Agnès, do look at what I have brought you! You have seen nothing like this before – jades so translucent you can almost see through them, and in the East they say that jade has magical properties.' Or else: 'I have received silken carpets that are as soft underfoot as the skin on your cheek, their patterns woven from the tales of a Thousand and One Nights; you must place them next to your bed or over tables.' He tempts her further with legends of jewels extraordinary: 'My lady, I have a new treasure you will love – emerald beads carved by a master many moons ago, and into each cut he wove a spell . . .' and of course she chooses to believe him – why not? It is he who conjures the magic of her days, just as the king does of her nights. And Jacquet knows, as does she, that her ever-generous lover will pay whatever she owes.

With such extraordinary lengths of beautifully woven cloth within her reach, she summons the court seamstresses and together they drape them this way and that for maximum effect. Her headdresses are the size of beehives; delicate wires give shape to the gossamer silks that lie on top, creating an effect of butterfly wings in shades of dawning: pale blues, pinks and yellows. Together with Marie de Belleville and Antoinette, she plays at shaping and inventing new ways to wear their gowns and head-dresses. She knows they cannot afford what she can, and constantly makes them gifts, including them in her extravagances.

Jacques Coeur knows that whatever Agnès chooses will be of the best quality – he will see to it – and she will set a style, a fashion and taste that the other ladies of the court will rush to imitate. Many are rich and can afford his splendour. Business is good, and Agnès is the best model he could wish for.

One of her greatest assets is a pretty décolletage, and she wants to show it for her royal lover – and for the others at court to see why he loves her. *No, that's not right – he loves me for myself, but he never tires of praising my breasts.* Charles has told her often that God gave them to her to bring pleasure, and she determines that they should. She cuts her necklines lower and lower, or leaves the front lacing undone to expose at least one whole breast.

This causes a sensation at court, but her kingly lover does not appear affronted at all; in fact he seems delighted and proud. She can see that many of the courtiers are shocked – or pretend to be – but she glories in the beauty God has given her for the pleasure of all. The looks and smiles the lovers exchange show they are oblivious to anyone else, and focused solely on their personal happiness.

As if the gift of the Château de Beauté and the other houses Agnès has received was not enough, following the birth of Charlotte in 1446, her royal lover presents her with Roquecezière, a mighty fortress in Rouergue, the ancient fief of the counts of Toulouse. This wonderful estate, which includes ninety-eight parishes, has always been royal property or belonged to a great lord. In addition, her love-struck king gives her the great fortified castles and estates of Vernon and Issoudun in Berry. 'You know, my love, Vernon was in English hands but was retaken in 1419 by none other than Jean de Dunois, my cousin and childhood friend, and another protégé of Queen Yolande. He has now become a mighty captain in my army, as we always knew he would.'

'My lord, I have met Count Jean several times and know of his closeness to my Lord René. I have a high regard for him, and this is not a property I would wish to have taken from him. Nor is he an enemy I can afford to make! Please, my dearest – it would cause me considerable discomfort if you were to induce Count Jean to give it up.'

'Nonsense, my darling, I promise I will make it up to Dunois.'

As for Issoudun, it has been royal property for generations and proudly displays the fleur-de-lys on the coat of arms carved in stone over the entrance. It is one of her lord king's favourite residences, rebuilt by an uncle of his after the fortress and belfry had been put to the torch. Now it is also hers to enjoy with him. But somehow she will avoid the gift of Vernon – Jean Dunois is too valued a friend to lose.

To the amazement of Agnès Sorel's many critics – and even some of her allies – she applies herself energetically to her new responsibilities involving her many estates.

Mistress of Beauté, and now of many other great castles and properties as well, she is realist enough to know that she can never please everyone, no matter how hard she might try. In the eyes of the majority, she is simply not worthy of the great gifts the king has bestowed on her. What has she done to deserve such favour, they ask, except to share his bed? Nor is it considered appropriate that he treats her openly as the queen's equal. Agnès can imagine how Queen Marie must feel, because she knows how *she* would feel were someone to take her place in her lover's heart. Every night she prays it will never happen – and she does all she can to ease the queen's quiet suffering. Nor does she ever allow herself to forget her place when in Marie's presence.

For some time, Agnès has known from notes passed anonymously to her household servants that the majority of Charles's subjects regard her as 'the other woman'. They say it is she who gives their much-loved queen her sad, resigned face; the one who spends their taxes; the one who has enslaved – no, *bewitched* – their victorious king. They call her a sorceress! Deliberately she pushes out of her mind the fate of the last fair young maid who 'bewitched' France's king. And yet at court, most are kind to her, and the others at least civil. There is still one notable exception – the dauphin Louis.

Ever since her arrival at Toulouse with the court of Lorraine, Agnès has been conscious of the way Louis looks at her, with a mixture of desire and disdain. He is the second in the land, after all, and accustomed to taking what he wants, yet he failed with the Mistress of Beauty. Had she given him the slightest encouragement, she knows he would have used her to shame his father. That she did not give him this opportunity has made him hate her. His revenge? He has taken a deliberately public stand in naming Agnès as the cause of his mother's humiliation, a position that gives him a legitimate reason to oppose not only her influence, but his father in general. While the dauphin plainly loathes his father and may indeed care for his mother, it is not as though he spent his early years by her side. In fact, he hardly knew her as a child, having been brought up elsewhere. Agnès is not alone in believing that he makes the queen's pain his justification for hating her and his father with a loathing so intense it blows like a hot wind in her face.

When she finds the right moment, Agnès speaks openly to her royal lover about Louis. His answer surprises her.

'My darling, this son of mine is so envious of my position that he wants my crown and anything that goes with it. That includes the fairest in the land: you, my Lady of Beauty.'

'Sire, my love, he has not had the slightest encouragement from me, and yet, he has been consistently rude to me since my arrival, and that pains me.' In fact, the dauphin takes every opportunity to humble Agnès in the presence of the court:

'Ah, I see before me the Mistress of Beauté, that great royal Château on the Marne that was the prize residence of my grandfather, the late King Charles VI. Now, do tell us of your own high and noble origins that entitle you to the best in France. You were born in a palace yourself, were you not, or did I mistake that hovel with a tower in Picardy for the great castle of your forebears?'

Wisely, she chooses never to reply to his baiting, always done expressly when his father is out of earshot. So it goes on, day after day, with some of the courtiers around the dauphin smirking, while others move away, depending on whether they are Louis' men or the king's. Agnès approves of the loyalty of the queen's ladies towards their mistress, but slowly her own isolation is beginning to weigh down on her.

The court has moved again to Razilly to prepare for another of Lord René's spectacular tourneys, with visitors arriving in large numbers. Charles is entertaining in the Great Hall, the queen has retired and Agnès is standing with some ladies near the king. She is most splendidly dressed in white satin, with wonderful pearls around her neck and woven into her hair. Perhaps tonight she looks too much like the king's lady – she will never know. Suddenly she becomes aware that the dauphin is marching towards her very determinedly, accompanied by two of his followers. As he draws near, his face twists into a hideous snarl and he almost spits at her while shouting in a loud voice: 'You whore, how dare you defile my mother before the court and our guests by your presence, your very existence!' And before she has time to recover from the shock of his verbal attack, he slaps her hard across her face in full view of his father and the assembled courtiers.

It is not so much the force of the blow that sends her reeling as the look in his eyes: *he wants me dead*. The king rushes to her side, supporting her. 'My dearest lady, can you stand?'

Somehow Agnès swallows and manages to keep her composure, assuring him she can, while turning to her attendants, who usher her from the room.

This is simply too much for the king. As she leaves the chamber, she can hear his voice, measured but clear:

'Louis, you are my heir, but from this day I do not want to see you at my court, nor in my kingdom. I banish you to your territory of the Dauphiné. You may not return until I bid you.'

The next day, Agnès hears from Pierre de Brézé that Louis turned white, bowed to his father, and stormed from the Great Hall with his entourage trailing behind.

Later, when her royal lover comes to lie by her and gently caress her swollen cheek, Agnès is at pains to have him be reconciled with his son. In her opinion, a breach with the dauphin, who represents the future, is not a wise move.

'My dearest lord, my love, I beg you to forget about my shame and forgive your son. Do not give him an opening to start plotting with your enemies. It will only lead to division within the country and enable the English to seize the advantage once again.'

He holds her gently in his arms for the rest of the night, anxious not to press on her swollen face, and considering her words.

Chapter Twenty-five

The summer of 1446 is marked by the arrival of three grand ambassadors sent by Henry VI of England to renew the peace treaty between their two countries, a peace that has proved most beneficial to both sides. Such an important occasion warrants – yes – another magnificent tournament! René d'Anjou, back at court and in the king's good graces once again, can be counted on to use his skills and experience to create an event even more thrilling than the last.

Good King René has never been one to disappoint his audience. The tournament is a brilliant sight: tents in bright colours surmounted with matching flags; pages carrying banners fluttering with the insignia of their masters; tiny bells on horses tinkling sweetly all around; and the knights – how bold and brave they look in their shining suits of armour, each sporting the favour of their chosen lady on their right arm. Etienne Chevalier proclaims himself to be Agnès's *chevalier servant*, her personal knight for the tournament, and he performs valiantly in her honour. However, the day is won by Lord René, who appears dramatically on a charger draped in black, he himself wearing a suit of black armour. Large silver tears, a popular device, are painted on his black shield displaying the motto: *With Fervent Desire* – and from the top of his shining steel helmet there bursts a riot of coloured feathers. The crowd and the court exclaim their loud approval of his effort and of the success of the tournament. Elated by his double triumph, he rides at a wild gallop around the tourney ground in a lap of honour.

Agnès is entranced by it all, and even more so by the crowd's surprising reaction to her. Many come and greet her, or hail her as if she is the star of the event. But when she notices she receives more salutations than the queen, she is disturbed. The last thing she wants is to give Queen Marie more reason to dislike her.

When she sees Pierre, she is emboldened to ask him: 'My friend, please tell me – I need to know. Does the queen hate me? Are you aware of anything she says that might give that impression? You know how anxious I am not to offend her, but my mere existence is probably enough for her to wish me dead.'

This last shocks Pierre. 'Oh no, my dear lady, you misjudge the queen. I have had the privilege of spending many years of my youth with her and her siblings, and I truly believe she could not hate anyone. Such an emotion is not a part of her make-up.' But Agnès is not convinced and will remember to ask Marie de Belleville when next they meet.

*

Queen Marie is pregnant with her fourteenth child, and it must be said, pregnancy does not suit her. The Mistress of Beauty can feel the queen's pain when forced to see her husband's young, beautiful, slender lover at her court when she herself is ungainly, large with child and looks worn and tired. For her sake, whenever she is in Queen Marie's presence, Agnès does all she can to appear modest and humble.

How many friends does Agnès really have at court? There are a few she can count on – Etienne Chevalier, certainly, and the dashing Pierre de Brézé; and she feels assured that René and Isabelle would stand by her, even if they retire from the court to Lorraine or Anjou for some of the time. Jacques Coeur is another – after all, she is his best customer; Marie de Belleville she trusts completely; perhaps even Jeanne de Clary, although she has not confided in her; and her cousin Antoinette – yes, she is sure she can trust her. As for the rest . . . since the death of the dauphine Margaret, Agnès is daily more conscious of her isolated position.

Although she sent for Antoinette to come to court to keep her company, she is always elsewhere when Agnès needs her, and besides, she has no power or influence. Her dear friend Marie de Belleville, who is well respected in the queen's circle, and by everyone in the court of Lorraine, is gentle and honest, but, as she told Agnès, she can hardly fight for her in the way the dauphine Margaret used to do whenever anyone criticized her.

'You know, my dear friend, the dauphine would simply not allow a word spoken against you,' Marie tells her one day.

'Really – how very kind,' replies Agnès, surprised.

'Oh, it was more than kind. She spoke very highly of you and said that anyone who thought ill of you could forget her friendship. Oh yes, she fought for your honour most fiercely! I believe she was genuinely moved by the love you and the king have for one another,' Marie added quietly. 'As you know, it was something she never experienced herself, but she could see how happy it made you both.'

At times, Agnès feels her seclusion from the intimacy others share at court binding her like a shroud. There is no category for the king's mistress; it is a solitary post. She is neither his family nor his wife, though she is closer to him than anyone else. However, she is confident that she has the love and protection of her dear, darling lord and master, whom she cherishes with all her being, and resigns herself that this alone must serve as her consolation.

On the evening of the last day of the tournament, there is a ball at Razilly. Jacques Coeur – that ever-faithful provider of luxury and servant of the king – comes to call on Agnès shortly before it begins. 'My Lady of Beauty, I want to be the purveyor of your magnificence for this ball!' Raising his hand, he stops her protest. 'Yes, it is something extravagant; yes, it will astonish everyone; and yes, I know the king will be pleased to give it to you,' he says with a twinkle in his eye and a merry laugh. 'I know how much you love jewels – what lady of the court does not? I have a surprise! The Dutch have learned to cut a diamond in a new way, with many facets, to make it sparkle and catch the light as if it had a fire within its heart.'

Whereupon, he produces a marvellous stone, and Agnès holds it in her fingers up to the light. It is true: the stone is breathtaking.

'But Jacquet, you know that only men have the right to wear diamonds at court.'

With a finger to his lips, he hangs it around her neck on a fine chain; there it sits, glowing in the hollow of her throat.

Agnès's arrival at the ball causes a sensation. 'It is the first such stone to be worn in the West,' whispers Jacquet as she enters the room, and everyone comes forward to admire it, or envy it, or hate her for having it. She pays them no mind, as she can see her king is delighted. 'Agnès, my love,' he tells her out of earshot of others, 'tonight you are the Queen of Diamonds!'

Both Jeanne de Clary and Marie de Belleville come and flatter her sincerely, and she notices to her relief that the queen is not present due to her pregnancy. The ball is another triumph for Lord René, and everyone dances till dawn.

When Agnès next sees Jacques Coeur, he has quite a different kind of surprise for her. Recently, a new card game called *piquet* has been introduced at court, and for the first time, face cards have been used – king, queen and knave for all four suits. Jacquet heard that the king called Agnès his Queen of Diamonds when he saw the stone flashing at her throat. This gave him an idea: he would see to it that in the new packs, the face of Agnès Sorel, the Mistress of Beauty, would be used for the card representing the Queen of Diamonds.

Chapter Twenty-six

With the new year of 1447, Agnès spends much time praying for the soul of her father, who died a month earlier. She hardly knew him but venerated him none the less. Neither he nor her aunt ever criticized her relationship with the king, despite it being strongly against their moral beliefs. At times, she imagines they were almost proud of her.

But there are other reasons why the last year ended badly, the dauphin Louis being the principal cause of their anguish once again. The king recalled his son from exile after some months, but it has not taken him long to begin plotting. One of Jacques Coeur's reliable agents has arrived with distressing information.

'My lady, my master wishes you to know that the dauphin has hatched a scheme to rid the court of the king's favourite, Pierre de Brézé, of whom he is insanely jealous. Somehow he has inveigled your loyal friend Antoine de Chabannes into his scheme.'

Alarmed by this story, Agnès goes at once to warn Pierre and to find Antoine as well, but that wily old soldier reassures her. 'Fear not, my lady, I know the character of the dauphin well, his good and his bad points. I will extricate myself from this treasonous conspiracy and show his father what kind of a son he has.' Happily he is able to do this in time, because as soon as Agnès tells the king of the intrigue, he summons the dauphin: 'Once again I have cause to accuse you of disloyalty to me and my crown. Speak now before I sentence you!'

'Sire, the plan was not mine; it was an idea put forward by Chabannes, and innocently I followed his judgement,' Agnès hears him say as she listens from the next room. But when Chabannes, who is well known to be an honest gentleman and an excellent soldier, is summoned to explain himself, he will have none of it and fights back.

'Sire, although I hesitate to say it about my lord dauphin, in this instance he is both a liar and a knave! His goal has always been to acquire your throne, and he will stop at nothing to get it. I have been his loyal friend for many years, but now he has gone too far. I am ready to divulge the whole of his wicked, avaricious plan, for there is no crime he is not willing to commit for his own ends.'

When he has heard it all, at last the king has had enough of this viper he has nurtured in his nest. Louis is summoned, and in a rage his father shouts at him: 'Ungrateful son, I have forgiven you time and again. Now I banish you from my court and my realm. I banish you to remain within the confines of your own territory of the Dauphiné. Do not leave it under pain of death!'

Once again Louis has failed to unseat his father, but

this time the tension has grown to boiling point, and his complete banishment is the wisest way of enforcing a cooling-off period – if there can ever be one.

That night, as she holds her beloved in her arms, Agnès can feel his heartbeat racing, and for once it is not on her account. Gently she rubs his temples and massages his shoulders, still trembling with suppressed anger, until sleep overtakes him.

The season has come for them to leave Razilly, where, apart from this drama, Agnès and her royal lover have been content and happy. Together with the entire court, their animals and servants, they embark on the gentle river Indre and travel to the royal Château of Loches in Touraine, the land of Agnès's birth. It is April, and the Lady of Beauty has come to lodge in her favourite house here. Bellevue is a charming villa given to her by the king after the birth of her second daughter, Charlotte. It stands close to the château itself and is built from the same honey-coloured stone, with three floors, a turret at each corner, and a pleasant garden. The spring flowers are already in bloom – daffodils and violets, wallflowers of every shade, and clumps of blue forget-me-nots. In the courtyard stands a large aviary. Ever since her time in Naples with Queen Isabelle, Agnès has loved to have songbirds near. Several white peacocks walk about freely in the garden, and there are golden pheasants and nightingales among the many varieties in her aviary.

Bellevue is not a large house, but it is furnished in the most exquisite taste, with beautiful tapestries, paintings by Dutch and Flemish masters, and the beds covered with soft furs. Aunt Marie brings Agnès's two girls, Marie and Charlotte, to stay with her. She finds them a delight and spends her days playing with them in the enclosed garden, lolling about happily on rugs and pillows placed on the grass, surrounded by the scent of flowers. They sit under the blossoming fruit trees and she tells them about growing up with her cousins. As yet, the king has not discussed his plans for their daughters, but Agnès is confident that eventually they will be sent to the house of some noble lady to be educated just as she was.

Pierre de Brézé comes to visit Agnès at her house, supposedly to see her little girls. It's a beautiful, lazy day, sun shining, bees humming in the flower beds, and Agnès is lounging under the shade of a tree. While he plays with her daughters, Pierre says casually:

'Dear lady, are you aware how the king has changed, even in the short time that you have been by his side?' She looks at him in surprise. 'The king you met when the court of Lorraine joined with his in Toulouse was not a fulfilled man, not a man who gloried in being alive as he does now. Admittedly, a little reserve has remained, but what France has now is a man in his element, a man who has achieved something to be proud of – the unification of most of his country.'

Agnès dares not interrupt – Pierre seems to have something on his mind.

'You were in Naples when his father died and he inherited his poor, battered throne. At the time, his country was being torn apart by enemies within and stripped bare by those outside. It was always Queen Yolande's great mission to heal the open wound of civil conflict: to unite the warring factions and make peace with Burgundy. Now, with a united France behind him, the king has pushed the invader out of France and into Normandy! Queen Yolande's other goal, her desire for his personal happiness, he has been able to achieve, my lady, through your presence by his side, inspiring him and giving him the kind of love he never experienced before.

'France is recovering – no, *flourishing* – after years of turmoil, devastation, plague and occupation. The king is jubilant and the people can see his satisfaction in them and in his kingdom. My Lady of Beauty, do not underestimate the part you have played in this remarkable recovery.'

'I am but a very small part of this *remarkable recovery*, I assure you,' she replies.

'No, my lady, your love for him has given our king his greatest happiness and comfort during these years of struggle, even if the people are not aware of what you have done for their sovereign.'

So that is what this is about. Pierre is trying to console her for the animosity she feels coming towards her from every direction.

'Pierre, dear friend, neither of us is a fool. You and I both know that there is no delight in my existence as far as the people of the country are concerned. Kings, great lords, have always had mistresses, but they have kept them discreetly out of sight and, to preserve an illusion of normality, officially married to a complaisant husband, especially if children were involved. As you have seen, our king wants me by him at all times; he behaves as if I am the very air he breathes. I cannot deny I am flattered, nor pretend that I would prefer it otherwise, but I only exist because of his love. Should it cease, I am nothing.'

While Pierre plays with the girls, her mind is whirling, contemplating the positives and negatives of her current life. In her efforts to ease her guilt, she has doubled and redoubled her donations to the poor, to the clergy, to convents, to anyone in want who approaches her. She gives to the sick, to abandoned children, to every worthy cause, and most of all, to the Church. But although her conscience is eased somewhat by the gratitude and warmth she receives in return, she knows she cannot stop loving her king. As long as she shares her life of passion with him, she cannot be forgiven by God.

Despite her acts of charity and ever aware that she should share her good fortune, she cannot deny glorying in the endless gifts showered on her by he lover. God and the king have given her so much; she reasons it is the least she should do to pass on some of her lover's bounty.

Another thought crosses her mind: for how long can she expect to remain so favoured? Her looks will fade soon enough, and the king's love? She finds it impossible to imagine he could cease loving her as he does, but she must be realistic: it *could* happen, and then what would be her fate? Or what if her lord king were to die? Her fall would be from a great height – perhaps fatal . . . But why is she even imagining something so dreadful? Charles loves her with all his heart and soul and she loves him as much. Fie on the rest!

Dismissing her racing thoughts, she smiles warmly at Pierre and, disengaging him from her two little girls, takes him by the arm. 'Come, my friend, and let me show you my garden, and my songbirds.' As he stands admiring them, she says softly: 'Am I, too, not a songbird, trained to sing for the king's pleasure? Safe in my aviary, my golden cage, supplied with every comfort I could desire? Better for me not to look outside, or concern myself with the insidious gossip of the envious. You too, dear Pierre, are much envied – for your position near the king, for your looks, your intelligence, your courage and military success, and for your closeness to the woman who has the ear of the king. Look out for *yourself*, my dear friend!'

They smile at one another, looking deep into each other's eyes, aware of the fragility of their favour, yet trusting in their king's commitment to them both.

Agnès has sent for Antoinette, ever organized and efficient, to whom she has given the charge of her girls' education. She has not seen her cousin for a while, and when Antoinette arrives at Loches, Agnès is taken aback at her changed appearance. Standing before her is a voluptuous red-headed woman with a plunging neckline and a most provocative demeanour. To her surprise, Agnès hears from her staff that André de Villequier, that courtier close to the king whom she has never liked or trusted, is the principle among her cousin's many admirers. *Oh well, good luck to her*, thinks Agnès. No doubt Antoinette appreciates that her own future depends on the continued favour in which the king holds Agnès.

Despite the splendour of spring at Loches, the Lady of Beauty must enjoy its pleasures without her darling king, since he is in Bourges, city of his youth and torment. His mission is to help solve the problem of the schism in the

Church that has resulted in there being two popes for the past hundred years or more – one in Rome and one in Avignon.

Eugenius IV, the Roman Pope, has died, and it is the task of the King of France to help adjudicate in the re-election. To assist him with this difficult task, Charles VII has turned to a man he trusts, a man of great sense and wisdom in the business of diplomacy and high office, namely Agnès's friend Jacques Coeur. Since the Pope in Avignon depends on the goodwill of the King of France, the incumbent has always been on the side of the French monarchy. The Pope in Rome depends on a number of supporters, usually the richest or the most powerful – the King of Aragon, for example, or the Holy Roman Emperor – and such sponsors have invariably been opposed to French interests.

Agnès receives almost daily letters from Charles, in which she can sense his frustration at the complicated negotiations, as well as his longing to be spending the spring with her at Loches – a longing she shares passionately. But besides missing his presence, Agnès bears another deep inner sorrow, a wound that will not heal.

Queen Marie left the court well before Christmas and journeyed to Tours, heavily pregnant. At the end of December, Agnès received a courier from Pierre de Brézé: 'My dear Lady of Beauty, I know what I have to say may grieve you, but I must tell it to you nonetheless. Our gracious queen has given birth to a strong, healthy son. The king is overjoyed and has immediately named him Charles for his father, and created him Duke of Berry.' The news completely stunned Agnès. Without knowing why, somehow it had been beyond her imagination that Queen

Marie could give birth to a healthy son. Perhaps her age, or that she had lost so many children.

In view of these great tidings, the court assembled at Tours for a celebration to herald this long-awaited second son of France. Bonfires were lit on hilltops to signal the report to all the country, fireworks exploded each night, and wine flowed from the water fountains in the centre of towns and villages. When Agnès arrived in Tours, she sought out Pierre de Brézé. How well she recalls asking him:

'Tell me, Pierre, my good friend, what does this mean? The king already has a healthy heir; why so much fuss over a second one?' He looked at her for a while and she saw how carefully he chose his words: 'My dear lady, do you not see? Now the king has an alternative to his unsatisfactory dauphin to offer the country.'

Agnès watched as the queen was carried into the Great Hall on a beautifully draped litter, holding out her new son for all the court to see and admire, a radiant smile on her face such as Agnès had never seen before. Yet far more disconcerting for her bruised heart was the look of sheer joy in her lover's eyes, a look she had not seen him direct at the queen before – a look of love for his wife that Agnès had not realized he felt either – and a sharp knife pierced her heart. Pierre was right. At last her royal lover could have hope for the future of his dynasty, and this hope, a second heir, was given him by his wife!

To mark the important event, Charles VII bestowed on Queen Marie, and in public, sumptuous clothes and a large amount of gold. But his greatest gift, and the one that pained Agnès the most, was the way he looked at her with devotion and deep gratitude – and in his lover's presence! Marie had done what Agnès, as his mistress, could never do. The queen for whom Agnès had felt such pity had won. She had transcended Agnès's love for the king.

Lost in her thoughts, suddenly Agnès became aware that Jacques Coeur was standing beside her. He kissed her hand and murmured: 'My lady, do not look so sad, all is not lost. Your king will return to you, I can assure you.' And with that little act of pity he disappeared. *Pity for me! I, who have felt such pity for her and for so long!* Jacques is someone Agnès trusts to confide in – perhaps she should seek him out more – ask him to tell her about his early life and relationships that have taught him such wisdom . . .

The christening of this second son of France is a most magnificent event – a state occasion with all the trappings that can be mustered. Lord René's brother, Charles of Maine, has been graciously forgiven his part in a recent fracas at court and invited to stand as a godfather. This the king does on the advice of Pierre de Brézé, who feels it politic to keep Maine where both he and the king can more easily watch him. Everyone who is anyone at court has come to the christening of such a long-awaited second heir, and there is as much grand regalia on display as for a royal wedding.

Attending as one of the queen's ladies, Agnès's place is near the font, and she does her best to look as lovely and demure as possible. She cannot help admitting to herself that even with all her new finery, the queen appears old, fat and tired, but from the look of adoration her lover gives his wife at the font, Queen Marie could be the goddess Diana herself. The pain is such that Agnès thinks she will faint, and is grateful for Pierre's firm grip on her elbow as they leave the cathedral. When she catches sight of Antoinette, naturally she expects a comforting word, but the look her cousin gives her almost suggests triumph at her discomfort.

When the royal party leaves the cathedral, the crowd bursts into spontaneous applause and Agnès sees tears of joy roll down her lover's cheeks! She must be alone. At the first opportunity, she runs to her room to bury her pain in her pillow to cry out her misery. She is truly glad for her dearest love – how could she not be? – but her heart is heavy knowing she can never please him as much, never give him so great a gift as this legitimate second son.

The dauphin Louis has been granted permission to attend the christening, and Agnès is not alone in her surprise that he has indeed come. He too witnesses the astonishing reaction of the people to the new royal son, and their elation can have left him in no doubt of his own unpopularity.

The day after the christening, Louis leaves again for the Dauphiné, uttering menacing threats of revenge against 'the one who has deprived me of my place at court'. Agnès knows he means her. No one dares take the dauphin's threats lightly – his temper is well known – but the happiness generated by the birth makes everyone forget the difficult firstborn – for the time being.

The hostile departure of the dauphin signals the loss of the king's peace of mind. To Agnès's dismay, he reverts to his former fearful self, always looking over his shoulder, even in his dreams. Dark nocturnal mutterings puncture their rest after lovemaking, and a deep melancholy begins to settle on her as well. How can this odious son cast such a shadow over their happiness? She knows the king comes to her for comfort and soothing, and, in a sense, mothering, even though she is half his age. His dependence on her is touching and his defence of her so violent that woe betide anyone he should hear speak ill of her!

When her lover clings to her in the darkness of the night and she can feel his angst slowly easing out of him, Agnès believes then that at least she is of some use to her king and country – as Queen Yolande had hoped she would become. She knows the king fears his elder son, as if he has the devil in him and intends them all some terrible harm, yet he cannot bring himself to restrain the dauphin completely. He has done all he can by banishing him, but he knows his son and his devious ways, knows him capable of anything, even regicide, and his mutterings in his sleep confirm it, as does his request for someone to taste his food and drink from this time onwards.

Chapter Twenty-seven

It is the spring of 1448. As the sun shines down on the Mistress of Beauty's walled garden at Bellevue, nature offers up her own riches for Agnès to enjoy. The strong scent from the borders of stocks and narcissi, clumps of blue for-get-me-nots, sweet violets, and pink, red and white peonies fills each breath she takes while playing happily with her daughters. Etienne Chevalier has become a regular visitor to her house here; loyal, faithful, sombre Etienne, who is invariably obediently on hand to keep her company during her lord's absences. Since the death of his beloved wife, his naturally mournful look has increased, and not even the fooling of the little girls manages to transform his sad mouth into a smile.

The girls are sleeping after their midday meal, while Agnès reclines on cushions under a tree, enjoying feeling lazy in the sunshine of the early afternoon. Etienne has arrived unexpectedly but to her pleasure.

'Come, my friend, sit here by me in the shade. Would you like some fruit juice? I am sure you have news for me, since you are one of my more observant friends, and if not news, then at least some merry tales to tell,' and she pats the cushions within reach. Etienne is unusually elegant in a bright-green doublet and hose, and sporting a jaunty hat with a long feather plucked from a golden pheasant. 'I must say, you do look remarkably dashing today – and that hat! It is a pleasant change from your usual grey outfits. And what is this gleam I see in your eye? What have you been up to? I have not seen a look like that from you for some time.' It crosses her mind that he may have met someone who has taken his fancy, but then she pushes away such a frivolous thought – not Etienne, and such a recent widower! And yet he is definitely on a mission; and then it tumbles out faster than he can control the words.

'Madame, my dear Lady Agnès, I have had a dream,' he begins almost in agitation.

Oh dear, not another one of his complicated dreams – they can be taxing on the concentration, especially on this lovely peaceful afternoon.

'My dream, dear lady, is to have a diptych painted for the chapel I have built and dedicated to my beloved wife. It will be placed over her tomb in the cathedral of Nôtre-Dame in Melun, my home town.' He pauses, and draws breath with an air of satisfaction.

'But that is a wonderful dream, dearest friend, and one that you can make come true.' What relief! Etienne is well known for his passion for the arts, painting in particular.

'Madame, I have met a most talented young painter named Jean Fouquet. He trained in Rome with the great artists of that city, and now he has established himself in Tours in his father's former studio. Have you heard speak of him, my lady?'

Agnès confesses she has not, while offering him more juice, but tells Etienne that he sounds ideal.

'Yes, I have visited him there and am convinced he is the one I should commission to create the diptych.'

'Well, that is settled then,' she says dreamily, ready to let him ramble on. She might even have allowed herself to doze off but for the fixed look in his eye – almost feverish in its intensity. He stands up and turns fully to face her.

'My Lady Agnès, I know only you will understand my passionate desire to commission a most talented painter to create a masterwork, since you know how much I loved my wife. I want to have a Madonna and Child on one panel; on the other, myself as the donor, together with my patron St Etienne.' By now he really is becoming quite overexcited and definitely needs calming.

'My dear friend, of course I understand, and I assure you I believe it to be a wonderful plan. Your dear wife in Heaven will be as delighted as you will be with the result,' she says, gently patting his arm.

He walks a few paces, then squats down quickly and falls to his knees. 'My lady, it is you – you who I beg on my bended knees to be the model for the Madonna, and with your baby in your arms.'

Agnès sits up sharply and is more than a little startled. *Mary Magdalene playing the Virgin Mary? The sinner posing as the saint? Poor man, his sorrow has confused his reasoning!* After a long pause, she says softly and sincerely:

'Dear Etienne, in spite of the great honour you are

paying me, I fear this suggestion may be viewed badly by many – especially the Church – and may even count as sacrilege.'

Etienne is unmoved. 'My lady, since your gifts come from God, you are but his creature. Therefore, to lend your beauty to represent His mother could hardly be considered inappropriate.'

Agnès is only half listening – the idea is completely impossible, and she shakes her head. Etienne rises slowly and bows, then leaves her, looking even more downcast than before. Agnès can see he is deeply disappointed. Watching his hunched back and bent head as he walks down her garden path, she sends a messenger running after him, with the promise that she will discuss the matter with the king.

Frankly, she wants to forget his request; to accept would be neither fitting nor appropriate. And yet to date, no one has painted her. Perhaps this is an opportunity to have her role in the king's life given a veneer of sanctity. No, that is going too far; but a veneer of *respectability*, certainly. Yes, she will ask him – or maybe just surprise him with the result. She will need to think about it carefully.

A messenger arrives: the king is on his way back to Loches from Bourges to spend time with Agnès and their daughters. May will now be a wonderful month after all, and she will share its delights with her lover and help him to forget his troubles. No, she will not bother him with a silly question about posing for her friend's painting. Charles has enough on his mind. She will accept Etienne's request and surprise her darling lord. No, she will not bother to ask Charles. She knows in her heart that her lover would agree if she spoke to him, since he too is very fond of Etienne and of his late wife.

Nonetheless, she writes to Jacques Coeur to ask his advice.

'My dear Jacquet, wisest of friends,' she begins, *'I have been visited by Etienne Chevalier, a dear friend of mine and of the king's – whom I am sure you know? Can you imagine, he has asked me to agree to be painted by a brilliant, new, young artist called Jean Fouquet. Do you know of him? I have not yet been painted. What do you think? Should I accept?'*

Jacques replies by return: *'Nothing could be more appropriate. It is a splendid idea, my lady, it is time we had a portrait of your beauty to admire.'* Agnès is pleased with his reply but thinks perhaps she should tell him what the painting would represent:

'The portrait of me is to be for one side of a diptych in honour of Etienne's late wife. It will be placed over her tomb in the cathedral at Melun, Etienne's home city, which he has personally helped to endow. For some time, I have taken Mary Magdalene for my particular saint – she seems appropriate in my position, and, as you know, I am as devout as I can be. But Jaquet, dear friend, what do you really think? Etienne insists that I pose as the Madonna of the Milk, with my baby, the king's baby, representing the Christ Child at my breast, and himself kneeling beside his patron saint on the other panel. I am not sure whether to be honoured or shocked. He wants me to wear a great crown as the Queen of Heaven, a blue cloak lined with ermine over my dress – and I am not at all convinced that I should agree to this spiritual elevation! I would welcome your advice since I feel I cannot trouble the king with such a question. Naturally, I refused Etienne when he asked me – I am sure you

can understand. Imagine me, the sinner, posing as the Virgin Mary, and holding the king's illegitimate baby daughter as the Christ Child! It is an outrageous idea and quite inappropriate, which I told him.

'But as I watched my dear Etienne leave my house, his shoulders hunched in sadness, I could not bear his distress, and sent a message promising I would ask the king. But I cannot – and I would love to be painted for him. Please tell me what to do?'

Kind and wise as always, Jacquet replies: *'Naturally you must be prepared for some criticism, yet if the king has agreed, it will soon pass.'*

Jacques can read between her lines and knows she is apprehensive, and once he sees the finished work, he is not surprised it causes a scandal, beautiful though it is. The subject matter of the Virgin giving milk to the Christ Child is a familiar pose of the time and is not the cause of the scandal – it is the fact that the baby is the king's illegitimate daughter and her mother, the king's mistress, is portrayed as the Blessed Mary, the Queen of Heaven – rather than as the sinful, but repentant Mary Magdalene. It is the role reversal, not the subject, that shocks the court and society.

Chapter Twenty-eight

In October, Agnès is with the court at Montils, heavily pregnant for the third time, when Marie de Belleville comes to her with a worried look. 'Agnès, my dear friend,' she begins, 'as you know, I never meddle in the affairs of the court, nor have I ever approached you with words against anyone.'

'Indeed, I know what a loyal friend you are. But tell me, what is it? I can see you are quite distressed.' Marie does indeed look agitated.

'Agnès, my dear, you are such an innocent, and I am deeply troubled that you are being pulled into a situation that does not concern you and may even harm you.'

Alarmed, Agnès asks, 'What do you mean?'

Marie looks at the ground like a young girl obliged to tell tales. 'I have it on good authority that some papers have been discovered in the possession of Guillaume Mariette, a man from the dauphin's circle I have never trusted or liked.' Agnès searches her memory but cannot place him. 'This man Mariette claims that he found papers while riding on the road from Montils. They take the form of a report from the dauphin addressed to the Duke of Burgundy in which the dauphin claims that it is Pierre de Brézé, with your connivance, my lady, who is in reality governing the country.'

Agnès has to laugh at that. 'Marie – stop; let us have Pierre come at once so that he too can hear this nonsense,' but Marie insists: 'My dear, I beg you to listen. This nonsense, as you call it, could have serious consequences for you.' She takes a deep breath. 'According to one of the documents in the packet, the Duke of Burgundy sent the dauphin some hunting dogs, but his gift was merely a cover to enable the messenger to inform the dauphin about the king's misgovernment under my Lord de Brézé's domination.'

Agnès summons Pierre, and they tell him the story so far. His outrage is deep and smouldering; nor is he even mildly amused by its clear stupidity as Agnès had thought. Marie continues: 'The writer of another of the documents, allegedly the dauphin, suggests that the solution is to rid the country of you, my esteemed *sénéchal* Pierre, so that he may take over the government in your place. My lord, you are depicted as being the greatest enemy of the dauphin, who asks for the Duke of Burgundy's help to eliminate you!'

Disbelief and shock mingle as they listen, and Marie is asked to continue.

'Alternatively the dauphin suggests to the duke that the king should be confined somewhere until he himself can return to France from his exile in the Dauphiné to take his father's place on the throne. Among the papers there is one that maintains the Duke of Burgundy agrees with the dauphin and is ready to finance him liberally to enable him to replace his father and impose a wiser rule on the kingdom.' As she finishes, poor Marie de Belleville looks exhausted, and Agnès tries to comfort her.

'What stupidity this is. No one could believe such a convoluted and absurd plot. But thank you, my kindest of friends, for your concern, which I treasure. You were right to bring this to our attention, but I assure you all will be well and you are not to worry.'

'My dear Agnès, you know how devoted I am to you, and I simply could not bear to hear any more of this plot without informing you of it. Not that it makes sense to me, but I wrote it all down so that I would not forget any of the details and become confused.'

The two friends embrace, and Marie de Belleville leaves, close to tears. Pierre looks troubled and pensive.

'Pierre, let us approach Jacquet for his opinion and advice. He always keeps a cool head and is astute in his, suggests judgements Agnès.'

Pierre readily agrees, and when Jacques Coeur arrives, they tell him Marie's story. He, in his wisdom, brings the tale to the attention of the king's advisers. Following careful examination by the royal notaries, it is soon agreed by everyone concerned that the letters are forgeries. And yet each of those allegedly involved – the dauphin Louis, Philip of Burgundy, Pierre de Brézé – come out of the story somehow tarnished, as if a hint of connivance still sticks to them despite their complete innocence. It was precisely this kind of damage caused all too easily by mere innuendo that Pierre recognized during Marie de Belleville's account.

'There are too many loose ends, too many possibilities, even probabilities,' he tells Agnès grimly.

For all she knows, Pierre *has* been in some sort of contact with the dauphin – nothing treasonable; perhaps involving preparations for the next reign. But what about Agnès herself? Is *she* thought to be involved or protecting anyone in this elaborate, long-winded tale? Could anyone really believe that she and Pierre de Brézé are plotting against the king? What possible motive could she have for that?

It does not take long to discover that Mariette has been accepting bribes from all sides and wrote the letters himself. Arrested in connection with another case of forgery, he manages to escape from prison and flees to the Dauphiné, thinking that Louis will protect him. Instead, he is arrested again, and the dauphin, desperate to return into his father's good graces, feigns outrage and delivers him to the royal prosecutor. Mariette's end is a foregone conclusion. Quickly tried and incarcerated at Chinon, then the Bastille, he is condemned and put to death at Tours. The dauphin has wasted no time in eliminating a double agent he can no longer use, especially one who might incriminate him – and possibly others associated with him.

However, Mariette and the dauphin have together succeeded in compromising the honour of the king's most trusted minister, Pierre de Brézé, and, by association, to a degree also Agnès. This Pierre realized at once from Marie de Belleville's telling, though at the time he did not want to frighten Agnès. Even Marie understood what Agnès in her innocence did not: that there was but one purpose behind those letters – to rid the king of Pierre de Brézé and Agnès Sorel! Who had the most to gain from that? One person – the dauphin Louis.

The court is at Chinon when Pierre arrives to meet Agnès in her chambers with serious matters to discuss.

'My Lady Agnès, please listen to me carefully, because what I have to say concerns your honour,' he announces gravely. 'The execution of Mariette is not the end of this sorry business, which has placed me under a dark cloud of suspicion. Further, I must tell you, much as it grieves me, it is being generally bandied about that you and I have been intimate; that we have been intent on deceiving the king in a number of ways and ruining the country; that we are traitorous in every respect.'

Agnès cries out in shock and has to sit, her breathing coming in gasps. How could this have come about? Her mind is spinning with disbelief. Pierre remains standing, pacing.

'For a man of honour – a *grand sénéchal* – and one who has taken an active part in the recent triumphant occupation of Le Mans, such a serious accusation is insufferable and cannot be endured. There is nothing I value more than the king's trust; it is my greatest pleasure to serve him. To lose his confidence would make a mockery of my life.'

Agnès turns to him urgently. 'Pierre, my friend, dreadful and false as these accusations are, you and I know that we are both victims of intense envy. I understand your desire to regain the king's trust, as that is all I live for too.

And I have been slandered with you in this regard. What can be done to restore my lord's faith in you, and in me – *if* he doubts me?'

For this all-powerful minister, the situation is intolerable. He has spent his life aligning himself in the right places and at the right time with the right people to achieve his pivotal position in the country. He will not allow his hard work to be thrown away because of the innuendos of an admitted double agent and liar. Pierre de Brézé has never lacked courage, and with his future at stake, he decides on a dramatic move to clear his name.

Agnès is watching as Pierre approaches the king seated on his throne in the Great Hall at Chinon, and hears him say loudly enough for all the court to hear: 'Sire, with your permission . . .' He bows low while Charles waves him on to continue. 'In view of the many accusations against me being uttered in private and even in public, I humbly beg you to demand that *parlement* be reconvened in Paris to put me on trial.' There is an audible intake of breath from the courtiers, who have all stopped to listen. 'I will not be satisfied until my case is judged by my peers. If they find me guilty, I will accept their judgement, but if I am found innocent, I request that my name be cleared completely of the suspicion and defamation that I have been obliged to endure.'

Agnès can see that the king is somewhat taken aback; he glances quickly at her, as if she might have some idea what this is about. But she is as surprised as he is. She wants to rush to his side, but he rises and looks at his courtiers gathered beneath him. Then, encompassing them all with his gaze, he praises Pierre de Brézé's courageous intention and declares that he will accede to his request. Voices rise. Nothing like this has ever occurred to anyone's recollection: that an important lord gives himself over to *parlement*, offering to be its prisoner; to be judged by his peers in order to clear his name.

That night, when the lovers are alone, Agnès discusses the situation at length with the king, and finally asks: 'My darling, is this move wise on the part of our dear friend?'

'No, my love, it is not, but it is what a real man like Pierre de Brézé feels he must do, and I cannot stand in his way. His is a bold but also a dangerous decision. Should there be sufficient members in *parlement* who find him too powerful, then he has given them their chance to get rid of him.'

'But surely the members of your *parlement* in Paris are all honest men,' she ventures, and her lover gives her a strange look.

'Well, of this you can be sure: Pierre is far more useful to me with our troops fighting the English in Normandy than sitting in prison awaiting *parlement*'s decision. He must return to the army while his case is being judged in Paris.'

Both Marie de Belleville and Antoinette rush to tell Agnès that the court thinks it a mad gesture on Pierre's part, and she has to agree. She knows that Charles is secretly proud of Pierre's courage and panache, and yet tucked away somewhere in the back of her mind there is a tiny inkling that perhaps her beloved king is not totally sure of his innocence. It will take the judgement of *parlement* to set his mind at rest, and she will concur with that.

There is also another important issue that must be

examined: Agnès too wants to be publicly vindicated. Naturally she is conscious of the sniping comments made behind her back; the envy and hatred that distresses her greatly. Both she and the king realize that Pierre is undertaking this hazardous procedure on her behalf as well, because when *parlement* declares him innocent of the accusations and implications against him, then she too will be exonerated.

Chapter Twenty-nine

Two months have passed since Pierre's departure for Normandy. The king is also with the army when Agnès gives birth to her third daughter, Jeanne, who, like the other two, is born without any difficulty. During her quiet recuperation, Agnès spends long hours thinking how she can clear her name of any incorrect involvement with Pierre de Brézé. No one at court can doubt her devotion to the king, but elsewhere, the story coupling her with the handsome *grand sénéchal* has been magnified alarmingly, and her name is being vilified from pulpits across the country.

By the time Agnès is fully recovered from the birth and little Jeanne is in the capable hands of her Aunt Marie and her usual attendants, Agnès has decided on as bold a resolution as Pierre's. She will go to Paris to help at his trial – perhaps as a witness in his absence – and in speaking on his behalf, she will be able to speak on her own as well.

The English have broken the truce; Pierre must remain

with the army in Normandy and cannot be in Paris to defend himself before *parlement*. For this reason, and for the first time, Agnès twists the truth of her plan when she asks the king if she might make a pilgrimage to Sainte-Geneviève in Paris, and on her return pass by her Château de Beauté to inspect the renovations she has commissioned. In her heart, Agnès knows that her beloved king does not believe a word of the rumours of her improper connection with Pierre de Brézé, but she needs to have it proved to the rest of her world.

Her dear friend Jacquet, who is privy to everything that happens at court, senses her anguish and offers his help, putting his Paris house, staff and agents at her disposal. Until recently, Paris has been in the hands of the Burgundians, allies of the English, and to find servants loyal to the king might not be easy without Jacquet's help. Once again, Agnès has good reason to thank him for his offer, though generous as it is of him, it would be naïve of her to forget that, as his best customer, she will be in a position to model his luxurious products in Paris to their fullest advantage.

In mid-April 1448, the Lady of Beauty's little cavalcade sets out for Paris, a city that she knows does not love any king's mistress. Her lord has instructed that she is to be accompanied in the same state as a royal princess, with all the opulence and elegance that requires. As always, Jacquet accommodates the king's wishes, and his efforts have her full of admiration. Etienne Chevalier attends her, which pleases her; she is less pleased that André de Villequier has also been appointed, as well as two other gentlemen of the court unknown to her. To her relief, her brothers, Charles and Jean Soreau, are also part of her retinue. At all times when she travels, her confessor, Father Denis, accompanies her.

Her entourage is both numerous and luxuriously attired. Her standard, a sand-coloured escutcheon bearing a silver elder tree, leads the way. Agnès chooses to ride rather than travel on a litter, and controlling her full-blooded little Arabian mare will keep her mind from wandering towards her apprehensions. Yes, she is afraid. She is afraid of the unknown; of a city where she knows she is hated on principle, a city not necessarily loyal to the king; and of a trial that might go against her best friend at court and thereby implicate her as well. And why has Charles included André de Villequier among her escort? Perhaps she is wrong about him; after all, he was another that Queen Yolande recommended to her long ago.

The journey from Chinon to Paris takes a week, passing through unfamiliar lush green country – forests, and fields with cattle or crops – until finally they reach the gates of the capital. What a sight meets Agnès's eyes: people scurrying in all directions, stopping, starting, chatting, dressed in every manner of costume; people shouting, waving their wares, pushing and shoving as their procession advances. She is used to the stares of strangers, but here it is not her face that draws amazement but the opulence of her entourage. Etienne and Agnès exchange glances and she can see that he reads her thoughts. A more modest entry would have been wiser. This way, they are attracting unwelcome attention – and she wishes she was wearing fewer rings!

Looking up, she can see an endless array of pointed

roofs on towers; shop signs swinging over doorways. All around her are women walking with baskets on their heads or arms; stalls selling everything one could eat or wear, and small live animals, chickens and birds chirping or singing in their cages; the smells of fish, of not-so-fresh meat, of leather tanning, of sweat; then delightful scents as they pass the flower vendors. There are students wearing satchels, throwing balls or their caps; artisans carrying tools; clerics and monks at their beads as they walk, heads down; even some bishops in red; dwarves, pilgrims, dealers in everything, musicians and – to be expected – beggars, many deformed and pitiful. She instructs her company to toss coins wherever needed.

This left bank of the river Seine is both frightening and thrilling. Blazing colours; and noise, such a jangle of different noises can be heard all around them. They pass water carriers, charcoal sellers, jugglers, child actors, merchants selling books, baskets, candles, hats, jackets, stockings. There are men repairing furniture; selling and mending carpets, chests, beds; metal merchants beating noisily at their wares, and shouting – everyone is shouting. There is so much to see and to take in. Hers is not the only cavalcade in evidence; they pass a number of beautifully painted litters and open carriages. Elegant people mix with the crowd, some on horseback, many more on mules, and they see heavily laden donkeys as well.

Naturally, they are noticed, and passers-by shout out asking who they are. Why, oh why, is she so luxuriously dressed? And yes, she is also recognized – and abused for her position by the king's side. Some of the names she is called shame her deeply. The cruelty of the abuse is alarming, and her guards move their horses closer around her. The name-callers have no fear of retribution, although any one of her guards could strike them. But their party is in no doubt that it would not be wise to allow themselves to be goaded by vulgar taunts.

Eventually they cross the river over the bridge of Saint-Michel, and come upon a completely different scene. Here on the right bank of the Seine there are gardens full of flowers leading down from elegant houses to the water's edge; they can see Nôtre-Dame, the great white stone cathedral of Paris; all around there are shops and merchants, but less noise, less shouting, everything more discreet, organized, respectable. They see many chapels, churches, convents, and steeple bells ring constantly. Agnès is still in shock at their rude reception that at first she fails to notice all the wonders above her, but at the urging of Etienne Chevalier she looks up to see the exquisite towers of the Sainte-Chapelle rising high before her. She knows it was built by King Saint Louis IX to house the Crown of Thorns and a piece of the True Cross, and inspired by these holy relics, she prays silently that the endeavour she has somewhat rashly undertaken may succeed.

They pass the Place de Grève with its gibbet standing empty in the centre, and a shiver runs down her back. Around them the populace is as numerous and as industrious as on the left bank, but tidier in their dress and more moderate of voice. The streets are cleaner too, and the Lady of Beauty feels less conspicuous advancing with her elegant suite. At last they reach the square of Saint-Antoine. The Bastille is nearby, but she focuses on the large area given to promenading and, at times, to royal tournaments. Here the passers-by notice them, nod with a slight show of respect for their obvious status, and move on about their business.

Finally they arrive at the royal manor of Les Tournelles; the king insisted that they stay at his own residence in Paris rather than that of Jacques Coeur. Agnès turns to Etienne with a small sigh of relief. 'How strange to be staying in the same residence the king and queen inhabit when they are in Paris.' But her royal reception does something towards compensating for the rudeness and wounding insults she encountered earlier along the left bank of the city. Did the king know how it would be? Most probably! Gates open as if by intuition, pulled from within, and they enter a huge courtyard from the rue Saint-Antoine through a portico surmounted by the three golden fleur-de-lys of France, supported by a finely carved stone angel.

During the occupation of Paris by the English, King Henry V, victor of Agincourt, appointed his brother the Duke of Bedford as his regent. Anticipating a long stay in the capital, Bedford greatly embellished the royal property. The building is more a palace than a manor house, and very large, with countless little towers and a number of pavilions attached to the main body of the building. Agnès is shown to a charming pavilion where apartments have been set aside for her and her suite. While her bags are being unpacked, Etienne takes her to explore her temporary domain. Among the pavilions, there is one for the queen, another for the royal children, and separate apartments prepared for important courtiers. There are several private chapels with cloisters; kitchens, stables, aviaries filled with unusual birds and a menagerie with even more exotic animals. There is a labyrinth appropriately called the Dédalus, but she doubts there is a Minotaur – or are the unusual animals free to roam there?

Inside, she is faced with supreme luxury and comfort. On the walls hang the most beautiful tapestries, and heavy gold-framed pier glasses. Beds are raised high with little steps alongside to climb up on to them. Thick silk hangs from the bedposts and the most luxurious coverlets of embroidered damask lie on top. The library contains many rare books and there are stands for examining manuscripts at one's leisure. Wherever she looks, her eyes feast on elegance and comfort, and slowly, slowly her composure begins to return after her frightening arrival in this hostile city. Agnès has brought along her portable altar, a unique possession, and with the help of Father Denis saying Mass, she knows she will regain her self-control and be able to prepare for the ordeal ahead.

While they wait for Agnès to be called as a witness in Pierre de Brézé's trial, Etienne proposes to show the king's lady what a satisfying distraction the thoroughfares of Paris can be. They dress with simple elegance and move into the streets, but without a steward carrying her banner before her they have more privacy. Now she can watch the animation of the people; appreciate the charm of the vendors of sweetmeats and other refreshments in the small passageways. On entering the great warehouses, she is astonished at the variety of goods on sale – every kind of fabric for clothes and furnishings; shoes, gloves, laces and furs. Nearby are merchants selling belts and jewels, headdresses and scents, books and herbs, flowers and even singing birds.

The variety and quality of everything enchants her; she is spoilt for choice. In addition, Jacquet has forewarned his merchants of her presence in Paris, and in no time they are calling on her, turning her head with an endless stream of desirable objects. Happily, their visits succeed in diverting her somewhat from her purpose in the city, since the prospect of appearing at Pierre's trial causes her constant nervous agitation.

For two weeks she waits, and every time she hears the ring of the great house bell, her heart begins to thump with anticipation: is this the call for her to go to *parlement* to be examined? No – yet another merchant to be welcomed with relief as he adds to the avalanche of enticing wares distracting her away from her devotions or the calls she should pay.

Each evening she walks with Etienne along the wide ramparts of the great walls surrounding the palace, looking down to the banks of the Seine, fretting that on the morrow she will be called upon to appear as a witness on her own or Pierre's behalf.

Then she receives encouraging news: the trial of her absent friend is progressing well. Each morning, Father Denis says early Mass for her; today she thanks God with all her heart for the good news. It is hot in Paris, and she longs for home and the countryside. That evening, when she has almost completed her walk with Etienne along the ramparts of the palace wall, the heady smell of lilacs blooming in the garden filling the air, she sees a footman come running with a message.

Tearing the seal, she opens the letter. Pierre has won!

She almost embraces Etienne in her joy and great relief. *Parlement* has found him innocent of all charges, innuendo, implications, everything. He has nothing to answer for. He has been completely exonerated. *And with him, so have I*, she sighs to herself. What good news she can at last send both to the king and to Pierre. Just as she promised, the next day she retires to the abbey of Sainte-Geneviève, to thank for her intercession.

Agnès Sorel leaves Paris without regrets. It is a city that has not welcomed her, regarding her only as a king's mistress, a being living a half-life. No one thinks to care if she makes their king happy, or improves the quality of his life in some way. The only people who are sad at her departure are the small army of salesmen in whose wares she has distracted herself.

Since Agnès told Charles that she would visit her Château de Beauté on her homeward journey, this she does, and with great pleasure. The air is cool as she walks down the avenues; watches the deer startle at her approach; breathes in the scents of the flowers in her gardens – the sweet-smelling jasmines, and roses already climbing the south-facing walls. She takes in the heady scent of a field of narcissi; marvels at the fountains shooting high, the light breeze stealing their fine spray. With what pleasure she inspects the vineyards just coming into fruit; the sheep with their fat lambs in the meadows; and the wild flowers – a carpet of pale-yellow primroses growing in profusion around the edges of the streams. How fittingly has this property been named!

She decides to stop there for several days, enjoying the

spring weather during the day, and her fabled library in the evening. She and her companions float down the little canals in small boats and picnic by the shady banks, allowing her bruised soul time to heal from the hostility of the Parisians. And all her constructions and redecorations have been carried out to her satisfaction and appreciation.

Thus refreshed and revived, it is time to leave this, her personal haven. Accompanied by her patient companions, her mission accomplished, Agnès sets out for Touraine and her king.

Chapter Thirty

She has arrived. Oh! and how her lover embraces her, smoothing her brow and doing all he can to make up for her anxiety and the distress the streets of Paris caused her. Has he missed her? She should not have worried. He showers her with affection and gifts: the most beautiful pearls from Jacques Coeur's warehouse; ivory carvings of people and animals; combs of tortoiseshell; and the books! Her royal lover gives her the rarest and most delicately painted manuscripts, as if nothing is sufficient to take away the shame of her reception in his capital. Naturally, he has heard already. She has to laugh at him, and tease that he must have a guilty conscience to spoil her so, and she begs to share some of her bounty with Marie de Belleville and her cousin Antoinette. He smiles a strange little smile, and she supposes he must find her very silly.

When Agnès sees Jacques Coeur, she feels the urge to unburden herself of the shame of her treatment by the

Parisians. She tells him that no matter how much his kind people tried, she felt ill at ease in the city, finding the Parisians unfriendly and lacking in respect.

'Jacquet, can you imagine, some of the women actually taunted me and made rude gestures as if to a harlot!' Her friend says nothing. 'You cannot know how their attitude shocked me. All my life I have only ever known courtesy, within my Lady Isabelle's court in Naples and Lorraine, and at the court of Queen Marie. I will let my lord the king know how much I dislike Paris, and I vow I shall never visit the capital again.'

Despite the beauty of the summer of 1449, dark clouds of war are gathering yet again. The English still refuse to give up the Anjous' region of Maine and other territories agreed in the marriage contract of King Henry VI with René d'Anjou's daughter Marguerite. The King of France must react, and sends his two most faithful and effective captains, Pierre de Brézé and Jean de Dunois, to subdue the rebellious towns. Everyone is sick of war, and now it is to begin again. One provocative incident from the English side follows another, and despite the king's best efforts to find a means of avoiding another conflict, people throughout the country let it be known that they are enraged and want the hated *goddons* finally out of France.

The court is at Chinon, that château much cherished by Charles VII. The summer is sweltering and Agnès has allowed herself to be lulled into a gentle languor by the sleepy, hot days. Once again she is with child and enjoying her own lethargy. No doubt her manner affects her royal lover, and he too is loath to rouse the army. It is Queen Marie who rounds on him one evening with a number of her ladies and urges him to retaliate against the English. Marie is well informed by Jacques Coeur, and knows the strength of the French professional forces – the superb cavalry, their archers, and the large number of well-trained artillery. It is true, the time is right. Still the king hesitates, and it crosses Agnès's mind that he is as comfortable in his inertia as she is – the stifling summer, the buzzing of the bees in the flower beds, their calm evening walks, breathing in deeply the scent of flowers after a little rain, their afternoon siestas and picnics, the slow boating on the river.

Since Agnès wants to please her lover, and also wants to please the queen, she makes a suggestion to suit both parties. The ladies of the court should accompany the king and his army to war, as was often the case in the past. Housed near the Front, the ladies would inspire their gallant captains, and entertain them too. They could be of use and share in the inevitable triumph of the French forces!

Charles VII is not an impulsive man, and he asks his senior courtiers for their views. The decision is unanimous – and Jacques Coeur agrees that the king's duty lies in bringing a final end to these effronteries by the English. Jacquet, Agnès's dear friend, who knows the cost of war, has been hoarding supplies for some time in case this might happen. In a gesture so typical of the man, he opens his generous heart.

'Sire,' he says before the assembled court, 'all I have is yours,' and Agnès knows he means it. The king is indeed well served by such a man, and she tells him so that night in his arms.

Once again, the nobles leave for war, and this time their elegant ladies follow them, in litters or riding. The knights are arrayed in their finery, armour shining, feathers bobbing on their helmets, banners aloft, horses caparisoned to the ground in bright colours – as if war was a tournament! They are all there, the favourites of Agnès and her royal lover – Jean de Dunois, Pierre de Brézé, the Counts of Clermont and Eu, the Count of Saint-Pol, Antoine de Chabannes, Etienne de Chevalier, André de Villequier and, most importantly, the Constable, Arthur of Richemont; all good men and most of them Agnès's dear friends. With the country's faith invested in these brave knights, the army is preceded for their spiritual comfort by holy relics in procession.

Only Agnès is not with the court following her lord the king to rejoice over his victorious army. This latest pregnancy has not been progressing as easily as the others, and the king's good doctor, Adam Fumée, will not allow her the jolting of the journey. After a touching farewell from Charles, Agnès makes her way slowly from Chinon to Bellevue, her beautiful sand-coloured stone mansion next to the Château de Loches. Her house was rightly named – a most lovely place indeed, and in a glorious position. There her children await her, three little golden girls whom she sees too infrequently. Her dear, uncomplaining, uncritical Aunt Marie has come to join her, and Agnès passes the hot, close days of August surrounded by those she loves.

She continues to do all she can to repay her good fortune,

giving ever more to the Church, to the poor and the sick, and begging God to forgive her if she has displeased him. The queen's sadness still affects her, since she knows she is its cause, and the awareness of her guilt lies over her like a spider's web tying her down. Surely her favourite saint, Mary Magdalene, would understand? She prays to her all the more for guidance.

The king wants to make Agnès a duchess, but she thinks it best to refuse – at least for a while longer. There is quite enough envy of her position as it is – the estates, the jewels, the size of her entourage, and now the king has sent her a new girl dwarf to amuse her at Bellevue during her pregnancy. She hears that gesture was not popular with Queen Marie, who wanted to take the dwarf to the Front to entertain *her*! More guilt, but Agnès is delighted to have the girl – she makes her laugh and forget her discomfort.

Inevitably, the favour the king has shown to her family has infuriated some – she is aware of that too. Her uncle, her aunt, her brothers, her cousin Antoinette – they have all been enriched and established well beyond any expectations. The advancement of her friends rankles with others, especially the honour done to Pierre de Brézé. He has served his king faithfully and well, earning his own advancement, but since he is *her* friend, that is reason enough for him to be scorned by some. *The king loves me – and such scorn is the price my family and friends have to pay.*

But will he always love me? she asks herself when alone in the dark of her chamber. *Will he not grow tired of me?* She notices how her voluptuous cousin Antoinette flirts with him when she thinks Agnès is not looking. *She knows*

I can have her sent home at once, yet still she dares . . . Has my lover given her any encouragement while I was away in Paris? No, surely not. But then Agnès knows she is not at her best when pregnant.

Something strange has happened. Because Agnès has Marie de Belleville with her, as well as Pierre's wife Jeanne de Brézé – another of Queen Marie's ladies – the queen has requested that Antoinette join her and go to the Front in place of Agnès. Since her aunt has come to Bellevue, Agnès has little excuse to pretend she needs Antoinette with her as well. Still, she is not comfortable having her cousin flirting with everyone at court when she is not beside her royal lover.

She finds this request of Queen Marie's hard to understand. Why would the queen want Antoinette near? Her own ladies are so very different in manner and behaviour. Nor would the king make such a suggestion. But if not at his suggestion, then whose? The dauphin's? Just to vex Agnès? She knows the queen; the last person she would want in her sober, staid court is a young woman as blatantly flirtatious as Antoinette de Maignelay. Then again, why should Agnès worry? Has the king not just conquered Vernon-sur-Seine from the English again and given *her* the city? What more could she have asked? And how can she doubt him after such a gift? Not only has he created her Dame de Beauté, but now also Dame de Vernon.

What is it that troubles her, pricks at her conscious mind? She has her friends around her. She has her most faithful dog, her levrette Carpet; she has her songbirds; musicians to distract her from her taxing pregnancy. And her funny, sweet girl dwarf! Is there anything more she could have asked for to help ease the discomfort in her belly? Before he left with the cavalcade, she was diagnosed by the king's doctor as having a flux of the stomach, a burning sensation and most uncomfortable. Her three daughters slipped into the world so easily – could this be a boy who kicks and rolls about with such rage?

Something is afoot – she can feel it; or does her condition make her more sensitive to her fears for the king's safety? The white liquid Antoinette obtained for her from Jacques Coeur and sent to Bellevue seems to be helping a little. How clever of her to have asked dear Jacquet for a remedy. He has often brought back new and helpful medicines from his travels for members of the court. When the queen hears of the difficulties Agnès is having with this fourth pregnancy, she sends her own physician, the fabled Robert Poitevin, who arrives with a new medicine from Jacques Coeur to add to the one she already has. It is a foul-smelling milky substance; thank heaven for the honey that Antoinette sent with him to sweeten it, or it would have made her retch.

Despite being in constant pain to a greater or lesser degree, Agnès tells them all she is blessed with the distractions she needs. She knows she is rambling – it is the heat – and she knows no one minds. In the evening, when they feel they can no longer bear the humidity, the clouds finally break with a clap of thunder, and then it rains and cools the air. The delicious scent of the flowers in her enclosed garden wafts up to her windows, and eventually she drifts into sleep.

*

Just as the summer has been one of the hottest in memory, the winter descends with an icy vengeance. The wind is sharper and the ground frozen sooner than in other years. The days are short and the cold more intense than any of them can remember. Fires are lit throughout the day and night, and some days Agnès remains in bed under her cover of beaver fur, asking her dear aunt to read to her; *how tiring and burdensome is this pregnancy*. She hears it whispered that strangers have arrived in the town of Loches, and one day, when she ventures out on a short walk a little way from her house, someone slips her a letter, passing on before she can stop him. The unsigned note contains a warning that there is a clear threat to the king's life – something she has feared for some time. '*To the Mistress of Beauté and Vernon*,' it begins. '*As a loyal subject I feel I must warn you of a plot against the life of the king. He is too near to achieving his objective. You are too powerful in your position for many to tolerate. I beg you to warn him. The danger comes from someone close to you both. Trust no one.*'

Agnès is deeply troubled, but she dares not say a word to anyone in her house, not even her aunt. She must think. Two days later, again she takes a short walk. This time a well-dressed woman approaches her with a small bouquet of dried flowers, a gift. It is not unusual. But when she returns home, she finds a second letter in the wrapping, written in a different hand. Again it is left unsigned; again it is a warning, though this time it ends: '*I regret to say a woman is involved as well.*'

Her heart is beating so fast that she feels sick to her stomach. She tries to remain calm. Perhaps she is merely being provoked by someone with ill will towards her. The king has achieved a number of victories recently – *too near to achieving his objective*? But how can freeing France of the English be anything but positive news to Frenchmen? His couriers bring her reports almost daily. City after city is falling to him, many without a battle, but with each new victory, Agnès becomes more afraid. How can she notify the king that he is in danger? How can she be sure that if she writes to warn him, her own letter will not fall into the wrong hands?

She frets and tosses this dilemma around in her mind for days and nights. Who can she trust? She decides to unburden herself to Father Denis. He has never failed her and has her total confidence. She seeks him out in his rooms and asks if they can be left alone for a while, telling the others she needs spiritual guidance, something that is normal in her condition.

'Good Father, please allow me to confide in you.' And he kisses her forehead as he always does, and sits her down beside him. Agnès tells him of her worries and of the letters, tells him she cannot sleep with anguish. Her greatest fear is that she knows if she does nothing, she will never forgive herself should anything happen to her king. He listens patiently, and looks into her eyes before speaking.

'My child, you are not well, but your worry is making you worse and I sense you have already taken your decision. What you want from me is my agreement and blessing.'

Father Denis is right. There is only one possible course of action, and she has already taken it in her heart. There is no other way. She must reach the king and warn him herself.

*

December of 1448 is the coldest in living memory, but nonetheless, Agnès bids farewell to her three little blonde angels and her aunt who must remain with them, and leaves the warmth and comfort of her favourite house. Everyone says she is insane to make this journey, but they all insist on undertaking it with her – Marie de Belleville and Pierre's sweet wife, Jeanne de Brézé; Guillaume Gouffier, who the king has appointed to her household; Father Denis and her brothers, Charles and Jean. She takes the medicine sent by Antoinette and also the one brought by Dr Poitevin, which will surely make her feel better. After all, both were sent by Jacques Coeur, who has produced such wondrous cures in the past from his Eastern contacts.

As well as the medicine, Dr Poitevin brought letters; among them she found the first two anonymous warnings and chose to ignore them. Then came the two from strangers in the street. There cannot have been a connection and these only serve to reinforce Agnès's determination to go to her king. The doctor prepares her for the expedition, and is adamant that he will accompany her. The dear man is really too old for such a journey, but he insists, telling her that Queen Marie instructed him to watch over her. Agnès shows him the medicine which Antoinette sent from Jacquet, and he agrees that it will surely help; a mercury-based remedy can only be good for her stomach condition. Everyone has such faith in Jacques Coeur, and the good monks whose honey Antoinette arranged to be sent are in her daily prayers.

They leave the comfort of Bellevue on a day when at least they have a little weak sunshine. There is a company of archers to guard them, and some baggage carts. Hardly a royal progress! Marie de Belleville shares a litter with Agnès. Its walls are of leather to keep out the wind, and the inside is lined, sheepskin wall to wall. Flat brass braziers filled with hot coals are slid under fur rugs to warm their legs. But it is not enough. Somehow the icy wind still slips in, and the horses slide unsteadily on the frozen ground, making the litter lurch from side to side, jerking Agnès painfully with every step. Marie hums to her in soft voice, stroking her cheeks, which is all that she can see of her, wrapped as she is from head to foot in a blanket of sable skins. Still she shivers, and hugs her round belly. In the litter behind is her dear young friend Jeanne de Brézé, who misses her husband as much as Agnès misses the king. Sometimes she and Agnès exchange looks, and each of them knows of whom the other is thinking – which creates a firm bond between them.

They move predictably slowly, the ponies slipping on the icy ground; how they sweat despite the cold as they strain for good footing. Even the riders have their boots encased in covers of wolfskin, and their light armour muffled with capes of fur. Would they be able to draw their swords if needed? Agnès thinks not. Happily, the English have been driven out, and they pass through friendly territory. Their goal is Jumièges in Normandy, where the king plans to spend Christmas feasting with the court before his next engagement: to repossess the harbour of Honfleur, a vitally strategic port.

Much territory has been conquered and reclaimed by the French forces; even the capital of Normandy, the great city of Rouen. Here the citizens were so ecstatic to see the

French approaching that they themselves opened the gates and welcomed their countrymen. It makes Agnès proud when she reads of the grand gesture the king made to Pierre de Brézé. After the long torment of his accusation of treason, his self-induced trial and acquittal, Charles gave instructions that Pierre was to be the first to enter Rouen, together with his lancers and a company of archers, and that he was to receive the keys of the city. *What a noble gesture on the part of my king to his loyal commander – the keys of his home city!*

In one of the letters the couriers bring her, she reads that when word reached Paris of the liberation of Rouen, the capital celebrated by staging a remarkable procession of more than fifty thousand people. The streets were decorated with archways calling Charles VII 'Le Roi Très Victorieux', and blue banners decorated with gold fleur-de-lys were hung from balconies along the processional route. How honoured she feels to be loved by this great king whose child she is once again carrying. *May God bless and keep him safe for his kingdom and for her,* she prays. Yet still she frets.

Pierre himself writes to tell Agnès and his wife how the king made his own formal entry into Rouen. He wore full armour, his parade helmet surmounted by tall ostrich feathers, his visor open to hear the triumphal shouts of welcome and to witness the pageants, the revelry, and the mystery plays performed on street corners in his honour. How proud Charles must be to have regained his capital of the north, and to receive the loyal acclamation of the population! Agnès glories in his success. She reads on that Lord René rode on one side of the king, his brother Charles of Maine on the other, and behind them, the three great soldiers who made that remarkable day possible: Jean de Dunois, Pierre de Brézé, the Constable of France, Arthur of Richemont, and riding with them, Jacques Coeur, who supplied the essential funding for their expedition.

These three outstanding generals, together with Jacques Coeur, led the prayers with the king during the solemn Te Deum in the cathedral at Rouen. It was wise of Charles VII to receive the nobles of the city, and even more so to assure them there would be no retribution for Rouen's disloyalty. 'The past must be put behind us,' he told them, but he did request an enquiry into the procedure of Jeanne d'Arc's trial, which Agnès knows still troubles him.

As her slow cavalcade continues the journey north, Agnès's determination remains strong despite the misery of their travel conditions. At Christmas time, she hears from the couriers sent by the king of his incredible achievement in subduing the cities of both Harfleur and Le Havre. And with the news of victory, more letters warning of a conspiracy against the king and his lady reach her. Who is sending these letters, always in a different but well-educated hand? Agnès shows them to Father Denis and he agrees that she must continue at all costs, despite the difficulties of weather and terrain. The letters are never signed – no doubt out of fear that they could be seized and the writer punished by the mysterious would-be assassin. She has still not told any of the others about their contents; she agrees with Father Denis – it is safer.

Their route north has taken them past Blois, Chartres, Dreux and on to Vernon, the city to which Agnès now

holds the title. The welcome she receives is most gratify-
ing and the citizens even appear honoured by her stopping
for two days. But despite their generous welcome and
comfortable lodgings, she continues to feel ill. Why has
the medicine she takes so faithfully not helped to ease her
discomfort? Is it like this with all boy babies, she wonders,
and why do women suffer so much before birth?

'Oh God,' she prays each day, 'please spare me any
more pain and anxiety.'

Wearily they carry on to Louviers and Elbeuf, but inside
her there burns a fire of pain from the flux and of necessity
– the urgent desire to warn her king of a traitor by his side.
She *must* make him believe her! By the time they finally
near Jumièges, she believes she has become a block of ice.
She takes more medicine; dozes and wakes and dozes on,
ever anxious, fretting, moaning in her discomfort, despite
the calm hands of the queen's doctor and her friend Marie
de Belleville, who nurse her alternately and gently wipe
her brow.

Then a shout from Guillaume Gouffier wakes her – they
have arrived! Is it possible? The good Benedictines of the
abbey where she is to lodge have surrounded her litter
and she is conscious of being lifted gently out and carried
into a great hall with a roaring fire. Jeanne de Brézé and
Marie de Belleville stand by her, as do her brothers, the
queen's good Dr Poitevin and Father Denis. Antoinette is
there to greet her sweetly, and goes at once to fetch her
medicine. They have laid her down on a bed of furs, still
swaddled in her sables, when she hears calls of 'The king,
the king!' *Can he be here?*

And he is, her dear, dear lord, who kisses her hands,

takes her into his arms, and holds her. 'How small you are, my dearest,' he says, despite her pregnancy and her furs, 'and so pale . . . You must rest.' She hears him tell the others, 'My Lady must be moved to a more suitable place.' Then he whispers in her ear, 'How foolish you are, my beloved, to come so far and so late in your pregnancy, on such a road and in such weather; but what a joy to have you with me!' She tries to stop his rush of words and kisses – she has to warn him. It is why she has come.

Everyone leaves them, and at last she can still her beating heart and tell him of the threats and her fears. But this changed, victorious love of hers brushes her terrors away as if they are no more than a few spider's webs – small irritants that come with success, with victory. He has not listened to her at all, thinking only of her comfort, and to where she is to be moved, since she cannot stay here with the good monks.

Back into her litter in the dark and the cold, but this time her lover comes with her. A large troop of guards accompany them, each carrying a blazing branch to light the way. *I must show him the letters . . .*

Agnès is installed in the charming small manor of Mesnil, a guest house belonging to the monks, and not far from their abbey. The rooms are well appointed, with high ceilings, and thick tapestries cover the walls and the windows. Sweet-smelling herbs have been thrown into the chimney pieces and a banquet laid out for her and her companions. There is warm wine with cloves, which soothes their chilled bodies, and delicious soups and pastries. Agnès hardly eats, but she is utterly content to be with her dear one, and assures the anxious faces around her that now all will be well. As soon as the others are refreshed and leave her room, Agnès turns to Charles to emphasize the danger he is in. He must be on his guard; post more sentries – do his servants still taste his food? – and take many more precautions. She shows him the letters and tells him of all her concerns that brought her so far to warn him – even at the risk to her life and the child's. But to her astonishment and consternation, he laughs, albeit good-naturedly.

'My dearest, oh how I love you for your concern,' and embraces her again, 'fear not my darling, precious one, I receive such letters almost daily. But it was your love for me that brought you here in this dreadful weather and your condition, and if it is possible, I love you even more for showing such concern for my safety,' and kisses her lightly and often. Charles makes it clear with tender gestures and his eyes looking deep into hers that it is *her* life for which he fears, *her* health in undertaking this dreadful journey. Then he withdraws and consults with Dr Poitevin. Agnès has to smile as she hears him upbraiding Father Denis and her escort for allowing such a foolish enterprise, but he understands they had no choice.

A colossal sense of well-being floods over her – perhaps some of it due to the mulled wine, but mostly because she is with her king and she can tell how he cares for her; all will be well.

Soon the doctor and her helpers are gone. Alone by the fire, Agnès and her king open their hearts to one another. How strong he looks, and self-assured after his many victories, and she realizes that no warning she can give him will have any effect. Queen Yolande taught her how to care for a delicate mind, a reticent king, a man of indecision and hesitation. But this man who holds her in his arms is none of these things. He is a conqueror, a victor, and the last thing he needs is Agnès to guard over him. No – she needs *him* to guard over her. And he does.

While they supped, everything has been prepared for her in a room on the first floor. Her own tapestries have been hung; her silk sheets cover the feather mattress laid over a number of white lambskins; and many soft down pillows await her aching body. She is washed and combed and scented, but tonight she refuses the foul-smelling medicine – tonight she wants to please her lord even if, Antoinette tells her sternly, she needs the medicine more! As she lies down in her chemise and is covered first by the silken sheet and then soft furs to her chin, her kingly lover holds her hand to his lips and watches as she falls asleep.

Chapter Thirty-one

Here at Mesnil, Agnès is happier than ever before in her life. Each day she spends mostly resting. In the evening, she shares her meals with Charles, who visits her full of stories from the camp and his people. And despite her pregnancy, the nights are filled with their passion. She cannot deny she is not herself – this pregnancy has been most uncomfortable, and her lover has such an anxious face when he discusses her condition with the doctors, but in this she only sees his love for her rather than any sign of serious concern.

Her dear Jacquet has not yet arrived, but Pierre de Brézé visits her when he can get away from the Front, as do Guillaume Gouffier, Etienne Chevalier, Antoine de Chabannes and her brothers. Marie de Belleville and Jeanne de Brézé take turns to sit with her. Antoinette is with her all the time and organizes the little house with her usual efficiency. One by one her companions come for short intervals and give her the news of the day, the stories of the trifling events of the abbey and the gossip of the court at Jumièges. She listens a little, dozes a little, smiles and thinks of her lover, and of the time to come when this child has arrived and the pain is behind her. But she wants to give him a son, and must be patient. Father Denis has taken over the writing of her journal, to her sporadic dictation. Long ago, Agnès promised to write her story for Jacquet, but now it has become a daily chore. 'Father Denis, you don't mind, do you? I hope it will not be finished for many years. Once the baby is born, I will continue myself, but until then I thank you for your efforts.'

Now and then, Agnès asks for the king's musicians to play in the next room. 'I am at peace even if the discomfort is great,' she tells Marie de Belleville. 'I know I must await the birth of this troublesome baby with all the patience and fortitude I can muster.' But silently and secretly, without a word to her good priest, she offers the pain to God to atone for her sins, sins of joy with her lord king.

Dr Poitevin, who was with her dear friend the dauphine Margaret throughout her illness, comforts her with his salves, oils and creams. *How gracious of the queen to have sent me her own doctor.* Agnès knows how devoted he has always been to Queen Marie, since the time she arrived in Bourges as a young girl waiting to marry the king. He has delivered each of her fourteen children, and seen how she suffered when most of them died. The queen and the ladies of the court are housed near Rouen, some distance away, and with the roads so icy, Agnès has forbidden any visitors from among them. Pierre's wife Jeanne has become a close and dear friend, gentle yet strong – very like Marie de Bellleville. Agnès knows in her heart that she can count on her discretion should she need.

The Lady of Beauty is quite unrecognizable; she has become very thin, but she tells Jeanne de Brézé that she is quite sure the evil-smelling cream Jacques Coeur has sent to Antoinette for her and which her cousin applies assiduously each day to her legs will help to make her well. *How can my lord bear to be with me when I am so unappealing?* But he assures her that soldiers smell far worse, and all the herbs and scented candles in the room take away the reek of the mercury ointments and unguents that have newly arrived thanks to dear Jacques. Agnès has been continuing to take a spoonful of honey with the thick white medicine Antoinette gives her while begging her to tell no one, as the honey is a secret gift from the Benedictines. Agnès cannot think why she should not speak of it, but since it makes the medicine go down more easily, she does not argue. Perhaps the good monks, or their flock, do not approve of helping a sinful woman such as herself.

Jeanne de Brézé has left for Rouen to spend time with her husband during his short leave from the Front, but Etienne, most loyal of friends, comes daily to visit her. Jacquet is still kept occupied with the army ordering supplies, but he passes by and wishes her well from the doorway of her room. More than anyone, she sees the queen's old doctor, Robert Poitevin. The good man has never hidden from her his grave concerns about making this journey during her difficult pregnancy, and in the worst winter for many seasons. He still does not know that among the letters he brought Agnès from Paris, two were threats to the king's life.

To her surprise, but not that of Dr Poitevin, her labour begins six weeks before her time. After such a journey she is told it is to be expected, but she can see the concern on the doctor's face. *Where is my love? He promised to return from the fighting before the birth. Better he is not here – this is not a joyous birthing.*

Her labour is the worst she has experienced. Hour after hour she cries out in pain, and she is too weak to help push this child into the world as she did her other three. After what feels like days, it is over. She is exhausted. The baby is a tiny stillborn girl. Poor little angel, already with God before she could cry out her welcome to the world.

Agnès wakes to find her ladies fussing around her, Antoinette, as always, covering her legs with that foul-smelling white cream that she promises will cure her. Agnès is in considerable pain and understands there is good reason for their anxious faces. Days pass and she is no better, no worse. More creams, lotions, unguents patiently administered. She drinks and swallows all she is given, mostly by Antoinette, and allows them to administer more evil-smelling ointments to her face to help restore her beauty for her darling. She insists, and they show her a looking glass. It is as she feared. Her skin looks grey; her pupils are greatly enlarged; her lovely face is gaunt, almost a skeleton with a little grey silk cover.

They wash and powder her, sprinkle rose essence on her

silken sheets, her pillows; herbs burn everywhere, as do the scented candles. Her lover has come to see her and she can feel his concern, his gentle fingers on her cheek. *I know men are bored by illness. I must get well . . . My baby, whom I put through this terrible journey, is dead. It is my fault. I have lost my freshness, my desire to laugh, my joy, and my pretty face is drawn and haggard. I have such pain in my stomach, and all the herbal drinks, the hot and cold compresses the doctor administers only seem to aggravate it. Can there be a worse pain than this?*

The days drag by; the bitter cold of January continues to chill everyone's bones, and Agnès begins to wonder if she will ever see the spring. News arrives of her three little girls asking about their baby brother or sister. She tries to rouse herself to be interested in their stories of their dogs and birds, their studies and the drawings they have made for her. She tries, and she fails.

Her darling king's visits are shorter – his smile cannot mask his anxiety. He wants her to rest. She is repelled by the smell of her own decaying body, so it must disgust him as well, despite his love for her. They talk again of her new title – finally she has agreed to become a duchess after all – and she tries to show him her appreciation and gratitude, but she has little interest in anything except sleep.

Dr Poitevin is exhausted. *He* has not slept for many nights. He asks to let a good woman he knows replace him at her bedside and tend to her. Agnès agrees – too weak to argue. Antoinette never leaves her, and she and the woman consult in hushed voices so as not to disturb her. It seems Antoinette is the one who recommended the woman to the fatigued doctor.

The pains are becoming worse, not better, despite more and more treatments applied by the doctor's woman. *I do not like her hands. My body burns, and smells of decay despite all the herbs in braziers around my bed. Will this torment never end?* Now the king's doctor, Adam Fumée, arrives to replace the queen's, even though he is not so well versed in the ailments of women. Agnès trusts and accepts all that is being done to her in resigned silence.

The king has been called to lead his army into battle. They look into one another's eyes and no words are needed. He kisses her forehead with the lightest of lips. *I know I mean everything to him; I am his salvation, his inspiration, his joy. He has told me so a thousand times. I cannot allow my lord king to revert to the half-man he was when I met him. I MUST NOT DIE.* Agnès's mind races as thoughts fly about inside her head, but she is almost too weak to speak.

The woman Dr Poitevin sent consults with Antoinette, and they both approach her bed with determined faces. She is told that her condition is so grave that they must give her a very large dose of a new medicine brought by Dr Fumée. It will take time to swallow it all, but Antoinette has managed to get hold of some special lavender honey that will make it bearable. When Agnès sees the size of the bowl full of the horrible thick white paste, she almost vomits, but every spoonful is dipped in honey and she swallows it down until the bowl is empty. *If this is the miracle cure, then it must be quick, for I fear I have little strength left.*

But there is no improvement. She is terribly weak and knows that she is dying. *The time has come; I must dictate my last testament.*

To her joy, Jeanne de Brézé has returned from Rouen to be at her bedside. Jacquet is here again, and he and Etienne will help her with her bequests. Even Dr Poitevin has come back, as if from the dead. The three men have agreed to be her witnesses.

Her instructions are simple, and Etienne writes them out for her. She asks for everything she possesses to be returned to the king. She also wishes for Charles, in his goodness, to accept the charge of her three daughters, under the supervision of her Aunt Marie. She knows she has no rights over them, since she is not their father's wife, but she entrusts them to his loving care. There are some bequests she wants made to her family, and to various charities; she has taken advice as to which of her staff in particular should be recompensed, and names them. It is soon done; she signs, as do her witnesses, and they withdraw. Agnès calls for her Book of Hours and asks Father Denis to stay with her to await her end. *I am glad that my king, my dearest love, is with the army – I do not want him here to be distressed. It is better so.*

Time passes slowly; it has been three days since Agnès took the bowl of thick white medicine with honey from Antoinette and the doctor's woman. She will allow only Father Denis to be with her, asking that Etienne and Jacques remain in a nearby room. 'I cannot let them see me again. Will you explain to them? I know my skin decays under my sheets. I cannot feel my legs – I think they are no longer there. I smell of something already dead, like a week-old lamb carcass one might find in the woods. The smell of my own decay is overpowering and makes me want to vomit.

My beloved lord and my friends must remember me as I was – radiant, laughing, content within the invisible cocoon of my king's love. Can you hear me, dear Father Denis? No one except you and the doctors may attend to me now. This is my last wish and must be obeyed.

'My life has been so blessed from many sides; will God forgive me my transgressions? I have a papal absolution among my possessions at Loches – it is in the little drawer of my altar. Will you believe me, dear Father, that my sins have already been forgiven? Can I die in peace? Having you kneeling by my side, even in my fever, comforts me as I pray.

'Ah! At last, a messenger from my beloved king. Father, look, he sends me his love and tender concern . . .

'I am so hot . . . Father, Father, I see my friend, the dauphine Margaret – can you see her too? Her lips are moving – she is talking to me but I cannot hear her. Can you? You were with her at her end. Can you recall her words? I can, so clearly. You told me, remember? As she lay dying, she lifted her sheet and looked down at her rotting body, as I do now. "What a slight thing, and base, and fetid, is my frailty"; dear Father, that is what she said – I whisper it again now, in her memory . . .' Then, with a sharp cry of pain, she falls back on the pillow and is gone.

The slow and painful dying of the Lady Agnès is a most distressing time for her family and friends. Yesterday Father Denis came to tell them that her pain was visible on her grey face, her eyes burning with fever, her mouth contorting with the writhing of her frail body.

The priest remains by her side, praying quietly. No

one speaks in the room next to hers. The three who witnessed her testament – Etienne Chevalier, Dr Poitevin and Jacques Coeur – sit looking at one another's faces, which hide nothing. At last Father Denis opens the door. As the doctors go to her, he enters the room and tells them:

'It is over. The soul of Agnès Sorel, the Lady of Beauty, left her body at six o'clock on this Monday evening, 11 February 1450. Poor, dear lady – her rotting body disgusted her, and she hated to offend – thinking of others, as always, to the very end.' With that he turns away, his eyes red from crying.

The friends and ladies of the Mistress of Beauty are all deeply affected by her death. How quickly such a vision of perfection disintegrated into someone unrecognizable. The king and Pierre de Brézé are still away at the Front, but Marie de Belleville, Jeanne de Brézé and Antoinette are here to grieve together. Jacques Coeur turns to Marie in a corner of the room and whispers:

'I am familiar with death, both violent at war and during peacetime too, but never have I been as disturbed as I am now by the death of this delicate, gentle lady, who gave unlimited joy through her many kindnesses and infectious gaiety. Always sweet-tempered, her company a guaranteed pleasure; in fact, quite childlike in many ways, despite being three times a mother. And oddly, very like her friend, the dauphine Margaret.' Marie nods and cries quietly beside him.

When Jacques Coeur sees Dr Poitevin again, the doctor tells him that the last words spoken by Agnès were the same as those of her close friend, the dauphine Margaret.

He had tried to save that lady with a similar treatment and medication, and was at the dauphine's bedside when she died.

Strange, thinks Jacques, the death of these two enchanting young ladies, one adored by the king and the court but hated by the dauphin, her husband – the other adored by the king and many of the court, and also hated by the dauphin. And both ladies were attended by the queen's loyal old doctor who had also presided over the birth of the dauphin and witnessed the pain of his mother, Queen Marie, as she lost one child after another. Thinking on these similarities, Jacques purses his lips in his thoughtful way.

Messengers are sent to the king at the Front and his instructions by return are clear and precise. Etienne de Chevalier, dear, true friend of Agnès, is charged by his sovereign to make the arrangements for a most sumptuous funeral at Loches. The Lady of Beauty is to receive the full honours normally reserved for a royal princess.

The king has left the army and arrives at Jumièges, and the effect on him of his beloved's death is painful to witness. She was his first real love. At the funeral his face leaves no one present in any doubt that his feelings for her were genuine. He created her a duchess the last time he saw her at Jumiège before she died, something several in the king's suite know he wanted to do for some time, but which she had resisted, fearful of inciting yet more envy. She believed there was a limit to the queen's tolerance, and that of others. Unlike many women who have been raised high, Agnès

Sorel never learned to develop a resistence to protect her against the calumny spread by those envious of her good fortune. She suffered visibly and consoled herself in prayer and by giving generously to the poor.

With her death, there is no restraint on the monarch in either his grief or his desire to honour his only true love. He orders her heart to be placed in a magnificent urn in the church at Jumièges. Her wasted body is to be embalmed by Dr Poitevin and then transported in state to the cathedral of Our Lady of Loches. Etienne de Chevalier is charged with leading the cortège there, while the king must return to the Front. On Charles VII's orders, the Lady Agnès is to have the most splendid funeral, with all the respect due to the duchess he made her at the end of her life. Further, the king commands that a magnificent tomb in alabaster is to be made with her effigy carved lying on the top. Around her head she is to have a duchess's circlet to show she received the most noble title a king can bestow.

Pierre de Brézé has asked his friend, the young poet Jacques Milet, to compose an appropriately charming verse to be engraved at the base of Agnès's memorial, extolling her beauty, gentleness and generosity. The magnificence of the monuments the king plans to raise to his beloved Dame de Beauté constitute a total break with tradition – never before has a private lady, let alone a mistress or concubine, been elevated to such a height, and officially. During her lifetime, the king honoured her and paraded her publicly, but the extent of the tributes from her royal lover that she receives in death comes as a revelation to the court. And, no doubt, to the queen!

With regard to the cause of her death, both the royal doctors agree that it was most probably due to puerperal fever, so common following childbirth. And what a dreadful confinement hers was. What torture she suffered! Everyone in attendance on her was aware of her pain both during and after the birth – and worse, of her decomposition. How it must have distressed this fastidious lady, not only the pain, but the disgust at her own decaying body.

After the funeral at Loches, Jacques Coeur escorts Marie de Belleville to Tours. On the way, they share their recollections of their dear friend. Jacques tells her how Agnès would exclaim: 'Oh Jacquet, how I love the beautiful things you show me. You and I know I do not need any of them; it is just my passion for beauty and the knowledge that my dear king will let me have them that makes me too weak to refuse.'

Marie smiles. 'Yes, she loved the luxury you provided – she made no secret of it. Nor did you ever hide the fact that she was your best client.'

Jacques recounts how whatever Agnès bought would start a fashion, and the rush of orders was often hard for him to fill. But there were times when her feelings of guilt would outweigh her natural self-indulgence and inspire her to give much of her fortune away.

'It's true, she was too generous, even to some who were ungrateful,' and Marie's voice trails away.

'My dear lady, may I ask you something? We were both her good friends, but I am convinced that a number whom she believed were her friends in fact were not.' Marie looks down, and he cannot see her expression. He continues: 'We are alone here, and fear not, I will never repeat what you tell me, but I myself have never been comfortable about her trust in her cousin Antoinette.'

Marie looks at him. 'Sir, I know you to be a loyal friend to my Lady Agnès and to the king, and so I will confirm what I told her myself when her cousin arrived. I did not and would not trust her, and I urged my lady to send her back where she came from, though it grieved her sorely, for she felt duty-bound to repay the kindess of her aunt during her childhood.'

'Then I must tell you what has been nagging at my conscience.' They ride on for a few more minutes at a walk before Jacques says: 'Do you recall coming from her room not long after my arrival at Jumièges and giving me a message from her? You told me she had asked you to let me know how grateful she was for the medications I had sent to her at Loches with the queen's doctor. You also told me that you and Dr Poitevin both obeyed my instructions to give her a spoonful night and morning.'

'Yes, yes, we did,' says Marie, nodding. 'The queen's good doctor was most careful to see she received it at the same time night and morning, even after we left Loches. It really was noble of him to make that journey with us, and at his age, but he assured my Lady Agnès that it was what the queen would have wanted. The dear girl was so grateful that Queen Marie should have gone to such trouble, and deprived herself of her own doctor.'

Marie says this in all sincerity, but it sets Jacques Coeur's mind whirling.

'Tell me, my lady, you did say, did you not, that it was

my medicine that the queen's doctor brought with him to Loches?'

'Oh yes, Dr Poitevin had heard from the king's doctor of the pains my lady was having already while the court was still at Chinon and diagnosed a flux of the stomach. Since Dr Fumeé was to leave with the king it was his suggestion that she should make her way slowly back to her house at Loches and rest. I went with her, and to our relief, the queen in her concern then sent Dr Poitevin after us.'

'And he brought medicine from me with him?'

'Yes, thank the Lord, and also a number of letters for Lady Agnès, but I do not know from whom they came – I assumed at least one was from you.'

'Thank you, dear lady, I wanted to be sure, that is all,' and he gives her a reassuring smile.

But it is not all! Jacques Coeur knows full well that he did not send any medications for the Lady of Beauty to Queen Marie; nor to her Dr Poitevin; nor direct to Loches; nor to Jeanne de Brézé; nor to Antoinette de Maignelay; nor to the king's doctor Adam Fumée. This is the quandary he turns round and round in his head.

No one was surprised at the Lady of Beauty's death once they had heard from the many honourable witnesses about the problems she was experiencing with her pregnancy, compounded by the long, cold journey to Jumièges. It all added up to the inevitable tragic outcome: the birth of a premature stillborn baby; the onset of puerperal fever; hallucinations; and then a painful, lingering death. But Jacques' suspicions have been aroused.

He, better than anyone, knows how difficult Agnès

found her role, balancing the pleasures with the pitfalls – the many luxuries he provided for her set against the pain of the slurs levelled at her. Hers was truly a charmed life, glorying within the nest of the king's adoration and sincere love, but it was an existence that was bound to attract as much envy and hatred as it gave him joy.

How the king will miss her, thinks Jacques – *and so will I*. She was a life-enhancer for the king and the court – in fact for anyone who had the good fortune to know her. *To whom will the king listen now that she has gone*, he muses? Doubtless Antoinette will waste no time in moving into her cousin's place – and her possessions, though he believes the king's love for Agnès was genuine, his first after all.

What Jacques Coeur does not see with his own eyes, his personel most certainly do. He recalls how the Old Queen, Yolande d'Aragon, had helped to put him on his path to success. When she recognized the king's need for a younger version of herself to become his life's partner and soul-mate, in her wisdom, she nurtured this girl they both had noticed in her son René's court, at first from a great distance, and then during her last year at Saumur. How well she understood her son-in-law, Charles VII – his passion for beauty in people as well as in all things. Had she not tried to instill in him the the right values – not that he adhered to her teaching as often as she would like? But she understood that her sensible, intelligent daughter, his wife and queen, could not inspire in him the passionate love he needed, as well as having someone unselfish and right-thinking to advise him – and replace her when she was no longer there. *The future*, thinks Jacques, *is such unknown territory now that Agnés is there no longer to whisper into the ear of Charles VII.* Not even his father's ring, given to Jacques by that great Queen of Sicily, could save him in his need any longer. No, Jacques Coeur will have to live on his wits more than ever to survive the new regime about to infiltrate the court of France.

Acknowledgements

As always I would like to thank my generous hostess in the Bahamas for allowing me the use of her guest cottage each year in which to hibernate throughout January and February, and for leaving me alone to write this Volume III of my trilogy. Also to the many friends there who respect my silence but welcome me when I need a respite and who responded so enthusiastically and generously to Volume I of this never-ending Anjou saga. May they please continue with their forbearance until the publication of Volume III next year!

My gratitude is due in great measure to my friends and fellow writers who have encouraged me to carry on during the seven years my trilogy has taken to date, in particular Philippa Gregory without whose urging I would never have dared make the leap into historical fiction in the first place. I confess the leap, though mentally huge for me, was physically small, since all the facts and figures I narrate are true to history. I have restricted the fiction to dialogue, details, dress, decoration, dogs – servants and spies – just as I did in Volume I, *The Queen of Four Kingdoms*.

My first editor, Susan Opie, must be recognised and thanked for her gentle criticisms, always to the point and most helpful. Also Andreas Campomar, my editor at Constable for his less gentle but also helpful corrections.

Leo van de Pas, genealogist extraordinary and possessor of the world's largest database, never fails to astonish me and provide unexpected genealogical data.

Most of all, my thanks go to my beloved brother Freddy who, among other invaluable advice, is always ready – and from any part of the world – to help me plot the course and length of my characters' travels throughout France, without road or rail and only the use of truculent rivers, their tides and storms guaranteed to hamper the gauging of time taken and distance covered.

Last and not least, I want to thank my husband for his unfailing support in all my literary and creative endeavours, his more than generous praise and infinite patience.

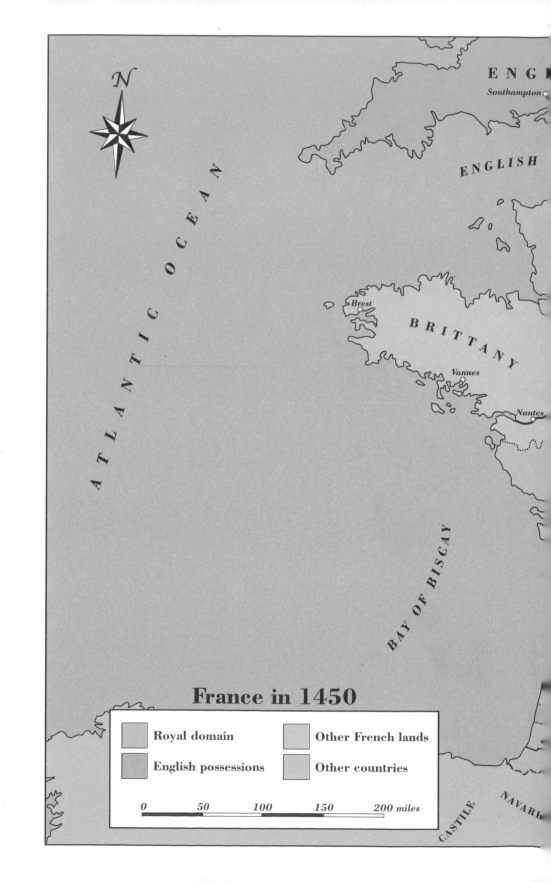

France in 1450

Royal domain
English possessions
Other French lands
Other countries

0   50   100   150   200 miles